WEAVER OF WORLDS

Carolyn Jongeward

WEAVER OF WORLDS

From Navajo Apprenticeship to Sacred Geometry and Dreams

◆

A Woman's Journey in Tapestry

◆

David Jongeward

Foreword by Frank Waters

◆

Destiny Books
Rochester, Vermont

Destiny Books
One Park Street
Rochester, Vermont 05767

LIBRARY OF CONGRESS CATALOGING-IN-PUBLICATION DATA

Jongeward, David.
Weaver of worlds : from Navajo apprenticeship to sacred geometry and dreams : a woman's journey in tapestry / David Jongeward : foreword by Frank Waters.
p. cm.
Includes bibliographical references.
ISBN 0-89281-270-2
1. Jongeward, Carolyn—Criticism and interpretation. I. Title.
NK3012.A3J66 1990
746. 1'4'092—dc20
[B]
90-45753
CIP

Photographs by David Jongeward

Printed and bound in the United States.

10 9 8 7 6 5 4 3 2 1

Destiny Books is a division of Inner Traditions International, Ltd.

Distributed to the book trade in the United States by American International Distribution Corporation (AIDC).

Distributed to the book trade in Canada by Book Center, Inc., Montreal, Quebec.

To Carolyn

Contents

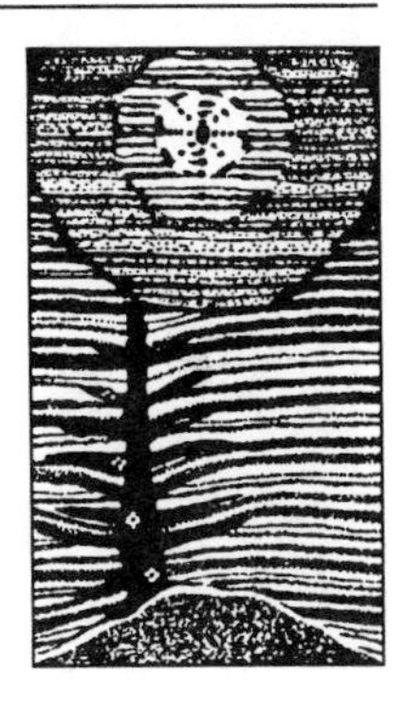

Preface

This book is about weaving in much the same way that *Moby Dick* is a book about whaling (which is quite a bit). The reader—weaver or non-weaver—is always aware that the reality of the craft is a metaphor for the unfolding of an intense inner journey, an odyssey of the soul. This journey shared by Carolyn and David Jongeward dives into the meaning of their lives, the nature of their art, and the discovery of their personal myth; it is paralleled by an outer journey into the world that is as faithful a supplement to the inner journey as one could find.

As a Jungian analyst, I try to encourage this process in my patients through examining their dreams and visions and searching for personal and archetypal meanings in them. David and Carolyn have gone considerably beyond this usual practice. They have not only examined their dreams and visions, they have, as far as possible in this intractable world, integrated them into their work and their ordinary lives, though actually their lives have not been ordinary. With no little sacrifice of comfort and security, they have traveled where their visions led them, finding through Carolyn's weaving and David's writing an ever-unfolding fulfillment.

The history of this myth-making really began on the Navajo reservation where, in the midst of a symbol-rich tribal culture, Carolyn's weaving took its first faltering steps. The old Navajo tradition of weaving made a wonderful nurturing medium for her early artistic development. In its own carefully separate, yet very intimate relationship with Navajo healing ceremonies and their heroic myths, Navajo weaving gave Carolyn the sense of how myths and traditions can be woven into abstract forms. After the slow and painstaking mastery of technical problems, her weaving of abstract forms began to reach beyond the Navajo culture, creating an expanding imaginal world that sought to include much more.

There were many other way stations on this journey: British Columbia, northern California, Los Angeles, and Taos, each of which contributed a new configuration and interpenetration of abstract values, giving rise to many more weavings. These weavings, some of which had begun to sell, were not only beautiful objects, but works of mythic art embodying the play of opposites from which they had sprung.

This play of opposites was strongly illustrated in two of Carolyn's major dreams: In the first was the appearance of the half-animal, half-human Deer Mother, an intensely emotional image filled with earthly warmth. The second was a dream of galactic space evoking the orderly processes of astrophysics and envisioning the universe as a gigantic loom. David says: "On the one hand, Carolyn's work is rooted in ancient traditions; on the other, her search is towards the mathematician/philosopher who reveals his Galaxy loom."

The play of opposites—the human versus the abstract, Being versus non-Being, Time versus Eternity—winds its way throughout Carolyn's work and David's writing (as in the chapter "Rain No Rain"), always moving toward an essential paradox, which, in the end, cannot be woven or written but stands behind them both. This book echoes Jung's words from his Kundalini seminar: "Individuation (a process of personal growth) is not that you become an ego; you would then be an individualist...that person would be a distilled egoist. Individuation is becoming that which is not the ego, what you are not, where you feel as if you were a stranger." (*Spring, 1975,* vol. 35, p. 31, parentheses mine).

But what a weaver's work it is to wrestle with this paradox and bring it into intense focus as David does in the last chapter entitled "Alchemy," "uniting the above and below, sky and earth, form and content, masculine and feminine. Uniting the part with the whole." Where can this devoted work lead them and us? Perhaps to the world behind the loom, "a world that is far away—nearby—and invisible," as Maria Sabina, the famous Mexican shamaness, described it, "A world where everything has already happened and everthing is known. That world talks." But it talks only in the language of art or mysticism, both of which are woven into Carolyn's work and this book that so faithfully and lovingly records it.

Donald F. Sandner, M.D.
San Francisco, California

Foreword

This book about weaving is a loom itself. It will entangle you in threads of visionary dreams and ancient teachings that are being woven into new patterns of compelling beauty.

Carolyn Jongeward is a master weaver. She learned the principles of her art while living with a family of Navajo weavers in a remote part of the Navajo Indian Reservation. Her first pieces adhered to traditional Indian designs. In the two decades since, she has been creating new designs that reflect her own emerging patterns of meditative and rationally inquiring thought.

This book describes the actual process of weaving: setting up the loom, handling warp and weft—the technical details. But its metaphysical dimensions far exceed the mechanical. The narrative is written by Carolyn's husband, David. It is his interpretative record of her inner journey to her deepest center, the transcendent Self, the ultimate observer, who weaves the cosmic pattern of all the forces of nature.

For these unusual tapestries, her Navajo weavers have been replaced as teachers by Carolyn Jongeward's own intuitions, dreams, and studies of the traditions of weaving, which may be the oldest art in the world.

Carolyn learned much also from the Egyptian, the African Dogon, and other ancient traditions which she embodied in her work. One of her most novel tapestries is now hanging on our wall. *Calendar* was modelled upon the construction of the Sacred Calendar of the Mexican Mayas, whose meaning and purpose is still unknown to us after nearly two thousand years. Unlike the solar and lunar Calendars, this 260-day cycle measured no natural time span. It was determined by the intermeshing of twenty "day signs," each ruled by a god, with a series of numbers from one to thirteen, forming a cycle that occurred every 260 days. To complete her long, narrow tapestry in proper color and black-and-white progression representing all aspects of this calendar, Carolyn wove nine rows for each of the days—a total of 2,340 rows.

For her large *Prism* tapestry she wove a geometric design based on the mysterious Golden Section proportions, which occur in patterns of organic growth at a rate expressed in the Fibonacci series of numbers.

Many other such examples illustrate the wide range of her studies and the mathematical precision with which she weaves some of her pieces. She has used the Pythagorean number symbolism; the hexagrams of the ancient Chinese *I Ching;* and the chakras, or psychophysical centers of Tantric Buddhism, each associated with colors and geometric forms.

Perhaps a more important source than these researched subjects has been Carolyn's dreams. She dreams often, records her dreams in a journal, and uses their themes and ideas in her tapestries. "Dreaming is a way of weaving," she explains, "and weaving is a way of dreaming. Both processes have ways of interrelating conscious and unconscious, masculine and feminine, dark and light, beauty and form. In weaving I touch the archetypes. In many ways the warp of weaving is like the collective unconscious in dreaming, while the weft is my personal experience woven into the collective experience." From these dreams come some of her most fluid woven images.

She has the facility for both right-brain and left-brain thinking, as we say. And sitting at the "place of balance," she reconciles, both on the loom and within herself, the polar opposites.

Surely, few if any other modern weavers have equalled the worldwide scope and symbolic depth of her extraordinary images. They are matched by the text of David Jongeward's book. Like the tapestries, it is rationally analytical, intuitive, and poetical. This book, too, is a record of a journey through the labyrinth to our deepest center, from which, if we can follow an Ariadne thread of transcendental guidance, we can emerge into a new world of light and beauty.

Frank Waters
Taos, New Mexico

1

First Threads

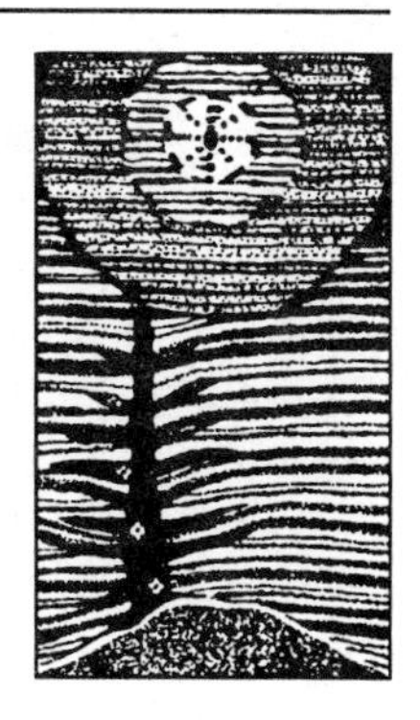

We climbed to a high point on a rock promontory near the Grand Canyon's North Rim. Piñon pine trees, mixed with a few junipers and scrub oak, greened the rolling hills behind us. A vast expanse of northern Arizona spread out before us.

"Indian country. Have you ever seen anything like it?" I asked.

Carolyn shaded her eyes. The gesture seemed out of character for her, a gesture rarely necessary in the Ontario lake country and northern woodlands from where she came. She had been a child of water and trees, familiar with deer and wild columbine.

"Strange country," she said.

A sun-drenched desert rippled out before us, empty of any signs of human life. Pools of white mirage shimmered in wind-washed flats and sandy hollows. To the east, grey-green hills gave way to stark formations of red-rock buttes, purple canyons, orange earth. In a corner of the turquoise sky, black thunderheads gathered, with silver rain streamers spilling out, lightly touching ground.

"Earth and sky," Carolyn whispered. "Maybe I've come here to learn about earth and sky."

We held onto a weathered old pine that twisted out of the rocky slope. I had not known Carolyn long, but long enough to know she looked for meaning in her journeys. She looked for links with the land.

Empty of humanity as the land appeared, a people lived there who would introduce Carolyn to the art of weaving. In the following few weeks, finely spun threads would be placed in Carolyn's hands by master Navajo weavers who know how to make manifest the invisible, creating designs from the elemental forces of Mother Earth and Father Sky.

This was my third trip to Arizona. During the previous two summers, I had come as an anthropology student from San Francisco to assist Donald Sandner, a Jungian analyst who was interviewing medicine men regarding their curing ceremonies. This summer I brought Carolyn, whom I had met in Vancouver in an anthropology course for which I was a graduate teaching assistant.

In one of our first conversations, Carolyn asked if I believed in something larger than individual consciousness, in unifying forces that connected the individual to ancient myths. I assured her that I believed in myths and all sorts of unifying forces. A few months later, I asked her to accompany me to Navajo land.

In July of 1969 we traveled south, entering Arizona by way of Grand Canyon country. We set up camp in the mountains outside a small reservation town called Lukachukai, beside a creek that trickled out of a spruce grove. We were soon meeting Navajo men and women in the trading posts and on the mountain. One day a rider galloped into camp to give his horse a drink. He wore turquoise earrings, a ragged red shirt, dusty trousers, and worn-out moccasins. He talked with a combination of incomprehensible Navajo and wild sign language. He was a blaze of color out of the past. Most Navajo dressed like cowboys, with only the older women favoring brilliantly colored velveteen or velvet blouses, ankle-length skirts, and displays of turquoise and silver jewelry.

Satisfied with our first encounters, we nevertheless felt we were waiting. Neither of us knew just what we were waiting for, but I was determined not to resort to typical social science research habits of hiring interpreters and knocking on doors. While waiting, we followed sheep trails into the mountains, or stayed in camp and read.

I introduced Carolyn to Carl Jung's *Memories, Dreams and Reflections,* a book which had been important to me for some time. During the years of my friendship with Dr. Sandner I had learned to look for recurring themes or patterns in my dreams, and to watch how these images changed over time. I recorded my most vivid dreams in a journal, and in Arizona, I suggested to Carolyn that she pay more attention to her own inner development. Before long, she purchased a notebook and recorded her first dreams.

Sitting out long days in the dust was not always exciting. In the July heat, we thought about water. Carolyn longed for the Ontario lake country, where most of her twenty summers had included weeks of swimming and canoeing.

"What am I doing here?" she asked.

The question terrified me. I thought Carolyn entirely capable of packing up and taking off. The trip was not turning out quite as I had hoped. We were not meeting medicine men.

Several years earlier I had purchased a four-harness loom, taken some weaving lessons, and woven a few pillow covers and wall-hangings. I had gone so far as to collect plant materials and dye my own wools, and I loved the creative sparks stimulated by weaving.

During my first visit to Arizona, I had seen many Navajo looms. The structure, often lashed to trees or built into outdoor arbors, was nothing more than a rough log frame held together by little more than rusty spikes, baling wire, and lengths of old rope. But the spread of finely spun threads, hanging down like a curtain of rain, completely absorbed me. An incredible sense of potential emanates from skeins of colored thread that wait to be woven into design. Equally compelling to me is the sound of weaving, hypnotic rhythms created by thread after thread being woven into place. The sound of weaving transcends time and space. It's a rhythm created by one of humanity's oldest art forms, and one of its most universal.

I described the process to Carolyn and encouraged her to ask the Navajo women we were meeting if they were weavers.

"Learn to weave," I kept saying.

"Why?" she asked.

"I know you would be a good weaver," I said.

"What makes you think so?"

"I just know," I said. "The least you can do is give it a try."

One blistering hot day, a blue pickup pulled off the dirt road and came to a stop beside our tent. Two men and two women occupied the front seat. Several boys clung to a goat in the back. A few minutes later the goat was tied to a tree. The older woman sharpened a butcher knife on a rawhide strap, while others gathered dry branches and hauled water.

Feeling like intruders in what appeared to be a family picnic, we decided to go for a walk in the mountains. We returned a couple of hours later to find the family preparing to leave. The older woman walked to our tent carrying a bundle wrapped in paper towels.

"*Ya-tah-hey,*" she said. "Where did you go? I plan to invite you for goat meat lunch, but you walk away."

She softly laughed and handed Carolyn a generous cut of goat leg. Mrs. Thompson introduced herself, her daughter Violet, and her sons and grandchildren. "Two days from now there'll be a singing at our sheep camp. They'll be dancing over there. You come."

The next day our old pickup truck wouldn't start, so we hitched a ride into town for supplies and mail. We decided to trek the seven miles back, and had gone halfway when a truck stopped beside us. The driver, a young woman with a thick braid of jet-black hair, told us to climb into the back. Beside her in the cab sat an old woman. We hopped into the back next to a skinny old man with a bent leg and a dirty head band.

"*Ya-tah-hey,*" he said, sounding like a bird.

It was the customary greeting, a happy, big-hearted expression used not only in greeting but whenever a situation calls for it. The old man gazed through the dust and didn't say another word until we climbed out of the truck at the creek.

"*Ya-tah-hey,*" he said, waving a weathered hand.

The driver called us to the cab window and introduced herself as Stella, and the old woman next to her as Mrs. Goldtooth.

"This old woman she say you two will be coming over to our sheep camp one of these days," Stella said. "We see you people camping here. The old woman she say 'They must really like it over here in Navajo country.' She want to know where you come from."

We told her and Stella translated to Mrs. Goldtooth. The old woman's face looked like creviced rock and her gestures were broad as a valley, but when she laughed, she sounded like a ten-year-old girl.

"This old woman she has bad legs," Stella said. "The medicine men, they'll be bringing a ceremony up the mountain four days from now. This old woman she say you two will take down your yellow tent and move on up to our sheep camp. You are welcome to help out with the ceremony."

Mrs. Goldtooth and Mrs. Thompson provided us with the invitations we seemed to be waiting for, and we gladly accepted both. We decided to move to the Goldtooth sheep camp for the next month, but frequently drove the ten miles of dirt road to the Thompson place. In both camps we were invited to participate in ceremonials the Navajo often call sings.

At the sing hosted by the Thompsons, we arrived along with hundreds of others who came on horseback or by wagon or truck. Wrapped in Pendleton blankets, Navajos huddled around small fires which formed a circle around a huge central bonfire. A drummer thumped on a hand drum with a carved oak stick. A chorus of high-pitched men's voices filled the clear cold night. Navajos not at the fires stayed among the trees, meeting with relatives, drinking bootleg wine, or trading gossip. Mrs. Thompson stayed by our side for hours, periodically whispering in Carolyn's ear. At least a head taller than the Navajo woman, Carolyn bent down to listen.

"That girl over there," Mrs. Thompson said, pointing with her chin. "That's my youngest daughter, Virginia. She likes the man she's dancing with. He'll pay her a little money for dancing, maybe fifty cents, maybe a dollar. She must be the same age as you."

The attractive couple danced by.

"Virginia is working with the weaving," Mrs. Thompson said. "Do you know about weaving?"

"No," Carolyn responded. "I've never learned to weave."

The next day, Mrs. Thompson took us to a large corral to show us her favorite lambs and kid goats. She led us to a stand of pines behind the family's one-room cabin and removed a heavy blanket from a log frame loom secured to two trees.

Mrs. Thompson sat on a sheepskin and asked Carolyn to sit beside her. Then she dug into a bundle of weaving tools and selected one of her weaving combs, a tool that looks like an oversize fork made of wood. There was a pack of kids around, chasing chickens or goats. I lent a hand to Mr. Thompson, who was repairing a cabin wall. Mrs. Thompson, matriarch of it all, took a thread and inserted it into her weaving. She pounded the thread into place with her comb.

"When she first asked me to watch, I was more drawn to the woman than to the weaving," Carolyn recalls. "Mrs. Thompson was never in a hurry. Even while introducing a thread into her design, she responded to the needs of her grandchildren. She was so gentle. She talked in a clear voice, just above a whisper."

A week later, Carolyn was beside the weaver at her loom for an entire morning. Mrs. Thompson's rug contained columns of triangles in alternating natural colors: black, white, and brown, set against a soft grey background.

"She giggled all the time," Carolyn told me that night. "I don't know what was funny, but she made me laugh too."

Carolyn played a wild harmonica. That night at our tent she let her long dark hair fall around her face as she leaned towards the fire to find her sound. When she looked up, firelight illuminated a smile a mile wide.

"Mrs. Thompson calls me 'little daughter,' " Carolyn said. "I wonder why."

Over at the Goldtooth camp, we participated in a spectacular five-day healing ceremony for Mrs. Goldtooth's aching legs. Crippled for years with arthritis, the old woman was no longer able to walk. She was heavy, and it was all Stella could do to move her from one place to another.

Removing a symptom is not the only purpose of a Navajo healing ceremony. Symptoms are removed as part of a process to restore inner and outer harmony, bringing the patient back into harmony with the natural world. Even though the ceremony was a private "family doings," Harry Anthony, Mrs. Goldtooth's oldest son, who was assisting the medicine man, told us that everyone participating benefits from the singing and prayers.

The Navajo are famous for their paintings made from colored sands. Each morning, Carolyn and I were invited into the ceremonial hogan, a six-sided log and earth construction, where the medicine man and his assistant artfully prepared sand depictions of snake beings and rain gods. The elongated stylized figures slowly took shape, formed over a fine layer of smoothed red dirt. The figures were surrounded by a series of guardians, or a circular rainbow that was open to the east like the hogan.

The ceremony included song cycles, prayers, hair-washing rituals, and daily sweat baths. When the sand paintings were complete, Mrs. Goldtooth was carried in and positioned in the center of the sand figures. After prayers, the medicine man chanted while transferring sands from the gods in the picture to various parts of Mrs. Goldtooth's body. The figures were soon erased and the sand was later removed from the hogan. The medicine men also massaged the old woman's legs, and it became obvious that all the effort was having an effect. She tried to stand, but this proved painful, even though she was too proud to say so.

Harry Anthony thanked us for our participation. His light-hearted nature was very ingratiating and he had seemed especially kind. He often played the clown, walking with the look of a man stumbling over logs. With Stella translating, he asked how long we intended to stay around. We told him we planned to head back to British Columbia in two weeks. Stella conveyed the information, then brother and sister engaged in a lengthy discussion we could not understand. Harry Anthony peered at me. I thought his eyes strange. He looked directly at me with one eye, but the other eye appeared unfocused. I often wanted to turn around to see what he was seeing behind me.

"He say you will be coming back next year," Stella said.

At the time I had no idea of the extent of that man's capacity for working his way indelibly into my life. We had no plans to return to the Southwest the following year.

During the next few days, I often rode horseback with Allen Begay, another of Stella's brothers, to track down stray cattle. Carolyn learned to make fried bread and mutton stew. She helped Nancy Begay, Allen's wife, to find good pasture for the sheep. The wiry woman moved around the mountains with the grace of an antelope. She usually carried a spindle for spinning wool, and a bundle of raw wool in a cloth around her waist. While herding her sheep, or while resting in the shade of a tree, she expertly spun the wool into the threads she would later weave into her rugs.

Late in the afternoons, Stella and Nancy fed firewood to an outdoor fire and waited for buckets of water to come to a boil, then added plant materials such as sage or rabbit brush and long skeins of wool to be dyed. Later, Nancy fished out the wool with a stick and asked Carolyn to hang the skeins up to dry. By early evening the surrounding oak trees were decorated with wool wreaths in hues of yellow, blue-green, and dark red.

We also helped with a four-day move down the mountain to the winter camp. The men rode horseback. The women walked, herding two hundred sheep and goats over twenty-five miles of trails. During the move, Mrs. Goldtooth, who was renowned for spinning wool into a strong fine strand, remained in the hogan. After the livestock was moved, we loaded firewood, sheepskin bundles, pots and pans, bridles, and saddles into the trucks, along with the old-timers. The hogan door was padlocked closed. Our three trucks pounded down the mountain road through clouds of red dust to the winter camp where the family would live until next June.

The impressive winter camp included three hogans, a cabin, and two corrals set near a windmill and water trough. Even so, the place seemed lost in the expanse of high plateau, dwarfed by the massive purple cliffs jutting up from a northern reach of the Chuska mountains. The area had provided grazing for Goldtooth livestock for generations.

One day during our last two weeks in Navajo country, Nancy opened the cabin door and asked us in. She spoke little English, but her blazing eyes and expressive hands did all the talking necessary. An enormous loom occupied most of the cabin. The uprights and crossbeams were made of four-inch pipe. Instead of the usual looped rope for creating tension in the warp, Nancy's loom boasted a chain and pulley system. When blankets draped over the loom frame were removed, we were in for a shock.

Several inches were woven into a rug that was well over four feet wide. When we asked how long the rug would be Nancy laughed, reaching a hand high above Carolyn's head. Initial design elements indicated that the rug would portray the tall, stylized figures of Navajo myth and sandpaintings called *yei-bei-chei.* Nancy used finely spun natural-dyed wools in a wide spectrum of colors. One thing was immediately clear: Nancy was a master weaver.

Nancy was capable of sitting at the loom for hours at a time, with an occasional break to share a laugh and a cup of coffee with Stella and Mrs. Goldtooth. Carolyn asked to watch her work, and Nancy welcomed her into the cabin, but she soon stopped weaving and covered the loom. Carolyn asked Stella about this.

"Maybe she think you will steal her design," Stella laughed. Then, growing serious, Stella added, "It is not good you watch too long while the *yei-bei-chei* are being woven."

The statement carried an impact Carolyn would never forget. "How can I describe it?" Carolyn wrote in her journal. "There is an incredible intensity in the weaver's work. They laugh. Weaving seems to be enjoyable, but at the same time, Nancy, Mrs. Thompson too, make me feel that weaving is as important as anything anyone could choose to do."

Weaving *yei-bei-chei* held special significance to the few Navajo weavers who attempted the complicated designs. The twelve *yei-bei-chei* are Navajo creator gods, powers who sustain the universe in its present form. The gods are not represented pictorially except in sand paintings, a medium which is temporary and removed from human sight soon after completion. Rug weaving is a permanent medium, however, and we learned that Nancy was careful to change details in her designs so as not to take power and meaning away from the gods' forms as depicted in sand paintings.

We also visited the Thompson winter camp, which was not far away. When we arrived, Mrs. Thompson took Carolyn by the hand and led the way into the main house. Violet was weaving on a large indoor loom. Kids darted around the house, staring at us with inquisitive black eyes. Carolyn was taken to a strange loom. A kitchen chair had been overturned and secured to a low table. Strung between the chair legs was a little rug, eight inches wide and about thirteen inches long.

"You watch now," Mrs. Thompson said.

Curiosity aroused, Carolyn watched as threads were woven to demonstrate details in the building up of a triangle. Like her larger rugs, this little one contained columns of brown, white, and black triangles over a grey background.

"Now your turn," Mrs. Thompson said. "You weave."

Carolyn is a great blusher. She outdid herself when taking the weaving comb in hand. Violet, Virginia, Mrs. Thompson, and a pack of kids all gathered around the makeshift loom.

Mrs. Thompson showed Carolyn how to work the various weaving implements. Into the strings which hung vertically from the loom frame, Carolyn awkwardly inserted a flat stick, called a batten, then turned it edgeways. She fingered in a length of wool. Carolyn was shown the correct way to hold the weaving comb. Mrs. Thompson was surprised when Carolyn switched the comb to her other hand.

"A left-handed weaver," Mrs. Thompson said. "I didn't know you'd weave with the left one. But you pulled the thread a little too tight."

Everyone laughed.

"I don't know how," Carolyn said.

She tried a few more threads, with instruction as to how to place each one. After a row or two, Carolyn returned the comb. Mrs. Thompson made a correction, then unfastened twine that held the little frame to the chair. She rolled the piece neatly up, and handed the bundle to Carolyn.

"Take the rug to Canada," she said. "You come back next year and show me how you finish the weaving."

She gave Carolyn balls of wool needed for the rug and a few other colors as well, all homespun wool. The next day we left Navajo land, heading north.

"They all say we're coming back," I commented.

"Maybe so," Carolyn said. "Whether we do or not, I want to finish the weaving Mrs. Thompson gave me."

In Navajo land we had waged a continual war against dust and sand. The following winter we battled British Columbia moss and fog. We lived in a large communal house in Vancouver's Kitsilano district, a house that was much too popular in our opinion, with six or eight guests often showing up for dinner to join our group of ten. Carolyn and I usually retreated to the relative quiet of our tiny third-floor room. During the hours when the clouds lifted, we enjoyed a view of English Bay, the Vancouver skyline, the deep greens of Stanley park, and the rugged north-shore mountains.

Carolyn rigged up a loom frame and secured her miniature rug to the loom's crosspieces. Mrs. Thompson had woven most of the rug's length. At the time, Carolyn was hardly aware of the fact that the last inches of weaving are by far the most difficult. Navajo weaving is accomplished with a fixed warp length, and the last section becomes increasingly difficult. Carolyn used a sacking needle to complete the remaining rows, and I thought she'd never finish. But when the little piece was removed from the loom, Carolyn was ready to weave another one.

The essential first step was to make a warp, a process Carolyn had not yet seen. She found descriptions of the entire process of Navajo weaving in Gladys Reichard's book *Navajo Shepherd and Weaver.* In tapestry weave, the term warp refers to parallel vertical threads strung between the upper and lower crossbeams of an upright loom. Weft refers to lengths of thread the weaver inserts into the warp horizontally so that they cross over and under the warp threads. In tapestry technique, the weft threads are packed down so tightly that the warp is entirely covered. This differs significantly from plain weave techniques, in which both warp and weft are clearly visible.

Carolyn followed Mrs. Thompson's precedent by using chair legs for a loom frame. The remainder of the weaving kit included half-inch dowels for securing frame to chair legs, cotton string for warp, chopsticks for heddle rods, a foot ruler for batten, and a kitchen fork for weaving comb. On this chair-leg loom, Carolyn learned to weave.

Initially, the process seemed uncomplicated. Carolyn inserted her batten into a space created by a shed stick, which separates alternate warps. She turned her batten edgewise to open the space, or shed, wide. She loosely laid in her weft thread and pounded it down with her comb. The batten was then removed. A second shed was created by pulling forward a heddle rod, which has the alternate set of warps attached to it by means of a looped string. Then the batten was inserted again and another weft entered and thumped into place. The process was repeated: alternate warps moved forward and back and weft inserted left to right, right to left, and pounded down tightly.

"It was all so new," Carolyn recalls. "Mostly I was concerned about technical details, but even in the first days I was aware of a kind of rhythm, a slow rhythmic building of thread after thread."

About this time, a big man with a big voice and a love of storytelling arrived on the scene. He was half Cheyenne and had come from reservations in eastern Montana; his name was Chuck Storm. He told us that as a boy he had been chosen by Cheyenne elders to become a shield maker. It was not entirely clear what Storm meant, but he described a process of shield painting for people who had completed a vision quest. Storm seemed to know the inner workings of the Plains Indian Sun Dance and led us to believe that the knowledge he shared was rarely revealed to outsiders.

He possessed an ability which at the time seemed nothing less than magical. After quietly talking with a person, he would sink into himself, then proceed to describe in great detail the person's animal medicine and associated medicine qualities. Someone was always knocking on Storm's door, wanting to know his or her medicine. Our Fourth Avenue neighborhood was soon populated by a menagerie of individuals: Fox, Snow Goose, Dragon Fly, Red Deer, Eagle, and many others. Storm was asked how he could divine medicines in people who had never accomplished anything like a Plains Indian vision quest.

Storm took his time lighting up a cigarette and appeared to study the blue curls of smoke that swirled up. "Everyone has medicine," he said. "Medicine is a gift from the Powers, a way of perceiving the world around you. All of you are seekers. You go to university to learn about life. Some of you do acid. You listen to Bob Dylan and the Doors. You talk about consciousness. You do these things because you want to know about yourselves. Your walk on Vancouver streets is part of your vision quest."

Storm's speaking voice commands attention. He talks with great deliberation and lets silence speak for him also.

"A Cheyenne vision quest is a ritualization of something every seeker undertakes. True, a formal vision quest can bring great power. It is good to fast, to pray, to experience solitude in sacred places. But you do not have to be Cheyenne to go on a vision quest."

It was a timely message for 1969. It struck home, and Storm quickly attracted a following. He decided to stay in Vancouver and finish writing a book, *Seven Arrows,* published under his Cheyenne name, Hyemheyhosts Storm.

Carolyn and I often discussed our Navajo experiences with Storm. He was particularly interested in Harry Anthony, the medicine man who had made such an impact on both of us. Storm stated emphatically that we *would* soon return to the Navajo. He said we'd been put on a path. We asked Storm to explain, but he laughed and motioned for Carolyn to sit down.

"Do you want to know your medicine?" he asked.

Carolyn readily agreed. Storm relaxed, and within moments his mood had changed as he seemed to withdraw into himself.

"You are a woman of the meadows," he said, slowly. "You know trees of many forests. You have tasted the waters of many rivers. You swim in the lakes. You swim in your dreams. You know the migration trails leading from the meadows to the woodlands, from the woodlands to the prairies. You hold your head high. You have the proud long neck of your animal sisters. I see lightning signs painted on your shoulders."

Storm passed a hand through his long hair, then continued.

"Your greatest pride is the spread of antlers you carry so high. But antlers are also your greatest problem. When you become careless or disoriented it's because your antlers are entangled in the webs of branches crisscrossing your path. Carolyn, you are Elk Woman. Now you know your medicine."

We were fascinated by his revelations, but I was unsure whether I was hearing poetry or witnessing an outright seduction. Whenever that hurricane of a half-breed Cheyenne came around I watched Elk Woman like an eagle. The dust eventually settled when Storm fell in love with a Red-Tail Hawk.

Carolyn had loved deer since early childhood. She often saw the graceful animals every summer in Ontario woodlands. Less familiar with elk, she nevertheless felt an immediate psychic connection with the larger member of the deer family. She wanted to learn more about elk medicine, and Storm told a story that was later published in his book.

The story was about a star that fell to earth. It shattered into pieces that changed into pools and lakes. A beautiful young girl went to the lakes, collected a handful of star-water from each, and distributed the water to every person in camp. For a time the people lived with the gift, until one man became angry and threw his star-water into the fire. Eventually other people followed his example, until only the girl retained the gift. She decided to return star-water thrown into the fire back to the lake, and to give her own to an elk. The elk became the woman's husband. They kept their star-water with them always. In time, the people who had thrown their star-water away recognized that they had forgotten to live in painted lodges such as Elk's and his wife's. When the people asked if they could have the gift again, Elk sent them to the four directions. But people who had gone north came back and tried to steal star-water from Elk. Those going south returned and tried to use trickery, while those going west returned and tried to take the star-water by force. Those who went east never returned.

"Elk and his beautiful wife left the camp," Storm concluded. "They took their star-water with them. And if you want star-water, you must follow Elk into the final direction."

Four days later, Carolyn woke up with a vivid dream. She dreamed of being transformed into an elk. Two companions were transformed into deer and a third became an elk with wolf's head. The four bounded up a mountain slope. Intensely aware of herself in an elk body, Carolyn experienced the sheer joy of graceful, big-bodied, sure-footed movement and tremendous strength. Then the dream changed. She was human again, and entered a dimly lit corridor which had opened up in the mountain. She came to a wall that separated her from a large room, in which a group of people, wearing white robes, were dancing or reading books. Hearing her name called, Carolyn jumped over the wall to join them. In an adjoining room, behind a glass wall, there were golden bulls and cows, some standing on hind legs and wearing white lengths of cloth over their heads.

Several years would pass before Carolyn realized that this dream had initiated an inner journey that would profoundly influence her creative career.

Carolyn returned to her little tapestry. She had chosen a simple stepped design using four colors, with the intention of learning to weave vertical lines. The final inches required laborious needle work, but eventually the piece was finished.

Storm dropped by for a look at the twelve-inch-square tapestry. His response was enthusiastic and entirely unexpected.

"You've woven a medicine wheel," he said. "You have woven your center and your four directions."

Figure 1: *Medicine Bag. Carolyn did her first weaving on a chair-leg loom, using kitchen utensils for weaving tools.*

Storm often described Cheyenne medicine wheels for us in his stories. The medicine wheel is an all-inclusive symbol; each of the four directions is represented; and each is associated with a color, a season, and an attribute of human life or human perception. For example, Storm associated the direction North with the color white, the winter season, and the thinking function. The color yellow, spring, and intuition or illumination were associated with the East. West included black, autumn, and introspection or dreaming. South included the color green, summer, and human feeling. Storm reminded us that it is the nature of a wheel to turn and not remain fixed, implying that no one set of associations was fixed to the four directions, and that each tribe and each individual have medicine wheels of their own. The basic representation is a simple cross with four equal arms. Add to this the circle and you have a cross-within-the-circle which Jung and others have found to be a universal or archetypal symbol.

When the little weaving was complete, Carolyn expressed her interest in learning more about weaving ways. We thought a lot about a return trip to Arizona, and I applied for a fellowship to study Navajo healing ceremonies. Waiting for the university's decision, we often recalled that both Harry Anthony and Chuck Storm had been convinced we would return to the southwest. Carolyn and I were married in Vancouver in the spring of 1970. Not long after, the fellowship was granted, allowing us to return to the Navajo for a six-month stay.

2

First Loom

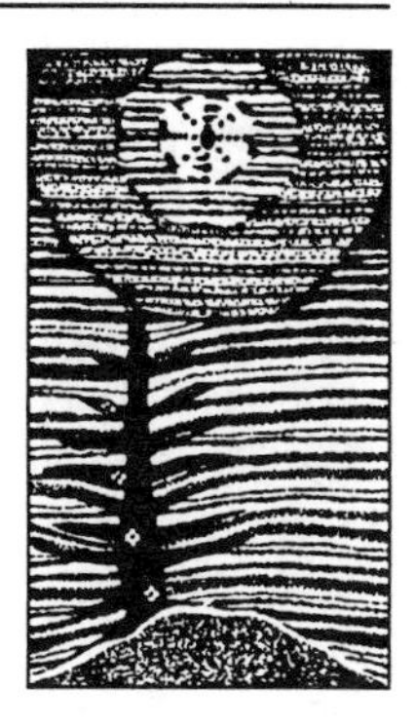

We arrived in Lukachukai on a sweltering August day when Navajo families were completing the annual move to winter grazing areas. Stella, Mrs. Goldtooth, and Nancy and Allen Begay welcomed us back to the pace of Navajo life by asking us to herd the sheep down the mountain.

Harry Anthony showed up the next day. He laughed when shaking our hands, unnerving me with his penetrating gaze.

"I knew you were coming," he said.

He invited us to live with his family after Stella and Mrs. Goldtooth were moved down the mountain. We gladly accepted. We moved in with the Anthony family, and Carolyn was pleased to see a small loom built into the south wall of the Anthony's central hogan.

The Anthony winter camp included three hogans and a newly constructed tarpaper-covered house. The house was built in a style introduced during the War on Poverty years, supposedly for the purpose of improving Navajo standards of living. Cheaply built by VISTA volunteers and unskilled laborers, the houses were impossible to heat in the winter and too hot in summer. Most remained unlived in but were used instead for storage or for winter sheep sheds. The older Anthony boys had learned carpentry skills, however, and added on some extra rooms to the tarpaper house. We lived in the smallest of three rooms and shared meals with the family in the central hogan.

We often felt closest to the family during the leisurely evening meals. Mary Anthony, mother of nine children, wife of an important medicine man, was clearly in her element when masterminding dinner preparations on the old wood-burning cooking stove. It was a pleasure just watching Mary move. She had managed to turn a pronounced limp into a fluid, wave-like motion, quite in contrast to Harry Anthony, who walked as if stumbling over every pebble in his path. We were served fried bread, mutton stew, and black coffee, the staples of Navajo cuisine. An atmosphere of light-hearted storytelling was sustained until well after the dishes were cleaned, and one of the older boys often volunteered translations for their *belagona* (white man) guests.

There were many days when nearly everyone was gone. The school-age children were bussed away to boarding schools and returned only on weekends, if then. The older boys worked away from home if they could find jobs. Only the oldest daughter, Mary Ann, remained home with any predictability.

Harry Anthony often asked me to drive him to a mountain or to one of the canyons in search of medicine plants. We were sometimes away for days when Harry Anthony conducted elaborate three- to five-day sings, sweat lodge ceremonies, or divination rites, in which he used crystals to diagnose an illness and decide on the appropriate cure.

During times of relative inactivity in the central hogan, Mary would sit down to her loom. She often welcomed Carolyn's company. Mary spoke no English and Mary Ann rarely offered to translate, so Carolyn quickly picked up words and phrases while watching Mary weave. The only light for the loom came from the open hogan door and the overhead smoke hole. In this semi-darkness, Carolyn sat behind the weaver for hours, watching the workings of heddles, weaving comb, and threads woven into angles.

Mary's rugs favored chevron designs expanding out from a predominant center. Her lines tended to be somewhat wavy and imprecise, and when running out of a color, she used wool that did not exactly match the original hue. After three weeks of sporadic work, a small rug was completed and taken to the trading post. Though the weaving was not of the best quality, we were shocked when Mary accepted only a twenty-five-dollar credit on the grocery bill in exchange for the rug.

Carolyn asked if she could watch the procedure for making a new warp and hinted at wanting a warp for herself. Mary responded with a careful evasion of the subject. We had become friends with the Anthony's second oldest son, Fred, and his wife Loretta. When it became evident that Mary seemed none too anxious to discuss anything having to do with the making of a warp, Carolyn turned to Loretta for assistance.

Fred was the only son showing interest in his father's medicine ways, and periodically accompanied us to ceremonials to act as translator. Loretta wove small pictorial rugs with considerable skill, but depended on her mother for warps, and her mother lived several miles away. Carolyn was advised not to count on a warp from that quarter.

One day after a long walk, Carolyn returned to the central hogan to find a new warp strung up on the loom. There was no sign of a second warp. Disappointed, Carolyn was nevertheless determined to weave. She asked for assistance in building a small loom that could be installed in our room. In a manner conveying great warmth and friendship, Mary invited Carolyn to sit with her at the loom. While weaving, Mary told story after story in Navajo. Mary Ann refused to translate, but the stories flowed like water for the better part of the morning. Carolyn understood phrases now and then, and shared in the mood of good humor. But later, Carolyn left the hogan with no assurance that the request for a loom had been acknowledged.

Always anxious to please, Carolyn complied with every request to help out with cleaning and cooking. From the beginning we were keenly aware of our outsider status. We were two additional persons for whom meals had to be prepared, firewood gathered, and water hauled from artesian wells ten miles away. We were tolerated as strangers to the mysterious something known as the Navajo way. We often discussed our kinship status. The medicine man had informally adopted us and always addressed Carolyn as "little sister" and me as "little brother." By contrast, Mary did not use a specific term of address, and her relationship to us seemed ambivalent. We wondered if Harry Anthony had stepped out of line when asking us to live with the family. Among the Navajo, property is inherited through the mother's side of the family. The hogans, sheep, and surrounding land belonged to Mary and her clan, not to the medicine man, whose relations lived miles away.

Depressed that her desire to weave seemed to be ignored, Carolyn began to feel like a household servant. Then, just when Carolyn's patience was running out, Mary became gracious, making every effort to insure Carolyn's relative stability of mind. When Mary accompanied Harry to an all-night sing, she asked Carolyn to go along. Carolyn welcomed the change from hogan duties and was able to see Harry conduct a ceremony for the first time.

After the sing, the tide changed. Carolyn was asked to clean the three-room house, then clean the day's mound of dishes. The chores were especially humiliating because the girls were home from school doing nothing except paging through Sears Roebuck catalogs and drinking quarts of Coca-Cola. I returned to our room late, after three days away, to find Carolyn reading in lantern light, tears streaming down her face.

"They treat me like a slave. The girls just gawk at me, and think up something else for me to do. You're never here. Nothing's happening for me."

The next morning, after an uncomfortable breakfast, Mary pulled a dusty old bundle out from under the bed. She unwrapped the bundle and handed the contents to Carolyn.

"A yeh heh," Carolyn said. "Thank you." She left the hogan with a dusty but apparently functional warp.

Later in the day, Loretta offered the use of a spare loom. By evening, the loom was installed in our room. Then Mary accompanied us to her sister's camp, where she negotiated the purchase of several balls of handspun wool. Before long we had strung up the warp to the loom crossbeams.

"My first loom," Carolyn rejoiced. "This is what I've been waiting for."

All that was needed now was the loan of the necessary weaving tools.

"Tomorrow," Mary said.

Joy turned to despair when no tools appeared. So, once again, she asked Mary for the loan of heddle rods, batten, and weaving comb.

Mary responded by sitting at her own loom and weaving, inviting Carolyn to watch. Feeling the imminence of her own opportunity to weave, Carolyn watched with renewed and excited attention. But after awhile, Mary stopped weaving, complaining of a severe pain in her weaving arm. Mary Ann suddenly seemed eager to translate and spared no detail in recounting the history of her mother's pain. Mary clutched her arm, grimacing with what appeared to be a throbbing soreness that was spreading up the arm into the shoulder even as she spoke. Carolyn sympathized and found herself wondering if pain was something every weaver experienced. Carolyn returned to our room feeling miserable, and with no weaving tools.

A few days later we found a grove of oak trees. We selected a thin branch and cut it. I peeled off the bark and sanded the branch smooth until Carolyn was satisfied the branch could serve for a heddle rod.

Using instructions from Gladys Reichard's book, Carolyn looped on the heddles. Having accomplished one further step, Carolyn studied the warp, thinking about design. She sketched a few ideas. She responded to a soft knocking on the door. Mary was brimming with incomprehensible news, delivered with much warmth and laughter. She noticed the sketched designs, then produced a batten and comb from the folds of her velveteen skirt. She left without another word.

After three weeks, everything Carolyn needed had finally materialized, including a sheepskin pelt to sit on. She inserted the first thread and commenced with the weaving of a dark gold band. The heddle rod worked reasonably well, and soon a bumpy rhythm established itself as row after row was woven in. Carolyn then entered a new color and wove a band of dark brown.

The first technical difficulty appeared in the form of pulled-in edges. The threads had been pulled too tight, just as Mrs. Thompson had noted in Carolyn's very first attempts. Instead of pulling the threads tight across the horizontal length, the weaver must allow little hills to be formed so that when thumped into place, weft can interweave with warp. It was one thing to know what to do, quite another to do it right.

A warp string broke. Carolyn showed the problem to Mary. Mary avoided the issue by complaining about all the work to be done with the sheep and goats. The pain in her arm had vanished, but she had not been weaving for days. Carolyn continued to weave, hoping the broken warp would somehow be swallowed up in the weaving. This was no solution, so Carolyn waited for Loretta's advice. Loretta demonstrated the tying-in of a section of new thread to replace the damaged warp.

A detailed design was eventually sketched out for the two-by-four-foot rug area, not large by Navajo standards, but an immense jump from the little medicine wheel design. Soon after the weaving was resumed, another warp broke. Carolyn tried repairs, only to find the repaired warp too loose compared to its neighbors. She fiddled with the knots, convinced herself the tension had improved, then continued working, only to discover that the edges were still pulling in. She tied strings into the warp and attached the strings to the loom frame, hoping to pull the warp back to its initial width. The effort was rewarded with two more broken warp threads.

"When a warp snaps it feels like something hitting me in the heart," Carolyn wrote in her journal. "I don't know what I'm doing wrong."

Harry Anthony indicated there were no plans for ceremonies for several days, so we welcomed the breathing space and headed off to a Hopi village to see a dance. We camped in Canyon de Chelly for a couple of days, then drove over to the Thompson's place.

We were welcomed with open arms. Mrs. Thompson repeatedly addressed Carolyn as "little daughter." For several hours, Carolyn received detailed instructions about the loom and weaving, generously given in fluent English—except on one point. When the subject of broken warps came up, Mrs. Thompson suddenly put away her weaving comb and left the loom.

"I don't know about that one," she said. "I wonder why the threads break like that."

Mrs. Thompson clearly wanted no discussion of broken warp threads. We had no idea why. The evasion produced new waves of doubt in Carolyn regarding her competency.

"Why am I weaving?" she asked. "What's it all about? Weaving is so important to Mrs. Thompson. She laughs, she plays with her grandchildren, she weaves. Then she says, 'Yes, weaving is the good way. Weaving is the Navajo way.' So who am I, thinking I can learn the Navajo way?"

Regardless of doubts, Carolyn came out of our three-day trip fired up, determined to weave on as best she could. Her sketched design included columns of triangles, derived from patterns favored by Mrs. Thompson. Sketching triangles is much easier than weaving triangles, however. The technique for achieving an angle with uniform slope presented further difficulties. Carolyn's angles looked flat. She needed a steeper slope. Loretta offered some help, but the design problems seemed to multiply. Once again, weaving stopped.

"I needed reassurance," Carolyn recalls. "Someone to tell me my problems were common, or, maybe I needed someone to tell me I was unfit for the demands of weaving. It was impossible for me to comprehend how the weavers could make their designs work out perfectly, with no advance sketches, no marks on the warp, no tape measurements."

Reassurance was not easy to come by in the Anthony hogans. One day when the girls were home from school, Mary led them into our room where Carolyn was puzzling over her design ideas. Carolyn was asked to weave a few rows. One of the girls pointed to the rug's uneven edges and giggled about the strings tied between warp and loom frame. Another girl noted the bumps made from knots tied into repaired warps. Mary Ann pointed to the rows of flat triangles. The room was soon choked with laughter. Mary Ann mentioned that her mother thought a big white box would be good for the center design. They were still laughing about the *belagona* weaving woman when they left the room.

I returned to the house that evening to find Carolyn fighting tears again. The suitcases were pulled out from under the bed.

"We're leaving," she said. "They're driving me nuts."

Long walks in a desert populated mostly by wild horses, sagebrush, and juniper trees have a way of soothing troubled souls. I asked Carolyn if Mary's suggestion for the design deserved any consideration. She balked at the idea of weaving a square into a design made of triangles, but later, after discussing various options with me, Carolyn faced the warp again and decided that a square would in fact greatly simplify things.

After several days of reasonable progress, Carolyn was treated to another of Mary's lengthy visits. Bubbling with warmth, exuding a seemingly boundless concern for the persistent weaver, Mary examined the woven white square, the new series of inverted triangles, and a black step design that marked the final stages of the design. Mary then loaned Carolyn all the tools necessary for completing the arduous last inches of weaving, including small combs, miniature battens, and heddle rods.

Mary's sudden, incomprehensible changes of temperament were deeply unnerving. For weeks, Carolyn had wavered between depression and elation, exhaustion and brief flashes of accomplishment. We had lived with the Anthony family for two and a half months when Carolyn finished the rug. It was a happy day when the last rows were needled in and the rug was removed from the loom. We brought the rug outside to clean off the wool fluff. When Carolyn shook the rug, edges frayed when more warps broke. Shaking a rug with a weak warp is certainly not the best way to clean it, and Carolyn spent two days of sewing to repair the damage.

The rug measured twenty-four inches at the bottom and less than twenty-one inches at the top. The edges were wavy, bulging in and out for the entire length. The design center, even with the addition of the white square, was nearly four inches below the center of the warp length. Several bumps from knotted warps pushed through the design. The length measured from forty-five inches to forty-seven inches, depending on where the measurement was taken. Within that rug was woven every doubt, every uncertainty, every frustration of a weaver weaving her first rug. Add to this the living situation and the nature of the instruction, and it seems now, in retrospect, something of a miracle that the rug was woven at all.

A week later, Carolyn informed Mary of her intention to weave a second rug. Carolyn wanted a new warp. Mary avoided the request with a quick change of subject.

Figure 2: *Carolyn's first rug, woven on a Navajo loom while we lived with the Anthony family.*

Then, after another week, during a day when the medicine man and I were gone, the kids in school, and the boys off to work, Carolyn found herself alone with Mary. Mary wanted everything cleaned out of the hogan, including bed rolls, furniture, and water containers. Carolyn wondered if another day of household work was under way, but Mary seemed especially kind. When the dirt floor was swept clean, Mary brought in four poles. She made a frame by lashing the poles together with baling wire. With the frame prepared, Mary brought out a big ball of warp wool. Carolyn was told to watch, but not to touch.

Humming softly, Mary passed the ball of warp back and forth between the crossbeams of the frame, which lay on the ground. Care was taken in maintaining equal tension with each round of wool, while also keeping equal distance between each set of warps.

Mary Ann returned from the trading post and a conversation began between mother and daughter. Carolyn understood enough to know they were discussing Spider Woman. As usual, Mary Ann was reluctant to translate, until Mary insisted.

"My mother she says this way of working with the wool is Spider Woman work. She says we must be careful to have only good thoughts today."

Mary Ann giggled, as if not impressed with her mother's words. "Spider Woman was here in the beginning. She was the one who taught the people about the weaving ways."

Mary Ann would say no more. But enough had been communicated to deeply affect Carolyn. In Reichard's book about Navajo weaving, there are references to the importance of Spider Woman in the Navajo creation stories; and Loretta had mentioned that during her "Becoming-a-Woman" ceremony, her grandmother had collected spider webs and put them all over her body before the medicine man prayed.

"The spiders help me become a good weaver," Loretta said.

That night, Carolyn wrote in her journal.

> Mary made four warps today. One is mine! Made with good strong cotton. Mary let me bind my warp thread to the dowels and was surprised I could do it so well.
>
> They talked about Spider Woman. Mary Ann seemed embarrassed by the talk. I wish she would have said more. But I have the feeling that making a warp, and the process of weaving itself, is somehow related to Navajo beliefs about the creation of the world.

A new warp! Sixteen by forty inches, made of sturdy cotton. While Carolyn strung the warp onto the loom, Mary brought in the tools needed to begin weaving.

I asked Mary if she knew where I could purchase good weaving tools so that Carolyn could have her own set. Mary abruptly remembered a task outside needing immediate attention. Then, a week later, she asked if I would drive her and Mary Ann to a relative. It was the first time Mary had ever asked me directly to take her somewhere without the presence of either Harry or Fred.

We drove on a dirt road winding through pine trees up to an old hogan hidden behind a hill, with grass growing on the domed earth roof. I waited at the door while Mary and Mary Ann entered. After several minutes, I was asked inside. The place smelled of grease and sheep. I waited until my eyes adjusted to darkness, then I sat on a sheepskin at the hogan's south wall. Pale light seeped into the hogan through a partially covered smoke hole. Mary and Mary Ann sat at the west side. There were two other women in deep shadows on the north side, wrapped in heavy blankets. One was old, the other ancient, and I could see neither very clearly.

In subdued tones, the four conversed in Navajo.The ancient one leaned forward, peering at me with beady eyes. Her face caught a shaft of dusty light and looked like gnarled oak. She drew back into the darkness and, giggling, pulled the blankets around her thin shoulders.

For a long while, silence permeated the hogan. I watched a wrinkled hand reach out from the blanket, holding a weaving comb. I looked at the hand, the comb, and Mary Anthony. Mary gestured for me to take the comb. The weaving implement looked nearly identical to the hand holding it— twisted, gnarled, cracked, but strong. The comb was smooth as silk, polished by wool oil and weaving hands that had used it for years. I pondered the age of the comb that was now in my hands.

Mary said something and Mary Ann translated.

"That old woman she say her mother give her the comb. Her mother give her that comb when she was twelve years old."

I imagined the old woman to be at least ninety. I tried picturing the scores of rugs that had been woven with the comb, but my thoughts seemed to spin away in a whirlwind. Then the hand reached out from the blankets again, holding a gently curved, finely carved batten. The oak batten was deeply grooved from countless years of use.

"This woman is too old to weave another rug," Mary Ann said. "She say you take these tools to your weaver woman."

They all cackled like a clutch of prairie chickens until it was time to go. Following Mary's suggestion, I wrapped the comb and batten as Christmas presents.

After the holidays, when telling Carolyn about the day I had obtained the tools, I found I could not recall the location of the old woman's hogan. I couldn't remember the road we had taken from the Anthony's place. The event had somehow lost its reality and become more dream-like. The medicine man had more than once shaken my sense of reality, but I found it strange to be unable to recount details of the trip with Mary. I wondered if the day was a demonstration of something Harry Anthony had said.

"There are many, many worlds," he told me. "One day you will see that the many worlds are separated by little more than a dream."

I could only guess at his meaning. But I had experienced an ancient hand emerging from folds of darkness to put a thing of great substance in my hand, in a gesture seemingly bridging the world of waking with the world of dreaming.

Dreams were of great importance in the medicine ways, and I attended a number of sings and divination rites given specifically for dreams. One night, when all of us joined Harry for an all-night ceremony, a woman who spoke English said that Mary wanted to know if Carolyn remembered her dreams. Carolyn responded affirmatively and took the opportunity to tell a dream dreamed several nights before.

After a long silence, Mary said, "Sometimes I dream like that. I get up early in the morning. I go outside with the corn pollen bundle. I raise my hand high and sprinkle the pollen before me. That way I give thanks to the rising sun for the good dream."

By mid-January, Carolyn's second rug had reached the halfway mark. The edges were slightly uneven, but weaving progressed relatively smoothly. She wove with white, black, green, and brown in a banded design that included a diamond form and columns of triangles, alternating with a ripple-like pattern.

It became increasingly clear that completion of the rug would signal the end of our stay in Navajo land. My grant funds were running low. We were uncomfortable about not being able to contribute as many groceries as before. We began hearing grumblings in the central hogan about diminishing supplies of firewood. Furthermore, Carolyn was experiencing another shift in her relationship to Mary, who seemed to be as unfriendly as the blizzards howling outside the hogan door.

One day a pickup truck arrived, picked up Harry Anthony, and drove away. After five months of participating in every ceremony he had given, this was the first time I had not been invited. I took it as another sign that our time with the Anthonys was coming to a close. The complex twists of emotions generated by life with the family had often been difficult to deal with, to say the least; yet it seemed impossible to confront the fact that it was actually time to leave. Harry suggested we take the unfinished weaving and move to the Goldtooth camp for our last three weeks in Navajo land. During a February snow storm, with half the family helping to push us out of deepening drifts, we left the Anthony winter camp.

In a small cabin near the Goldtooth hogans, Carolyn unrolled her weaving and strung it up to one of Nancy Begay's old loom frames. Within a few days, we knew that Harry Anthony's suggestion to move had been carefully considered and planned.

Nancy was weaving one of her enormous *yei-bei-chei* rugs. She completely dropped her former reluctance to have Carolyn beside her at the loom. Carolyn was suddenly enjoying the undivided attention of a master weaver. We marveled at Nancy's weaving speed, the complexity of her designs, her expertise in handling every technical

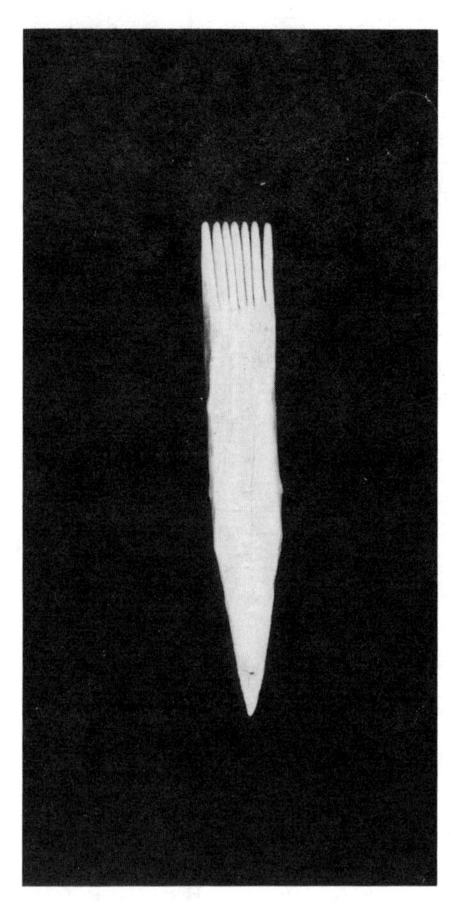

***Figure 3:** The oak Navajo weaving comb—possibly one hundred years old—which Carolyn still uses.*

difficulty. She wove tall, stylized figures with multicolor kilts, feather streamers, elaborate headdresses, and intricate medicine pouches and belts, all surrounded by delicate rainbow guardians. She sat tall and proud at the loom, her weaving comb drumming threads into place with an efficiency that left us speechless.

Stella was weaving also for an hour or two every day after returning home from her job at the local school. It was the first we had seen of Stella's work, and her weaving was superb. Old Mrs. Goldtooth rested on a thick pile of sheepskins in Stella's hogan, busily spinning her fine warp wool.

Carolyn was free to weave for hours every day, with Nancy and Stella coming by in the evenings to offer advice and a continual stream of commentary. Carolyn was elated by the supportive atmosphere. As she approached the last, tedious inches, Mrs. Goldtooth gave Carolyn a set of finishing combs and battens and told her to keep them for her

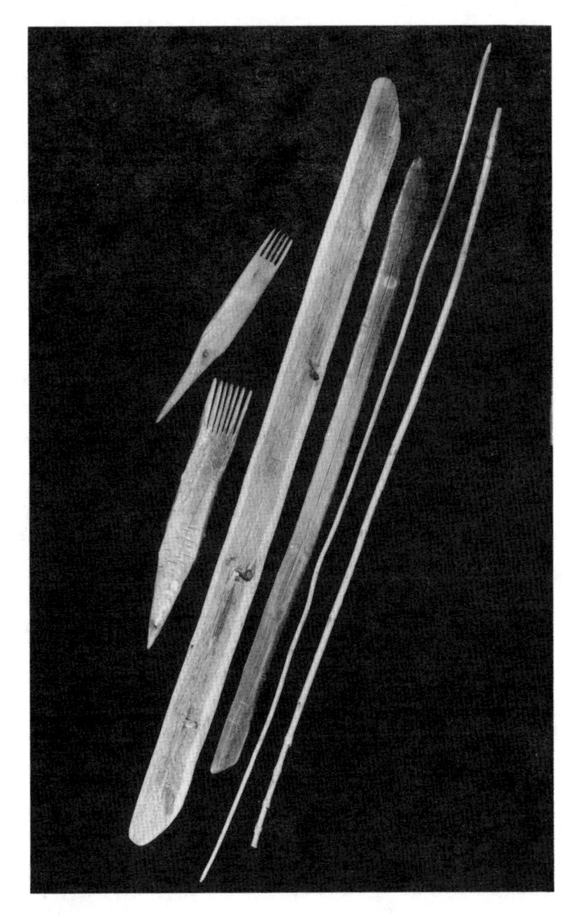

***Figure 4:** The basic weaving tools for Navajo weaving. The smaller comb and the batten are used for finishing the last difficult inches. The reeds are used for separating the sheds.*

own weaving kit. Every problem encountered was worked out on the loom with Nancy's supervision.

The rug was nearly complete when we were invited into the main hogan for a feast of mutton stew, broiled sheep ribs, fried bread, and salad. Later, Mrs. Goldtooth asked Carolyn to sit beside her. The old woman's face looked like rock, but when she talked, she always sounded like a girl.

"A weaver must watch out for the enemy," Mrs. Goldtooth said, with Stella translating. "Every weaver must watch out for the big enemy Anger. When the weaver gets angry, the threads go wrong. The weaver forgets her way."

Carolyn felt the words burning their way inside her. Stella continued translating.

"What this old one say is that a good weaver must find the harmony place. That is the white people's word for it. The place of harmony. Weaving is a way of sitting still within the harmony place. That's what my mother says. In the harmony place there is no room for the enemy. That is what my mother tells me to tell you."

When the rug was finished and removed from the loom, Stella, Nancy, and Allen Begay came into the cabin for a look. Carolyn held up her rug and I stood aside, trying to make sense out of the lighthearted laughter and the indecipherable comments. The rug was apparently a success.

"They'll give you seventy-five dollars at the trading post," Allen teased.

We wanted to show the rug to Mrs. Thompson, so we tested our luck with soggy roads and only got stuck twice on the way to the Thompson's place. Carolyn's work was warmly praised, and Mrs. Thompson gave her a much-used, good-quality spindle, along with a bag of raw, unspun wool. Learning that we were packing up to leave, Mrs. Thompson invited us to live with them next time we returned.

Our bundles were ready for the road when Harry and Mary Anthony, Mary Ann, Fred, and Loretta came to Stella's for a visit. The medicine man broke out into a wide grin when he saw the rug. He was his usual comic self, playing tricks and making us laugh. By contrast, Mary offered no comment about Carolyn's achievement.

After another feast, Mary told stories. We understood enough Navajo to know Mary was talking about our five months at the Anthony camp. But no one chose to translate, so most of what was told passed us by.

"She did it again," Carolyn said to me later. "Everyone was having a good time, yet Mary didn't give me more than a passing glance the entire evening."

Carolyn felt she owed Mary apologies for having been so demanding and imposing on the family for so many weeks. We decided to drive by for a final round of thanks and farewells. The reception was cold, the visit short. Only Fred and Loretta seemed interested in conversation. We left feeling tangled in a hopeless web of contradictory impressions. We had been issued our exit visas from the land of purple mountains and orange earth.

We headed north and west, relieved to be putting distance between ourselves and a place where life had often been less comprehensible than the language. Nevertheless, our Navajo experience seemed unfinished and incomplete. We approached the Canadian border convinced we would return to Arizona within a year or two.

3

Emergence

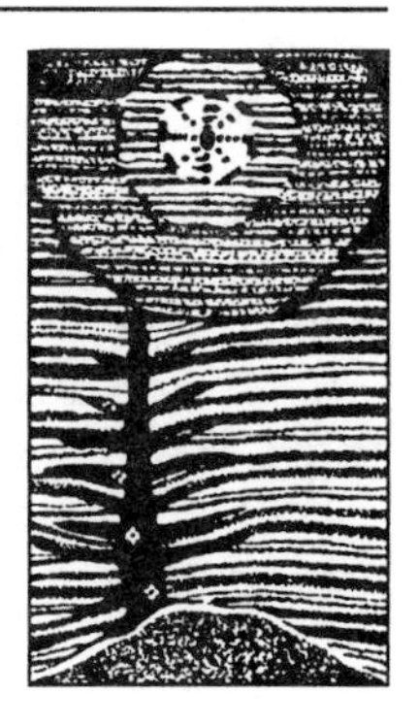

Outside Vancouver, where suburban sprawl was beginning to penetrate forest and farm land, we rented an old two-story house on five acres. Dense bush covered most of the property. Great blue herons nested in the red cedars. Deer periodically emerged from nearby mountains to graze in the meadow-like clearing back of the house.

We hauled truckloads of firewood to feed our wood-burning stoves. We plowed a large garden area, and in the spring planted seeds. The soil proved to be fertile and the garden produce abundant, and a seasonal cycle commenced that was to last four years.

I was teaching cultural anthropology and comparative religion courses at a new community college and was involved in a full schedule of day classes, special curriculum development, committee work, and adult education programs.

I painted our kitchen sunshine yellow. Friends joked about Carolyn's Cosmic Kitchen. She ground wheat in a grain mill, and every day mixed up a batter for biscuits, buns, pancakes, and whole wheat bread. She made candles and a strange variety of soap. She put up jellies, jams, chutney, preserves, and sauces made from the apricots, peaches, apples, cherries, and plums we picked in the Okanagan orchards of interior British Columbia.

The home industry and conservation streak surfacing in Carolyn astonished me. The industry was not confined to the kitchen. In some respects we could have called our place Camp Navajo North. I was asked to paint the wool room forest green. Carolyn learned how to spin wool with the spindle Mrs. Thompson had given her. She used onion skins, walnut shells, marigolds, plum tree bark, fireweed, and rock lichen to dye wool various shades of green, yellow, brown, and beige. She rediscovered knitting needles and knit thick sweaters with homespun wool. I installed a Navajo-type log loom in the green room, and Carolyn picked up comb and batten to weave pillow covers, curtains, and floor rugs. She wove herself a winter coat. From time to time she worked on a tapestry.

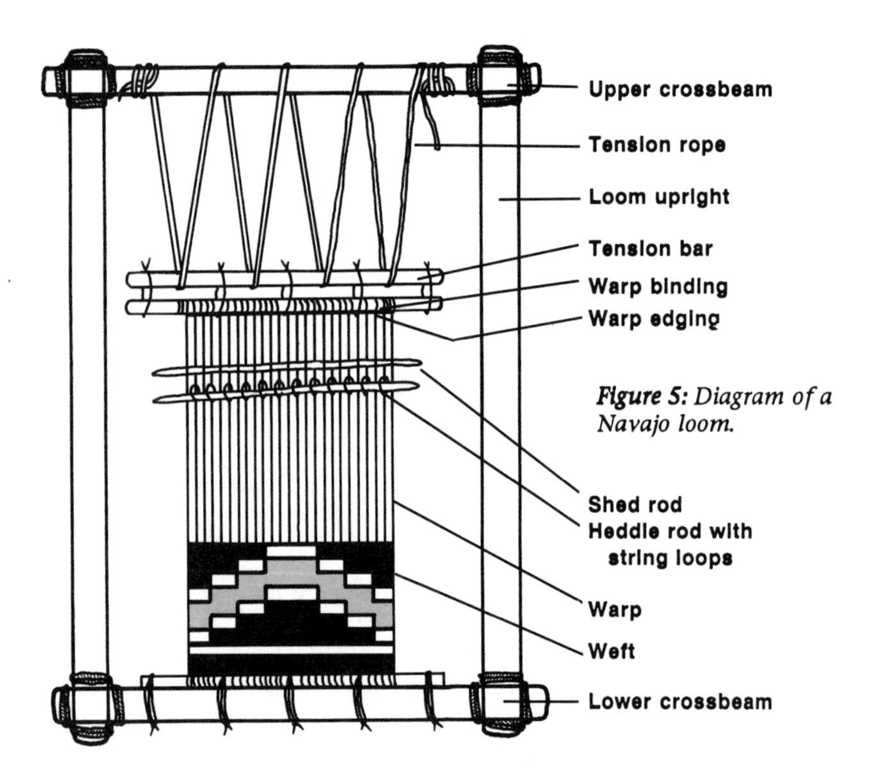

Figure 5: Diagram of a Navajo loom.

The first priority for tapestry work was to learn to improve technique. The initial work reflected design ideas inspired by Mary Anthony or Mrs. Thompson, and each rug demonstrated increased facility with the tools and techniques. Carolyn also developed a habit of keeping journal notes about design ideas, color choices, technical difficulties, and discoveries.

On the fourth day of January, 1974, the telephone rang, bringing news that would initiate another dramatic change in our lives. A social worker informed us that in a few days we were to fly to the Queen Charlotte Islands, seven hundred miles north of Vancouver, and complete adoption proceedings for a baby girl born three days after Christmas.

A large tapestry occupied the loom. Carolyn knows the precise thread woven in when the call came. The tapestry was patterned after an old-style Navajo design known as *Chief's Blanket*. Carolyn removed the half-finished rug from the loom and quickly strung up another warp. In the days before our journey north, Carolyn devoted every spare minute to a papoose wrap, woven with handspun, plant-dyed wool. Two woven sections were sewn together during our air flight and finished during a barge ferry ride across Queen Charlotte Sound, the same day we were to meet the ten-day-old girl for the first time.

That night, we told our baby her name: Crystal. We celebrated the event with a sleepless night. Carolyn wrote in her journal.

> Suddenly, a baby!
> Tiny. Sleeping. Waking. Crying.
> Born from the universe.
> A baby awake, a living dream.
> All memory, potential, all life,
> Everything inside and outside is united
> In her, all one.
>
> Nourishing. Caring
> Awakening to a new direction.
> A new idea. A new life. A new way.
> Who am I, mother of this new one?

Crystal's presence added new dimensions to the various enterprises of Cedar Road farmhouse. Her energies were irresistible, her demands unmistakable. And her arrival coincided with a renewed attention to dreams.

"Dreams contain a symbolic language that I believe to be a direct expression of my inner Self," Carolyn wrote in her journal. "When I attend to dreams, I realize it's up to me to make a choice. I could ignore dreams, dismiss them as meaningless fantasy. Or, I accept the challenge and relate to dreams as teachings. I have decided that however horrifying or enlightening, a story is to be found in dreams, and the author of that story is me."

> I am in tall grass beside the garden at sunrise. I walk through long

healthy rows of corn plants, then see large white birds flying up.
A beautiful, fair-haired young woman appears beside the garden, holding a large egg. She tells me she will take good care of the egg and not allow cutworms to kill the unborn white bird.

The egg is an archetypal image; within its shell is all the knowledge and potential of a developing life. The egg seems to be symbolic of an imminent birth of consciousness, a creative potential about to break through and take flight. The cutworms suggested the need to protect from harm the emerging inner life.

Carolyn began weaving a new tapestry, and birds again entered into her dreaming, accompanied by a sign.

People are silhouetted against a background of night sky and the ocean. I am lying on my back feeling wind in my hair. Something strong moves through me. I know something big is about to happen.

The silhouetted people turn towards the crescent moon. A crescent moon rises above a star cluster which forms a triangle. An inverted triangle is reflected in moonlit water. It's a star-water sign. And then I see a water lily in full bloom.

I am beside a tapestry loom. I have begun a rug with brilliant colors: red, orange, green, white. I notice a perfect circle in the weaving which turns out to be an opening. I reach through and pull out a long, blue-grey feather which uncoils as I pull. I lay the feather to one side, then find more feathers, and baby birds with long feathers. I watch the little birds moving. I see them growing, growing bigger, becoming stronger. I watch them for a long time until they fly away in a "V" pattern.

I go to the side of the loom and look behind. A corridor, adjacent to the weaving, leads to a doorway. I see that there was plenty of room for the birds to grow there, and realize they must have flown away through the doorway.

The art of tapestry was giving Carolyn more than woven designs. There was life and movement *behind* the art of tapestry, growing within her, learning to fly. Tapestry was also linked to the full bloom of the water lily and to qualities suggested in the star-water sign.

When Crystal was five months old, she laughed out loud for the first time. We decided to follow a Navajo precedent and celebrate the event with a feast. We invited our friends, and as part of the celebration, we passed Crystal around our circle. She screamed her protests, exactly the reaction we had seen in a Navajo First-Laughs-Out-Loud ceremony. After everyone had gone home, Crystal laughed again.

The harvest moon arrived and the garden's yield surpassed our expectations. We packed away all we needed, with more than enough potatoes, pumpkins, squash, and onions to give to neighbors and friends. With the arrival of winter, Carolyn found more time for her loom, and time also to renew her attention to dreams.

When looking into our own dream images, we leaned towards a Jungian point of view, looking for recurring themes or patterns that might reflect what Jung called the archetypes found in the ancient myths. Jung believed that each of us possess an inherited memory of the whole of human endeavor and history which influences our behavior and personality in a variety of ways. This vast memory rarely makes itself evident consciously, but we retain it nevertheless in what Jung called the collective unconscious, vestiges of which appear in our dreams. Intriguing as Jung's ideas are, Carolyn and I were not looking for conclusive interpretations. Dreaming is a turning of the eyes inward and offers an invaluable reflection of aspects of waking reality. We entered into the world of dreaming like children, gradually becoming more familiar with the strange inner landscape.

During that winter, Carolyn worked on a tapestry called *Seven Stars*, spending an hour or two a day at the loom and making slow progress over a period of months. The design seemed to be associated with a slowly unfolding awareness of inner life, as revealed in dreams, and also with a realization that completion of the tapestry was coinciding with Crystal's learning to walk. Carolyn wrote in her journal:

> The tapestry is nearing completion.
> I am familiar now with the weaver's tools.
> My hands, my concentration, my time,
> These are the tools I also need for weaving.
>
> Weaving reveals patterns in my movement.
> Does *Seven Stars* know the nature of my journey?
> Does she have the patience to wait for me,
> While I weave her into being?
> Born in the spring, she has seen the seasons change,
> Watched the seasons move in me.
> *Seven Stars* knows my every breath
> And now has a life of her own.
>
> It is the way of the unborn
> To surprise when formed.
> With knowledge and care,
> Beauty is there.

Crystal takes her first free steps today.
She lightly clutches air,
Moving cautiously, yet boldly,
Balancing, testing her world.
She ventures a step or two, then goes down,
Returning to the security of a crawl on all fours.
Her excitement, my excitement, to find a new way,
Standing up, walking alone.

When *Seven Stars* was removed from the loom, the edges proved to be even, the design center corresponded to the tapestry center, and the angles were woven with uniform slope. A basic Navajo design idea had been developed into an overall pattern of Carolyn's own creation. The creative child was asserting itself, learning to walk. Like Crystal, who grounded herself on all fours before taking a stand, Carolyn knew herself to be firmly grounded in the traditions of Navajo weaving.

I could see the progress Carolyn made with each tapestry. The sound in the house produced by the weaving comb seemed to me an essential sound. The drumming seemed the echo of my own heartbeat. Without it, the house lacked something necessary.

"Weave more," I said.

"Crystal needs my time," Carolyn argued. "And what am I going to do with all these apples?"

"You're an artist and everyone knows it except you," I said. "Weaving deserves a priority at least equal to applesauce."

Carolyn stoked the fire and put four more loaves of whole-wheat bread into the oven. "Who would ever want to buy one of my tapestries?"

"Forget about selling," I said. "Just think about weaving."

Carolyn's perception of herself as an artist was given a substantial boost when a friend, noted Haida artist Robert Davidson, suggested a trade of one of his silver bracelets for a tapestry. Carolyn had given many of her woven items away as Christmas presents, and sold two fine tapestries for less than one hundred dollars. The next time Carolyn asked herself who would want her work, all she needed to do was look at an exquisitely crafted bracelet, traded for a tapestry called *Lightning Mountain* (see Plate 1).

Carolyn wrote a lecture to herself.

You could weave, Carolyn. You could begin a weaving business. You're not weaving now—too much to do. You think you don't have enough time, enough room, enough experience. Yes, you are good, I suppose, but you must study, gain skill, grow. You only have the surface stuff of weaving. . . .

Wait. Your time, what you do is valuable. That's what they're telling you, isn't it. 'Take pride in what you do,' they say. 'Why don't you stop hiding,' they say. 'Can't you see yourself?'

You give another tapestry away and friends ask, 'What are you doing? You can't give your work away forever. Why don't you value your work?'

'Stop apologizing,' they say. Say 'Yes,' once in a while. Say 'Yes, you're right, the work is okay. I appreciate the compliment.'

But no, you remain hypnotized. All knowing inside is flooded away by the outside shoulds, oughts, doubts, uncertainties, fears. So where does real knowing begin?

I feel movement.
Yes, movement within my heart and mind.
It is beautiful to perceive.

I take a step on a path,
To follow my heart.
I take steps in my mind,
Wanting the path to be clear,
With beauty surrounding.

The song of the earth is my song.
I want a song to herald the beauty,
To be beautiful indeed.

After Carolyn's lecture to herself, she strung a new warp, intending to produce a tapestry for the marketplace. Carolyn prepared a traditional Navajo saddle-blanket weave, thinking a saddle blanket the most practical, saleable item she could weave. An acquaintance who had recently purchased a horse heard about the project and came by when the weaving was completed. She loved the work immediately, but the price Carolyn asked was higher than what the woman had paid for her horse. As a compromise, Carolyn sold a large floor rug for twenty dollars, woven two years before in a first attempt at saddle-blanket weave. The new blanket would have to wait for another buyer.

We had been living in the Cedar Road farmhouse for four years while the area was rezoned for residential and commercial development, allowing suburban swell to surround us. Local farmers moved, leaving behind their homes, horse sheds, and chicken coops. The stand of cedar bush in back of our property was leveled, destroying the nesting trees for the great blue herons. We received a notice to vacate. A week before moving, a man in a hard-hat knocked on our kitchen door and asked permission to park his bulldozer in our garden. We moved into a Vancouver apartment but returned to Cedar Road a few days later to recover a few odds and ends. We found the house leveled, the five acres of trees and meadow ripped up and reduced to mounds of rubble, roots, and broken boards.

Figure 6: *Carolyn's first tapestry for the marketplace was a traditional Navajo saddle-blanket weave.*

I built a new, modified Navajo loom to install in the Vancouver apartment. Carolyn commenced design work, committed, at least in principle, to make the move from Cedar Road to city, a move into new priorities for her time. The result of this decision was a tapestry of delicate design and gentle colors called *Emergence*. The tapestry completion was followed by a long dream, vividly recalled, offering further confirmation of the directions in which Carolyn's artistic emergence would go.

> I am in a large hall with a Chinese master. He is light, agile, and wears a two-piece, loose-fitting, dark blue silk suit. He teaches me several T'ai Chi movements.
>
> His hands are black. He has more than five fingers on each hand, and the center finger of his left hand is forked. He has supreme control over the independent movement of each of his fingers. The movement is a kind of dance of the hands.
>
> Many adults and children arrive in the hall. The master begins

moving his fingers in such a way that they each divide. This division continues until there are enough fingers for at least thirty children to hold on to. The master's black fingers grow longer, becoming spider-like, bending in the middle, slowly rising and lowering. Each child holds a finger and the master dances, maintaining a position in the northwest corner of the large, square hall. Completely in control of the spider-finger dance, the master oversees the surrounding circle of children.

I am in the southeast corner of the hall. A young, yellow haired boy begins singing in a high, clear voice. "Beauty indeed," he sings. Others join in, singing "Beauty indeed."

Everyone leaves the hall except the master and myself. He teaches me new T'ai Chi movements and I follow his lead.

I see a woman in the far east side of the room. She has short, yellow-brown hair, and is dressed in sand-colored silk slacks and a fawn-colored quilted silk jacket.

The master introduces me. "This is your mother," he says. His voice is full of pleasure and warmth. "This is your Eternal Mother."

I lie down with her and rest my head against her breast. Her silk jacket envelops me. She smiles. Waves of feeling for her sweep over me. I seem to dissolve, merging with her smile. I become one with her.

Then I am high above, seeing us lying on the center of a large rug that completely covers the hall floor. Many designs in black are either woven or written into the sand color background. The rug looks like a Navajo sand painting, but the design also suggests Chinese characters. The design seems to be a form of writing about ancient history and civilization.

4

Beauty Equals Harmony

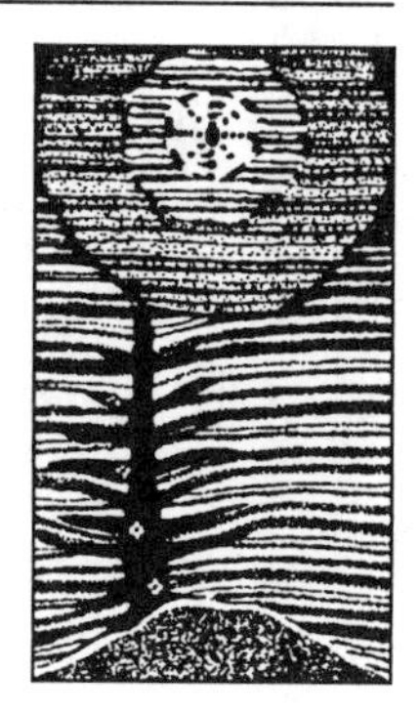

"Beauty indeed," sang the yellow-haired boy in Carolyn's dream. The boy's song echoes a fundamental principle of Navajo world view found in their prayers, myths, and ceremonials.

Navajo weavers introduced Carolyn to much more than weaving tools and techniques. Their world view permeates the entire weaving process. By introducing Carolyn to their way of understanding beauty, they laid the foundation for her approach to design.

The Navajo regard the universe as supremely beautiful and intrinsically harmonious. They view humanity as part of nature and in no way separated from nature. Beauty to the Navajo is not an abstract concept, not something perceived as external or as something to be searched for by an appreciative viewer. They believe beauty to be an intrinsic quality of Being, experienced by living a good life and especially by creating beauty continually. Three Navajo words, repeated in songs and prayers, best describe their perception of humanity. They can be only approximated by English phrases, and have been translated in this way:

With me there is beauty.
In me there is beauty.
From me, beauty radiates.[1]

"In the beginning God created heaven and earth," describes the biblical Genesis. For the Navajo, Genesis might read, "In the beginning and in this very moment, the gods and humanity, working together, create the sky and the earth." Creation is perceived as an ongoing, ever-present, living process, and as much in human hands as in the gods'.

It has often been said that in our society we have more art critics than artists, more collectors than creators. In Navajo society, it is the exceptional individual who is not involved in creative activity of one kind or another. Creation of beauty is seen as both natural and necessary, the destiny of a person who follows the Navajo way.

Navajo conceptions of beauty are perhaps best expressed in their Blessing Way, also called the Walks-Within-Beauty Way. Blessing Way forms the backbone of the entire ceremonial practice, as all the healing rites derive from it. The Blessing Way ceremony itself lasts from one to three days and is used during a girl's initiation, or Becoming-a-Woman ceremony; for the marriage ceremony; for the opening of a new house; and during the conclusion of the major healing ceremonies. Its ultimate purpose is to ensure well-being. In a characteristic Blessing Way prayer, a person is asked to recognize the beauty before and behind, beauty above and below, beauty surrounding, beauty everywhere, until

> It is completed in Beauty.
> In Beauty I am restored to Harmony.
> This day, I am restored, I say.
> With happiness becoming mine again, I say.
> It is beautiful indeed.
> It is beautiful indeed.[2]

I recall Harry Anthony telling me, with his son Fred translating, "Blessing Way maintains good mind, a good heart, right activity, right relations. Following that way gives us long life and happiness and we find harmony." Blessing Way is much more than a ceremony when discussed by Harry Anthony. It's a way of life.

According to Navajo creation mythology, the first Blessing Way was created by the Holy People and given to Changing Woman, who in turn instructed the Earth-Surface People whom she had created to be her companions in the present world. Changing Woman personifies mysteries of birth, life, death, and transformation and is the embodiment of a fundamental Navajo equation, that Beauty equals Harmony, in both inner and outer forms.

To the Navajo, a mountain perceived out there also has an inner form which we do not see with our normal vision. Everything we know has this inner form, or unseen essential quality. The sunrise has inner form, as does water, wind, each plant and animal, and every human being. The loom also has inner form.

According to a creation story, "Spider Woman instructed Navajo women how to weave on a loom which Spider Man told them how to make. The loom's crosspoles were made of sky and earth cords, the warp sticks of sun rays, the heddles of rock crystal and sheet lightning. The batten was a sun halo, white shell made the comb."[3]

A Navajo loom looks like a rough assemblage of logs, rope, and wire, and it may be set up in a shelter with little protection from roving goats or dust, but every weaver knows her loom's inner form represents a marriage of Father Sky and Mother Earth. The offspring from this marriage is the woven design, and that design is an expression of Beauty equals Harmony. The highest standards of excellence to be found in rug designs and weaving technique are reflected in this equation.

There are many ways to determine quality in a Navajo rug—for example,the fineness of the threads used, the quality of colors, the straightness of edges. A good test of quality is to fold the rug in half and see whether the middle of the rug corresponds to the middle of the design. Another test is to look for correspondence in color and design details above the center with those same details below the center. In either case, the test is for symmetry: harmonious relationships between parts and whole. A good-quality rug contains the essential fabric of Navajo philosophy.

The loom has inner form—so too does the weaving. It can be said that a woven design's inner form is the weaver's mind, or her entire attitude when weaving. To say it another way, the completed tapestry is the outer form of the weaver's mind. A mental image guides the entire weaving process. Of great importance, however, is the weaver's relationship to the individual row of thread. Though a design is conceived as a whole and must be held in mind, a completed pattern depends entirely on the correct placement of threads in every single row of weaving. These single rows are like steps a person takes when following a path. For the Navajo, patterns in life also depend on appropriately taken individual steps. When steps go wrong, a responsible person resorts to ceremony and transformative measures to ensure a return to walking in the Blessing Way.

Life rarely reflects the perfect symmetry found in woven design. The greater share of Navajo ceremonials are given to restore balance, to recover health and happiness that have been lost. Even a common accident like falling off a horse is perceived by the old-timers as a consequence of inappropriate behavior either during the horse ride or some time earlier. Anything from a headache, to bad thoughts or bad dreams, to terminal cancer signals a wrong move made somewhere, sometime, a stepping away from the teachings and practice of the Blessing Way.

Today, medicine people still offer a pinch of corn pollen to the sunrise with a prayer to honor the arrival of a new day, but they do so entirely aware that the climate of the times reveals increasing disharmony. Some Navajo attend ceremonials caring more about the availability of wine and less about the presence of medicine bundles. Tribal councils bow to the demands of oil and coal companies and rake in the revenues while relatives die in Gallup, New Mexico, streets. The pain and sadness run deep in medicine people who see their own sons and daughters pay homage to a stranger's greedy god, sacrificing creative energies to the money-centered, consumer-oriented values of the larger society.

The pervading climate prompts native prophets to emerge from their centers of silence to reveal what they foresee. Whether Navajo, Hopi, Cheyenne, or Cree, the message is the same. Like the people, Mother Earth is ailing, and moving towards profound change. Signs everywhere reflect a world gone crazy.

Every part is related to the whole. The above mirrors the below. So say the medicine people. Modern philosophers and ecologists say much the same, repeating corollaries of the beauty/harmony equation known to native Americans for generations.

This relationship is referred to as mirror symmetry. Symmetry is also to be found in subtle relationships between weaver and weaving. A design of quality reflects a weaver of quality. A weaver's care and discipline, her creative capabilities, her rapport with both inner and outer forms all reflect symmetrical relationships between weaver and weaving.

In a Blessing Way prayer, the outer form of the individual for whom the ceremonial is being given is identified with the outer form of the earth, and in the prayer's second section, the individual's inner form is identified with the earth's inner form, then the inner form of mountains and various deities. Perhaps weavers recall the song while drumming threads into place and watching their work slowly take on life of its own.

Earth's feet have become my feet
    by means of these I shall live on.
Earth's legs have become my legs
    by means of these I shall live on.
Earth's body has become my body
    by means of this I shall live on.

Earth's mind has become my mind . .
(Repeat as before)
Earth's voice has become my voice . . .
Earth's headplume has become my headplume . . .

Hózhó (beauty/harmony) has been restored.
Hózhó has been restored.
Hózhó has been restored.
Hózhó has been restored.
It is surprising, surprising . . .
It is the very inner form of Earth that continues
to move within me, that has risen with me,
that is standing with me, that indeed
remains stationary with me . . .

(Repeat, naming mountains and deities)[4]

This process of ritual restoration and returning to a state of hózhó, or beauty and harmony, must occur within a weaver also as she drums her threads into place and watches her work slowly take on a life of its own. A weaver must learn mental discipline, a level of paying attention which Carolyn sometimes refers to as loom attitude. We often wondered what Mrs. Goldtooth meant when she said, "Weaving is a sitting still within the harmony place."

Weaving tapestry is not accomplished from a physically comfortable position or posture. In Navajo land, weavers sit cross-legged on the floor or on a sheepskin pelt. Light in a hogan is often very poor, but even in good light, dealing with hundreds of threads puts strain on the eyes. Work with the comb requires a vigorous motion to pound threads tightly into place. This tires the arm and shoulder. Pulling heddle rods and inserting the batten in a warp that is fixed with very high tension takes its toll in the shoulders and lower back. The body also registers tension generated by the mental concentration. Carolyn now weaves on a modern tapestry loom and sits on a bench, but the entire process is still very demanding.

Physical discomfort, however, is taken into account in the whole importance the Navajo give to the weaver's spot, and every weaver learns she must adjust to the position regardless of body aches and pains. Once a weaver sits down at the loom and takes the weaving comb in hand, her mind must become ready, her attention focused. Experienced weavers make this transition look easy, as if work at the loom is just another thing to do during the day, but even the weaver who has mastered her technique knows she must achieve a rapport with her work. The weaving spot is sacred ground in the sense that a special activity is engaged upon once she begins to work. In spite of physical discomfort, the weaver must find harmony within, harmony without. The colors must be entered correctly, the design built up appropriately, and the weaver must keep track of all the threads, row after row.

Carolyn has often asked herself why Navajo weavers choose geometric patterns to best express their principles of beauty/harmony. Weavers did not discuss with us the symbolic meanings in their designs. When asked, they usually said, "I don't know about meanings to it, my mother taught it to me this way." Later, we realized the response was more than it first seemed. Kinship terms referring to the biological mother can be extended by the Navajo to include Mother Earth. In a sense, what we were being told in the characteristic response is that the earth is the true source of all design.

Looking for meaning in her own emerging art, Carolyn also wondered how the Navajo determined factors of size and proportion in their designs. These questions relating to geometry, size, and proportion became a starting place for Carolyn's search for relevant design ideas that could express a beauty/harmony equation of her own. A dream helped her on her way.

She dreamed she told an art instructor that she wanted to study art through the ages. The instructor opened a large book with gold leaf cover and referred to a reproduction of a seventeenth century masterpiece. It was a portrait of a marriage painted in chiaroscuro lighting. A radiant, light-haired woman wore a richly jeweled, magenta dress. The man was dark haired, focusing all his attention on the woman, and seemed to be offering payment, perhaps for her lavishly elegant dress. The instructor then found a footnote reference to another book, titled *Art Through the Ages.*

From this dream, Carolyn derived one of the first principles of her art. Woven art, like the painted portrait, must convey the principle of marriage. Carolyn sees in the portrait a marriage of beauty and form, with form acknowledging beauty.

For Carolyn, dreaming is a way of weaving, and weaving is a way of dreaming. Both processes interrelate conscious and unconscious, masculine and feminine, dark and light, beauty and form. "In weaving and in dreaming," she says, "I touch the archetypes. In many respects the warp in weaving is like the collective unconscious, and the weft is my personal experience woven into the collective. The warp is also like a medicine wheel, the weft my way of exploring the four directions, the cross, the circle, the center."

The dream inspired Carolyn to begin researching artistic expression around the world and through the ages. No doubt this research will last a lifetime, but while weaving her tapestry called *Emergence,* Carolyn discovered two books which were very important for the next stages of her work. In D'Arcy Thompson's classic *On Growth and Form,* and Matila Ghyka's *The Geometry of Art and Life,* Carolyn found that the Navajo were not alone in their appreciation of a beauty/harmony equation.

Like the Navajo, Plato believed that the universe exists in a state of perfect harmony. Platonic schools emphasized four areas of study: astronomy, music, arithmetic, and geometry. Their conceptions of beauty or aesthetics were derived from a sense of harmony in the universe and a belief in mystical properties of number. Centuries before Plato the Pythagoreans had arrived at a similar explanation of universal harmony. Pythagoreans believed that the source of knowledge could be found in number. They derived their philosophy in part from the Babylonians and Egyptians. Carolyn discovered that relationships of numbers and geometry, harmony and beauty, have deep roots in ancient civilizations.

Symmetry was a key ingredient of Platonic and pre-Platonic aesthetics. For the Greeks, the definition of symmetry extended beyond static symmetry, or the infinite repetition or duplication of equal parts in a whole; symmetry was related to proportion, or what they called *anologia,* meaning consonance between part and whole. The relationship of unequal parts in a whole, or dynamic symmetry, better expressed their view of symmetry.

There is a particular proportion, found throughout classical Greek art and architecture, which describes a unique relation of two unequal parts in a whole design or form. This proportion, revered by Pythagoreans, regarded as supreme by Plato, and called divine by Kepler and da Vinci, is known as the Golden Section, or *phi,* and is expressed by the notation Ø. Its most renowned application is in the Parthenon. The proportion was believed to reflect cosmological principles, and because the human body was seen as a reflection of the cosmos, Greek sculptors devised complete anatomical descriptions of the ideal human skeleton in terms of the proportion. The proportion reappeared in Renaissance times when architects and artists rediscovered the powers of numbers and geometry to reflect cosmology and principles of harmony. Knowledge of the proportion crossed continents and oceans; it can be found, for example, in the Citadel of Teotihuacan in Mexico.[5]

D'Arcy Thompson described the role of the Golden Section and *phi* in terms of the patterns of growth and form to be found in the natural world. He has shown, for example, that a geometric curve called an equiangular or logarithmic spiral precisely represents the principle of growth that governs the formation of spiral-shaped seashells. It can be expressed by a simple law which states that the shell grows longer and wider according to an unvarying proportion, the *phi* proportion; i.e., the shell grows larger in size without changing shape. This law accounts for spiral growth in animal horns, distribution of leaves around a stem, arrangement of seeds in a sunflower, growth patterns of flower petals, and the development of animal and human bones. Thompson demonstrates that mathematical laws, including geometric proportions such as *phi,* characterize the action of inner forces that shape the outer form of living things. Though stated differently, Thompson's discussions echo Navajo conceptions of inner and outer form.

The unique relationship between two unequal parts in a whole can be shown in a division of a line into what is called the Golden Section or Golden Mean. The line is divided according to the following principle: A is to B as B is to A + B, or, said another way, the small part is in proportion to the large part as the large part is to the whole.

In a Golden Rectangle, the shorter side is the Golden Mean of the same rectangle's longer side. This rectangle has the unique property that if a square is drawn inside the rectangle, using the rectangle's shorter side as the side of the square, then a new rectangle is formed outside the square which is also a *phi* or Golden Rectangle. This subdivision can be repeated into smaller and smaller squares, and smaller and smaller rectangles outside the square, and each new rectangle is still a *phi* rectangle.

In the five-pointed star or pentagram, each line crosses the other at the point marking the Golden Mean of the line. It was of interest to Carolyn that the five-pointed star was used as a badge by Pythagoreans to symbolize heath and inner harmony, and pentagonal forms are often found in nature, especially in flowers.[6]

Phi is related to an additive series called the Fibonacci number series. In the series, 1, 1, 2, 3, 5, 8, 13, 21, 34, 55, etc., each element is equal to the sum of the two preceding elements. Ratios derived from any two consecutive numbers in the Fibonacci series approach closer to *phi* values the farther the series is extended.

The Pythagoreans and Plato had stressed the powers of whole numbers and their relationships to one another, but the Golden Section was regarded even more highly because it could not be expressed in whole numbers. It's an unending decimal, 1.618. *Phi* is irrational, incommensurable, transcendent. The Fibonacci series comes close to a whole number approximation of *phi,* but *phi* can be derived only

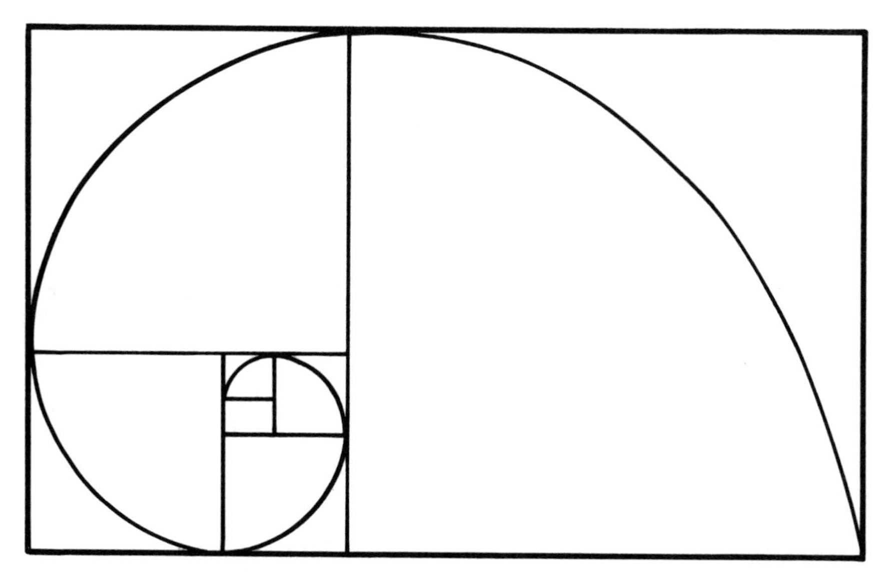

***Figure 7:** The discovery of the Golden Rectangle allowed Carolyn to move beyond the influences of Navajo weaving into new areas of design. The related Golden Section, Fibonacci number series, and Logarithmic Spiral enabled Carolyn to find her own sense of symmetry and harmony in her tapestry designs.*

geometrically, not arithmetically. Nevertheless, as Thompson emphasizes, *phi* principles appear in nature and growth patterns at very elemental levels.

The realization that mathematical laws underlie the processes of nature and harmonious patterns in nature was just the key Carolyn needed to move into new areas of designing. Learning properties of the *phi* proportion and the related Fibonacci series allowed her to move beyond influences of Navajo design to find dynamic symmetries appropriate to her developing artistry.

Carolyn's tapestry *Emergence,* though Navajo in its essential design concept, represented a departure because its overall dimensions and design content were conceived in terms of *phi* proportions. In *Spring Pollen,* woven after *Emergence,* each design unit was arranged according to the Fibonacci number series. Color areas were defined in height and width by successive numbers in the series. Still retaining the principle of mirror symmetry, the tapestry nevertheless represents a move further away from Navajo design in her use of color mixing technique. Each area was composed of more than one color and woven

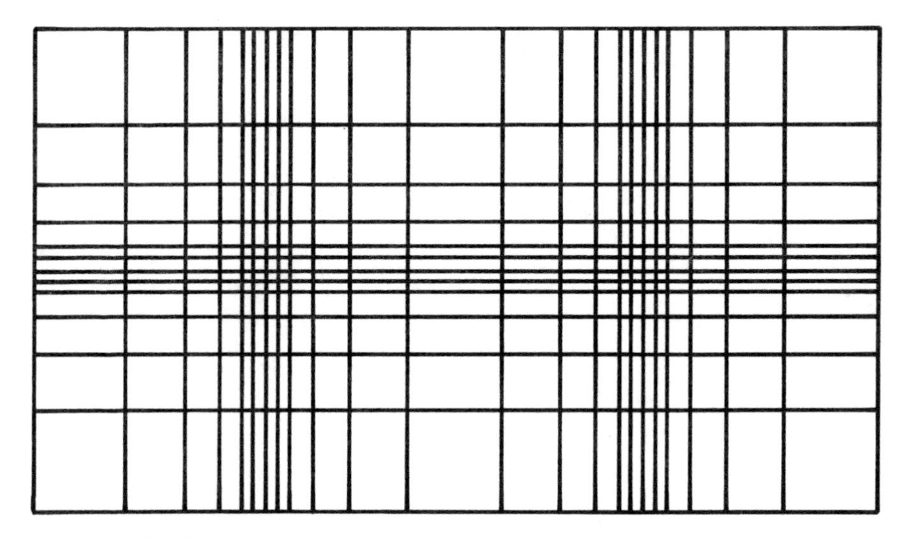

Figure 8: The design elements for Carolyn's tapestry Spring Pollen *are arranged, both vertically and horizontally, according to the Fibonacci number series.*

according to a count of rows. *Spring Pollen* proved to be the most technically difficult tapestry Carolyn had attempted, and it demanded new levels of concentration.

Carolyn's awareness of the importance of mathematics in weaving led her to further explore the potential of mathematics for tapestry design. She began reading math and geometry books, and looked up equations for graphing lines having various slopes, then studied algebraic formulas by which she could plot points for curved lines.

In her next tapestry, Carolyn found a means of translating points plotted on graph paper to points on the warp. In *Four Looks East,* tapestry dimensions and design proportions were again determined by *phi* ratios. The design included her first curved lines, as well as slopes she had never attempted before. The tapestry's asymmetrical center was found by intersecting vertical and horizontal golden means of the warp's length and width.

If art was to be a marriage of Beauty and Form, then perhaps mathematics was one of the tributes Form gives to Beauty. Carolyn wondered if ideal beauty could in some way be achieved by uniting art and mathematics. Whether such an ideal could in fact be achieved did not preoccupy her, but rather motivated her more than ever to relate to each new tapestry as a challenge to technical facility and her growing sense of design.

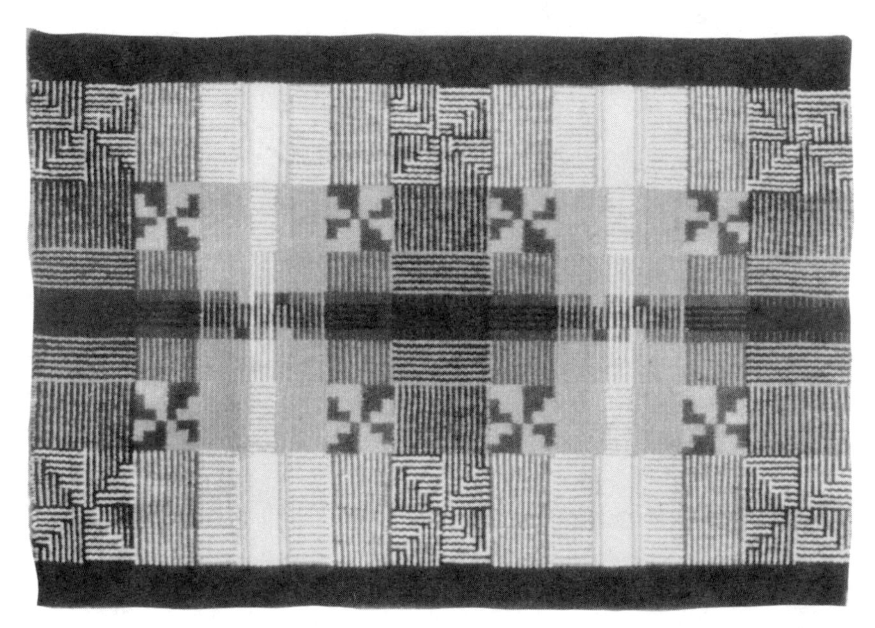

***Figure 9:** Spring Pollen*

Four Looks East includes a woven surprise. Carolyn departed from her carefully conceived, mathematical precision to allow a spontaneous element in the design. She wove an eye into the tapestry's northwest quadrant. When completed, it seemed as though something behind the design were looking out through the eye. The eye reminded Carolyn of the design she had dreamed about earlier, when through an opening in a weaving she saw birds growing up and flying away. This eye seemed to reveal new growth behind Carolyn's art. By becoming more familiar with her sitting-still-within-the-harmony-place, Carolyn was beginning to discover a beauty/harmony equation of her own.

5

Wings in Gold

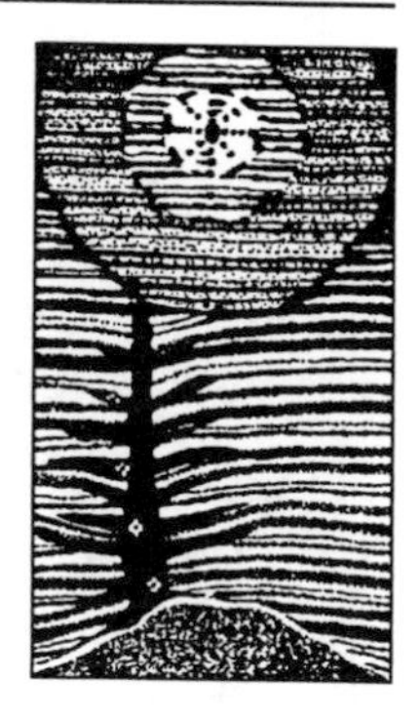

Carolyn made a pledge. She decided she wanted to create a design that would stand alone as a symbol of her intention to become a tapestry artist. This idea gathered momentum during the autumn of 1976 as Carolyn worked harder to find the meeting point between research, dream, tapestry technique, and woven design.

Carolyn was particularly drawn to Jacob Bronowski's discussion of Arab symmetry in his book *Ascent of Man*. In the tiled domes, walls, and floors of the great mosques, designs utilizing mirror, bilateral, and rotational symmetry reflect ancient systems of mathematics. Carolyn dug deeper into a study of the various kinds of symmetry. In preliminary drawings, she worked with an idea associated with the Pythagorean definition of the right angle: a principle of rotation is established for the ninety-degree angle, which, when turned around on itself four times, returns to the same point.

Carolyn had often found that frustrations generated by technical difficulties in weaving had to be overcome before a day's work could progress. She recalled Mrs. Goldtooth's warning about a weaver's enemy. "Keep the big enemy Anger away," she had said. The advice had proved invaluable. Anger could be a relentless adversary, provoked also by circumstances outside the weaving itself, including family pressures and world news. The enemy had to be dealt with before

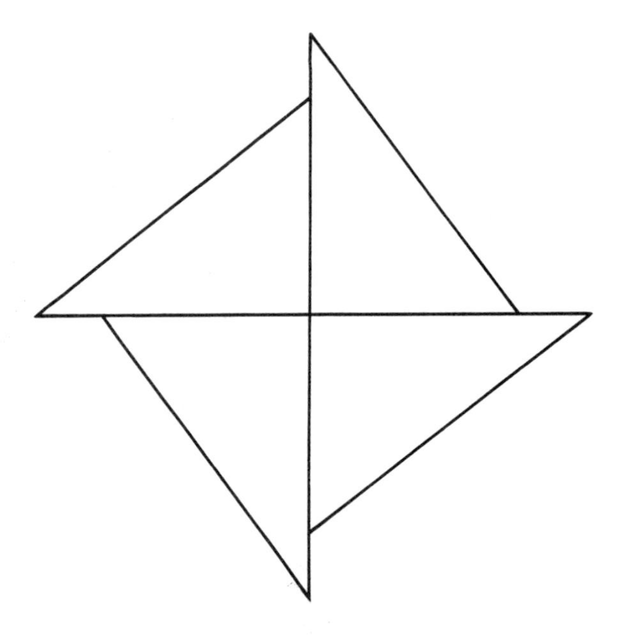

Figure 10: *In preliminary drawings for her tapestry* Wings in Gold, *Carolyn worked with principles of rotational symmetry generated by the ninety-degree, or right, angle.*

concentrative work could continue; otherwise, as Mrs. Goldtooth had said, "The design will go wrong." Carolyn now wondered what the old woman would say about another enemy, doubt.

Doubt was hanging over her shoulder whenever Carolyn contemplated design ideas outside the fundamental concepts taught by her first teachers. Doubt was ever-present when Carolyn considered bringing her work into the marketplace. It was a debilitating enemy, which struck whenever she felt the least bit vulnerable. But one day a break-through occurred as a result of picking up a pine cone.

"Something in me woke up when I saw the spiral rotation in the growth pattern of a pine cone," Carolyn said.

Carolyn realized that even though her designs appeared to depart from Navajo traditions, she would always be linked with her first teachers. She shared with them an appreciation of the earth as the Great Mother of all design, manifesting in countless forms, more than she could hope to weave in ten lifetimes.

We recalled a discussion with Chuck Storm about Plains Indian Dog Soldiers, especially disciplined warriors who were committed to individual pledges. To explain Dog Soldiers, Storm had asked us to imagine a circle of lodges in the prairie. The camp was located near a good source of water in promising hunting country. We were asked to imagine the people living in that circle. Mothers would organize camp activities while caring for the children. Hunters searched for food. Medicine people prayed for well-being and health. Warriors told their stories. Old ones taught the young. The circle of lodges remained a vibrant wheel of life.

Seen from the eye of a soaring eagle, however, the lodges appeared small compared to the vast surrounding prairie. The people understood a paradox of great importance: the prairie was at the same time provider of life and destroyer of life.

The Dog Soldier's society pledged to die in defense of the people. Danger assumed many guises in the camp: marauding bears, hungry wolves, and winter starvation; subtler dangers included camp jealousies, factionalism, doubts, and individual fears. The Dog Soldier placed himself between the people and whatever threatened them.

"Internalize the teaching," Storm said. "That is what the stories are for. A circle of lodges on the prairie is also a circle of lodges within me, within you. The prairie of everyday life nourishes, but also threatens. We must awaken the inner Dog Soldier, protector of the inner circle."

The teaching was precisely what Carolyn hoped to include in her design.

"My creative center will need its defender," she said. "I must weave a tapestry which will stand as a symbolic defense of my intention to follow a creative path." The task was to find a weavable image to convey a symbolic Dog Soldier.

No sooner had Carolyn made her pledge than a host of adversaries reared their heads. Doubt swept in again, and, in any vulnerable moment, frustrations and excuses of every size and description. What an army. Carolyn found, curiously, that her troop of problems withdrew when she plunged back into designing. Hard work and attention to purpose proved to be the best defense.

She found, for example, a preference for rotational symmetry generated by the pentagon. She had been attracted to Thompson's discussion of pentagonal symmetry, and after a few pentagon drawings she recalled another conversation with Storm. He had mentioned that the Cheyenne pentangle was both a star design and the sign of the human. Two points touch earth. Two extend out, like arms uplifted to touch the sky. The fifth or center point is the human head.

Dog Soldier. Pentagon. The human sign. The ideas were there. Carolyn continued drawing.

Extending the lines of the pentagon's sides to a length determined by the Fibonacci series established new points from which lines could be drawn to form a new pentagon. Repeating this process produced points and lines of larger pentagons that revolved around the original pentagon. Carolyn knew her design center would convey the sense of rotation. Many of the drawn lines now seemed right. But something else was needed.

During the slow unfolding of design details, Carolyn came to recognize her most formidable enemy, the source of all the forces that hammered at her pledge and stopped the work: fear. Its all too frequent appearance made Carolyn feel like a pretentious fool. I reminded her of a situation described in Carlos Castaneda's *Tales of Power* when the brujo Don Juan stated that a warrior accepts knowledge, however frightening or awesome. In Castaneda's "appointment with knowledge," fear was singled out as a great enemy to anyone choosing a path of heart. To battle such a foe required a warrior's clear intent, a disciplined mind and heart.

Returning to Bronowski's *Ascent of Man,* Carolyn found a picture of a Japanese sword maker. He was following ancient techniques of hammering steel softened by white-hot fire with the intent to fashion a perfect *samurai* sword.

"My design needs a weapon," Carolyn wrote in her journal.

She needed a warrior's weapon, but perhaps what she really wanted was a warrior's stance. She looked for it in T'ai Chi. Carolyn was practicing the movements regularly, having found an affinity with the system's inherent balances of strength and gentleness, advancing and yielding, motion and stillness. In T'ai Chi, the five points of the human—hands, feet, and head—must achieve maximum effectiveness with each shift of position. Carolyn studied the postures, looking for the right stance to suggest points and lines applicable to her emerging design.

One night she dreamed of a deep-sea plant that was part plant, part animal, a fish-like fern. The fern filtered its food, transforming it into a gold dust. The gold dust arranged itself into feathered forms having an appearance of moth or butterfly wings. The feathering grew until it became a yellow fabric that formed by absorbing plant-produced gold dust. Carolyn carefully folded the fabric and awoke, thinking, "It will be my robe. And I can use the gold dust any time to create gold material."

The dream indicated the strong alchemical processes within the unconscious that were continuing to grow while creative energy remained a focus of attention. The image reminded Carolyn of another Castaneda reference. The Yaqui sorcerer states that moths are heralds and guardians, depositories of the "gold dust of eternity."

Color ideas were clearly suggested in the dream. Gold, in combination with white, grey, and black, provided one of the concluding steps of designing. Points and lines had been found, colors chosen. Only one step remained.

To weave the sign of the human. Dog Soldier. The warrior's stance. The moth. Gold dust. Light. Dark. Symmetry.

All in one tapestry? I admitted to certain doubts, a grave error on my part. I came home one evening to find the house in a mess, no signs of activity in the kitchen, and an intensely unhappy Crystal. As for the woman of the house, I barely recognized her. It was the first time (but not the last) I found the weaver woman utterly absorbed by her work. She was virtually untouchable, as if surrounded by a circle of shields.

The next morning, Carolyn removed the blankets that covered the loom. She entered her weaving spot. She picked up the gnarled old comb and began drumming threads into place. Threads for a design of her own creation. Threads of carefully chosen colors. Threads of a pledge.

The weaving situation itself soon became another obstacle. We had moved from Vancouver to a second-floor apartment in New Westminster, within walking distance of the college where I was teaching. A typical British Columbia winter arrived, bringing freezing rains and wind. The apartment's heating system proved to be inadequate. Sliding glass doors overlooking the concrete playground did little to keep out the drafts. Carolyn battled the flu, complained of cold feet and hands, and woke up one day with swollen purple fingers. She sat at the loom regardless, and waited for lulls in playground noise before entering threads into the warp.

The ominous army, which seemed now to take on the appearance of a rampaging mob, attacked from new fronts. I had decided the autumn semester of teaching was to be my last.

"Write,"Carolyn often told me. "Weave with words."

She sounded almost like my own voice, reminding me of what I already knew. I had postponed a decision long enough. It was time to make a pledge of my own. We would soon be faced with the prospect of no secure income.

Carolyn continued weaving, determined to complete the tapestry before New Year's Day, when we planned to move. "Thump thump, thump thump," drummed the weaving comb. The rhythms established a first line of defense as thread after thread of changing colors was woven in.

Unforeseen technical difficulties emerged. The design's center section proved to be particularly demanding and slow, with up to twenty-two thread changes required in a single woven row. Carolyn kept weaving.

On Christmas morning we opened our presents. Crystal ran circles

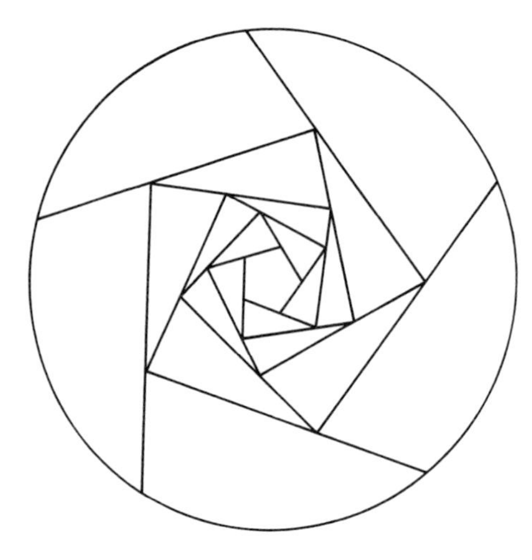

Figure 11: *As her design ideas for* Wings in Gold *progressed, Carolyn experimented with rotational symmetry generated by the pentagon.*

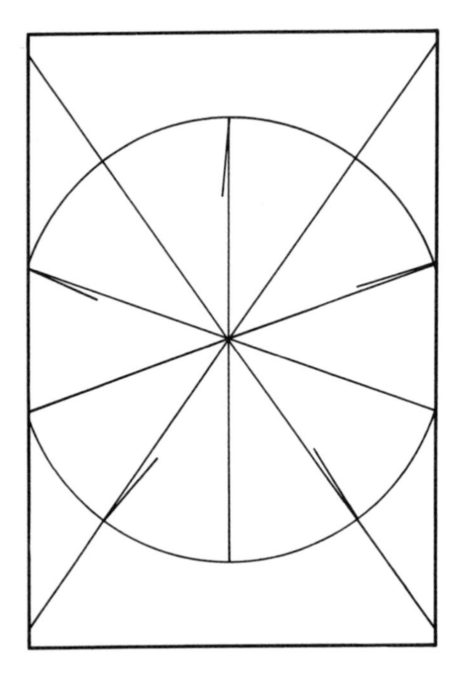

Figure 12: *The next step in designing was to find points and lines that would suggest a weapon. Carolyn was interested in a warrior's stance she had found in T'ai Chi movements, and also the five points of the human body—hands, feet, and head.*

around the apartment for the rest of the day. In the afternoon I began to pack boxes and decide what was to move with us and what was to be left behind. "Thump thump, thump thump," went the weaving comb.

Two days later, an unannounced visitor, Carolyn's younger brother Jim, arrived on holiday leave from pilot training with the Canadian Air Force. Intrigued by the loom and the weaving, Jim watched his

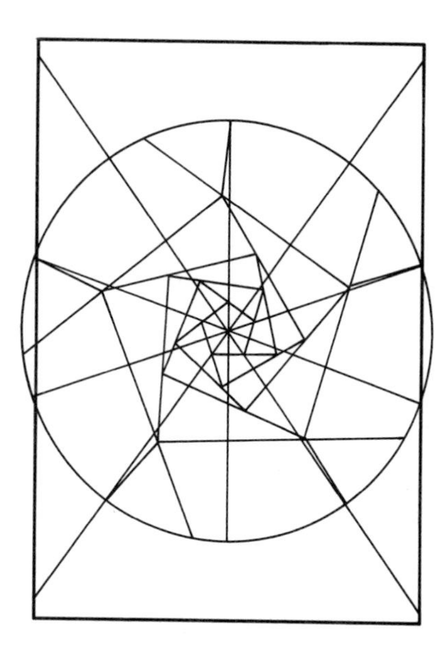

Figure 13: *Carolyn combined design elements from the rotational symmetry of the pentagon with the lines and points derived from the warrior's stance.*

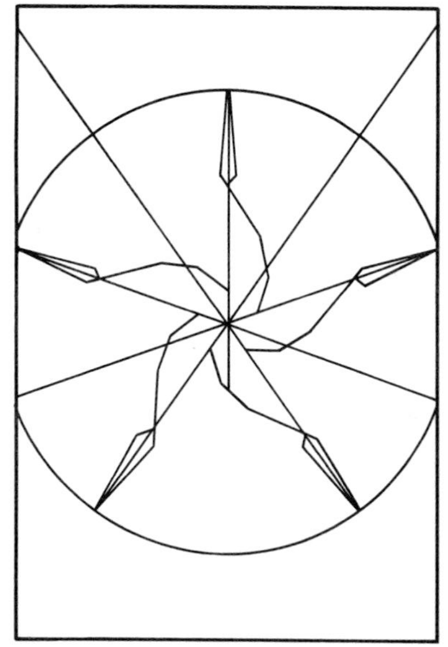

Figure 14: *These are the final lines and color areas chosen for the* Wings in Gold *design.*

sister for hours as she worked on the difficult last inches. When the tapestry was finally finished, we celebrated, and gave it a name, *Wings in Gold* (see Plate 2).

"What's the meaning of the design?" Jim asked.

"It's about flight," I said. "It's about taking off and flying well defended."

Jim wrote out a check for a down payment. "I'll buy it," he said.

Designed to be the defense of a pledge, *Wings in Gold* sold the day it was removed from the loom. This financial confirmation, sponsored by the Royal Canadian Air Force in the person of her younger brother, held ironies and promises that greatly pleased Carolyn. With the sale, we were ready to move into a new life at a new location. For the moment, fear and its army of doubts and excuses were nowhere to be seen.

We were packed and ready to go by New Year's Day. The tapestry traveled with us to northern California, where we rented a cabin in the redwoods. Three months later, we were preparing the tapestry for mailing when the telephone rang. Storm was on the line, suggesting a meeting in Menlo Park, and we kept the tapestry to show him.

We walked with Chuck and his wife, Sandy, around a pond in a spacious park outside Menlo Park. The spring day was beautifully warm and sunny. The Storms asked to see the tapestry. Carolyn produced *Wings in Gold* and held it high, as if the tapestry were the precious gold fabric she had dreamed about. Chuck and Sandy stood back, whispering to each other while enjoying a good long look. Chuck asked to hold the weaving himself so that Carolyn could take a look from a distance away.

With tapestry in hand, Storm walked uphill while a gentle breeze rippled through the knee-high grasses. Near the summit, Storm unrolled the weaving and let it catch the late afternoon sun that filtered through the trees with a soft yellow light. He lightly touched the design center and the points radiating out from the central image. Then he held the tapestry in such a way as to hide himself from our view. The piece was long enough to hide most of him. The grass hid his lower legs and feet.

The tapestry appeared to dance. It moved slowly along the hill crest. Then we heard light, high-pitched singing. The tapestry danced in tune with the rhythms of the song and continued moving slowly downhill.

Sandy was the first to respond to what happened. Her eyes were wide as she glanced my way. She pointed towards the dancing tapestry and then I saw the strange movement also.

Large moths, the size of the central image in the tapestry, appeared to be emerging out of the design. The tapestry was not only dancing while accompanied by song, but was giving birth to huge insects, whose wings appeared speckled with gold dust. The moths fluttered out one at a time as if feeling the use of their wings for the first time.

Each insect hovered momentarily above the design, then winged off, only to quickly dissolve as it fluttered across the orb of golden evening sun.

The vision lasted but an instant. Sandy and I were left looking at each other, while Carolyn asked what all the excitement was about. Then the song melted away. The dancing stopped when the tapestry was directly in front of us. Storm's easy laughter rippled around us, then he rolled it up, and with a quixotic grin, handed the bundle back to Carolyn.

We put the tapestry away in our pickup truck, then joined Sandy for a walk up the hill where Chuck had danced. We followed Sandy's example by leaving a gift of tobacco on the hill. It was a Cheyenne gesture of respect for a place "where a gift has been received." We stayed on the hill to appreciate the last glows of sunset. Storm played hide and seek with Crystal, and we heard her squeals of delight all the way from the hill top.

6

Rain No Rain

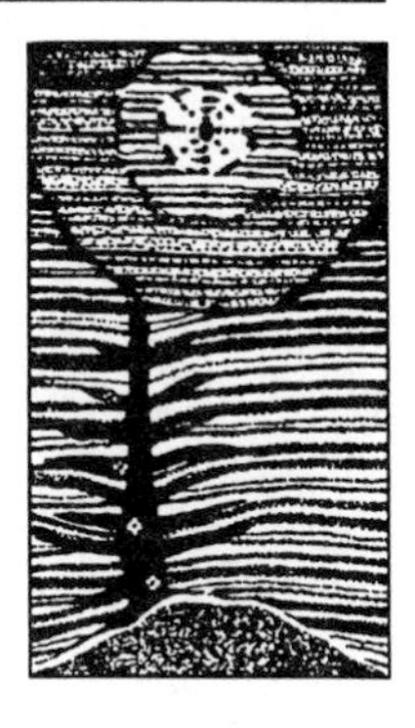

Crystal chased sandpipers and played with the foaming waves. Carolyn and I contemplated the shimmering ripples that spread over the bay.

"I want to weave water," Carolyn said.

"Water?" I asked. "Woven water?"

With bare toes, Carolyn made a series of patterns in the beach sand. "Zen priests weave water by raking sands. There must be a way of weaving water with wool."

Several months earlier, when completing *Four Looks East,* Carolyn had shown the tapestry to Stephen Cummings, a friend and Vancouver poet who was also an authority on the Japanese art of *bonsai.* We had often been intrigued by his ability to see—as one of his poems conveys—mountains in the gardens, multiple worlds of conjecture in a stone. Stephen was especially responsive to the tapestry "eye" in *Four Looks East,* which he saw as a Zen surprise emerging from an otherwise formal design. He suggested Carolyn meet Roy Sumi, creator of the Japanese garden at the University of British Columbia.

We had visited the garden often. We loved the garden's brilliant winter textures, its flowery exuberance in spring. Sculpted pines, gracefully arching bridges, stone lanterns, pebble paths, and quiet pools blend harmoniously into an environment of great serenity. We welcomed an opportunity to meet the garden's designer and caretaker, known for Japanese gardens he has created all over North America.

Roy Sumi invited us to his small home outside Vancouver. We talked with him in his private garden, surrounded by a maze of azaleas, rhododendrons, and meticulously pruned plum and cherry trees. When Carolyn held up her tapestry, he said, "Ah yes, I see you study Japanese raked gardens, is this true?"

We were soon conjuring up images of monks preparing ground, planting stones, pouring sands, and slowly raking out sand patterns under the watchful eyes of a Zen master. I recalled photographs of dry gardens, which include sand and stone arrangements designed to convey an impression of the presence of water.

"Did you know?" Roy Sumi asked. "The process of raking sand into water patterns is best translated from the Japanese, 'to weave.'"

After leaving British Columbia, we moved to the Russian River area in northern California. The area was suffering from severe drought. Water was making headlines daily with reports of damaged vineyards and orchards, lack of drinking water, and impositions of strict water rationing. The river was running at record lows. The annual salmon season was threatened.

Always thirsty even in the best of years, the redwood giants around the cabin were looking thirsty. The creek was reduced to a trickle. Within a month, the trickle was gone. The only signs of water in the creek bed were rippling textures of sand.

Water. No water.

"I want to weave water," Carolyn had said.

During warm winter days with no rain, Carolyn commenced designing a new tapestry. For a drawing table, Carolyn used the sandy creek bed. Her pencil was a pointed stick. Initially, Carolyn used the stick to retrace sand patterns left behind by water. Soon she began to experiment with patterns of her own. In textured sands, which sparkled like quiet pools in midday heat, Carolyn learned to appreciate the remarkable affinity of sand and water.

Sandwater. Watersand.

We found library books on Japanese gardens and landscaping. Paging through the photographs was a great pleasure and opened our eyes to the Japanese way of creating worlds with trees, stones, and sand. In many dry gardens, sands were raked into elliptical patterns. Intrigued, Carolyn looked up the formula for the ellipse, a geometric form she had not yet attempted. Once the formula was found, it was necessary to find a way of translating the mathematical equation into the language of weaving.

"Preparing this design is like preparing ground for a garden," Carolyn said. "Once the ground is prepared, Zen priests rake the sands into place. For me, wool must be woven into the prepared ground of a tapestry design."

Waterwool. Woolwater.

Then, in a biology textbook, Carolyn read about chemical bonding in the water molecule. Of particular interest was the 105°angle formed by the bonding of the two hydrogen atoms with the one oxygen atom. Carolyn became preoccupied with the problem of translating the molecular bonding of water to woven design, by means of the ellipse.

I set up a writing table in the cabin attic, and initiated my first efforts in writing fiction. One day, wondering why the house was so quiet, I took a break and headed downstairs. A note informed me Crystal had been invited to a neighbor's place. The loom was uncovered, a new warp stretched taut between the beams. The weaver woman was missing.

Weaver. No weaver.

Making myself comfortable on the couch, I recalled a dream of the night before. I had dreamed of making dresses for four women. A forest green dress perfectly fit a young woman who was my first lover. A sky blue dress, with pearl color floral patterns, was worn by an incredibly beautiful woman whom I very much desired. This second woman seemed remote, almost unreachable, and I tried deciding how I could approach her most successfully, eventually thinking, "it's just a question of time." The third woman reminded me of my mother but was larger, much older. I was aware that this woman would die, that I would have to accept her physical mortality, while realizing that "mothers never really die." She wore a luminous yellow dress, possibly silk. I dressed the fourth woman in a black outfit. This woman was dangerous. She could witch me. She could unravel her dress, making her naked and all the more alluring, and then use the thread to weave a web that would "trap me and take my life."

I woke from the dream thinking I had been presented with an inspiring—and somewhat frightening—challenge to "unravel the dresses" of each of these women. Jungians speak of a psychological woman to be found within every man. The inner woman, or feminine self, is called the anima. The masculine self, or man within the woman, is called the animus. My dream seemed to describe four aspects of the anima.

The dream was asking me to understand my relationship with my anima. Inner world and outer interweave in the psyche, and for a man, particularly in the anima. Women in a man's life influence the nature of his anima, and conversely, the women in his life are often projections of his anima. Carolyn, and all women, embody in varying degrees aspects of the feminine I dressed in the dream: lover, goddess, mother, witch. Clearly, coming to terms with the anima has its risks as well as its attractions. Aspiring towards the spiritual feminine must be balanced by warnings to watch out for the negative feminine. Whatever her nature, anima work begins at home. I decided to give closer attention to my web weaver wife.

I looked for her outside. I figured she was still working in the creek sands. I didn't find her, but trails of her designing were easily followed. A series of concentric ellipses, linked to others before and behind, all interwoven with sand patterns, flowed down the creek around a bend out of sight. Sunlight striking the designs gave them a shimmering, watery appearance. I suddenly felt rather peculiar, as if I were wading around in little whirlpools.

A quarter mile downstream, I found a barefoot Carolyn bent over the sand with her stick, studying more ellipses carved into sand. Brushing aside waves of hair streaming down her shoulders, Carolyn looked up at me ecstatically.

"I've found my design," she exclaimed.

"Where?" I asked.

"Here," she said, pointing with the stick. "I followed the trail of my designing downstream until I found my peacekeeper, and now I have."

"Your what?"

"I've woven a warrior tapestry. Now I'll weave a peacekeeper."

"I thought you wanted to weave water."

"Calm water," Carolyn said. "My perfect peacekeeper."

I took a closer look. To me, the elliptical sand whirlpools at her feet appeared virtually identical to the swirling myriad of others flowing a quarter mile down from the cabin. But I didn't argue. I've learned it's best to take a weaver's word, once she has found her design. The least a man can do is to honor a woman's creative life. Otherwise the bonding, not unlike the chemistry gluing together hydrogen atoms with oxygen, might come unglued, producing confusion to say the least, utter chaos most likely, just possibly the end of the world as we now know it. I took Carolyn into my arms and gave her a kiss. Then I looked down at my feet, and tried to shake the odd sensation that I was standing ankle deep in water with my shoes on.

Creek bed designing had to be translated to prepared warp. The 105° angle turned out to be the means of holding design ideas together. Tapestry dimensions were determined by invisible triangles, 105° at the apex, with lines extending to upper and lower corners of a warp with predetermined width. A woven water molecule, including two hydrogen atoms linked to the oxygen by means of the angle, was to be bonded to a second molecule by weaving the two central oxygen atoms along the tapestry diagonal.

Initially, the idea was to weave with several colors. Two days before actually sitting at the loom, Carolyn changed her mind. If the intention was to weave water, no water, with wool, then a similar principle could be applied to color. A natural white, a neutral grey, proved to be all the color necessary.

For several days the weaving progressed relatively smoothly. A section of border design was completed. In preparing for the first ellipse, Carolyn chose not to mark points on the warp to guide the weaving. Instead, calculated points derived from the formula of the ellipse were translated to the warp threads and weft rows in terms of measurements made by counting. The elliptical curve could be achieved by devising a sequence for weaving a known number of wefts before advancing the design to the next warp.

Even with a specific numerical approach, technical problems multiplied. More than once Carolyn would weave for hours only to discover a mistake made early in the day, or find herself unsatisfied with a particular approach. In either situation, the perfectionist in her would allow for no error. What was woven had to be unwoven.

Weaving. No weaving.

Unweaving is a shattering, heart-breaking task. Occasionally, when several hours of work needed undoing, I was asked to assist. I sat at the loom, unweaving woolwater, while the weaver went to the creek to bathe her feet in sand whirlpools. Unweaving reminded me of my dream. Was I caught in the web? I resisted the thoughts. I thought about time.

The process of weaving inspires a special relationship to time. The rhythmic drumming of thread over thread produces a sense of movement, or flow, quite unlike usual perceptions of time. In tapestry time, a woven design emerges. The design is like a woven net cast out to catch a fleeting image: fluttering moth, a splashing rain drop. The image, idea, or dream caught in the net is held in time, out of time. Unweaving, however, reverses the flow. While removing the threads, I was reversing the flow of water, the flow of time. It's an ominous feeling, unweaving time.

In time. No time.

Carolyn developed a technique of weaving a background area to form a bowl-like outline for her ellipse. She inlaid weft-pairs of alternating white and grey into the bowl. The technique worked, but only

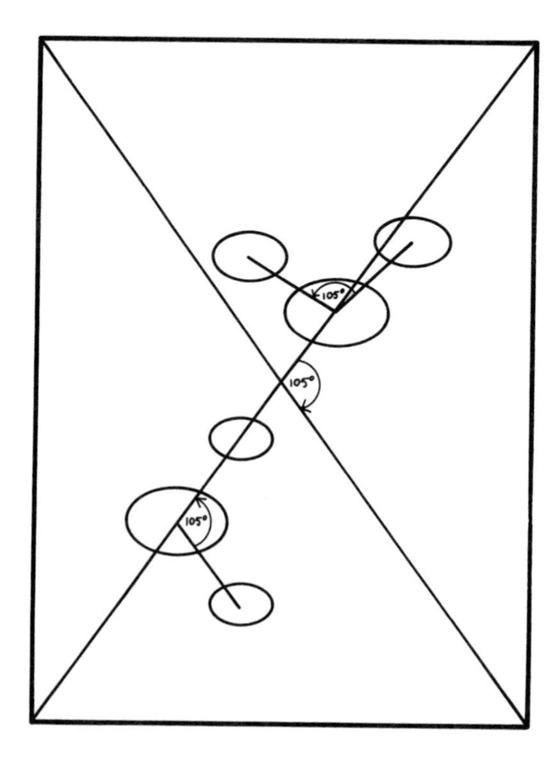

Figure 15: *For her tapestry* Rain No Rain, *Carolyn's design ideas came together in the 105-degree angle formed by the bonding of one oxygen and two hydrogen atoms.*

to a point. Other obstacles arose which were eventually resolved by changing from inlaid threads to verticals, woven in the alternating colors.

The problems were not over. The number sequences, derived from the formula for the outer ellipses, did not apply to the inner ellipses. With smaller major and minor axes, the inner ellipses needed a different set of calculations. New numbers were not difficult to obtain, but the unforeseen dilemma aroused confusion, and questions about what she was hoping to accomplish.

Weaving water. No water.

Designing and weaving required three months of full-time work. When finishing touches were completed, the tapestry was finally ready to come off the loom. And then the loom appeared enormously empty. The loom, as a structure that facilitates the catching of time, transforms time into design. When the design is taken away, the loom becomes a vacuum, occupying a time-space of its own in a profound state of rest, as if waiting for the arrival of another design, another piece of time.

"Does the design work?" Carolyn asked. "What have I woven?"

Figure 16: Rain No Rain

"In this weaving, I walk through a quiet garden," I said. "We toss pebbles into the pools."

Clouds built up over the hills the following day. By noon the winter's first rain was wetting the grass. By late afternoon the rain fell in sweeping silver curtains. The redwoods drank deep and asked for more. In the evening the rain stopped, but the creek was flowing. Sand patterns, all the swirling whirlpools drawn in the creek bed, washed away.

By morning skies had cleared. A cool California mist clung to the redwoods. Crystal splashed in the puddles while the weaver and I contemplated the no colors woven into the tapestry. Looking very carefully, we found little rainbows hidden within the patterns. Carolyn gave her new tapestry a name.

Rain No Rain.

7

Return and Give Away

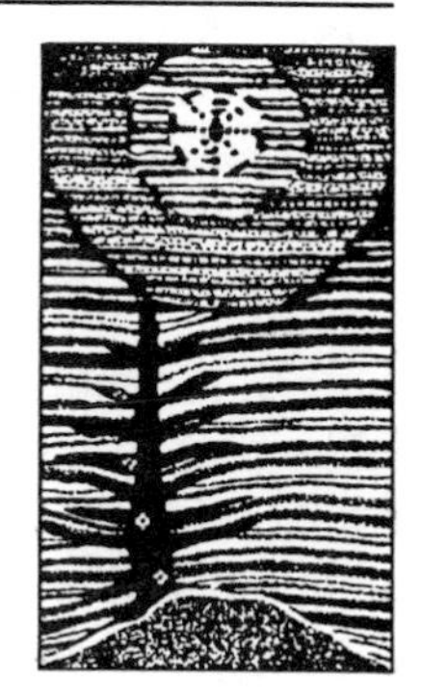

Crystal often asked, "When are we going to Navajo land?"

She had heard our stories. Every summer we discussed the possibility of a return trip, but there always seemed to be reasons for postponements. Native American philosophy continued to inform and inspire our respective arts, but we no longer felt the urge to live with the Navajo for another length of time. Nevertheless, we could never shake a sense of being in debt to our native teachers, even if we could not imagine just how that debt, whatever it was, could appropriately be settled. Perhaps the real reason for the delayed return was the complex of ambivalent feelings aroused by memories of our southwest experiences.

About seven years after our time in Navajo land we received a telephone call that would initiate a journey to Arizona and beyond. Chuck Storm invited us to a Crow Sun Dance in eastern Montana.

We arrived at the Sun Dance when the ceremonial lodge was being constructed. We assisted with preparations and stayed with Chuck and Sandy while they took their last drink before spending three nights and days in the lodge with nothing to eat or drink. During a pause in the drumming and dancing, Storm introduced us to Mary and Solomon Hall, Lakota Sioux medicine people from Manitoba. After the Sun Dance, the Storms and Halls planned to drive to British Columbia for a private ceremony on an island in Georgia Strait, and we were invited to travel along.

During the trip, we became acquainted with the Halls, with whom we felt an immediate rapport. On Galiano Island we stayed with a Salish Indian fisherman and his family. While Solomon prepared for a pipe ceremony to honor eagles, Mary asked to see tapestries.

Storm had heard our Navajo stories before, but listened with renewed interest as Mary Hall learned about our living situation with Mary and Harry Anthony and our times with the Thompsons, Begays, Stella, and Mrs. Goldtooth. Carolyn described the difficulties encountered in her first rug, especially the broken warps, which had aroused so many doubts about learning even the simplest skills associated with Navajo weaving.

"Mary Anthony was testing you," Storm said. "The medicine woman gave you a rotten warp, and she did it on purpose."

Storm's response came as a complete shock. Carolyn had always blamed her own lack of skill for her problems. Even when suspecting that the warp was in poor condition, we had not imagined Mary Anthony would intentionally give Carolyn a rotten warp. Furthermore, we had regarded Mary Anthony as a complex woman, but not a medicine woman. I asked Storm for clarification.

"Behind every medicine man there is always a medicine woman," he said quietly. His tone left no room for further questions, and Mary Hall confirmed his statements. "The medicine woman was your true teacher," she said, "testing you every step of the way. When you return, thank her for giving you that first warp. You completed a weaving on a shredding old warp, and that is why you now have your great skill."

We let the words sink in.

"You were young when you journeyed to the Navajo," Mary said. "You only had your innocence to carry you through. The medicine woman sensed something about you. Maybe she said to herself, 'I wonder if this young white woman really wants to learn. I wonder if she can work with the weaving.' Maybe the medicine woman was thinking about you in that way."

Mary passed her fingers over the colors and designs in the tapestries. "Weaving is a very ancient way," she continued. "As ancient as the people. Weaving goes all the way back to Spider Woman. That's why the medicine woman tested you. That woman cannot give her knowledge away easily. She had to know you were not just looking for something to do while David was working with the medicine man. She made you cry. She made you angry. She made you think she was a cold woman. She even let her daughters order you around and humiliate you. But all the time, that medicine woman watched you closely."

"Don't you see how much the medicine woman cared for you," Mary said. "Always giving to you, little by little, first the tools, then the skills, then the patience you need to become aware of a weaver's way. This woman was right when she sensed something about you. You dream with your weaving. Your weaving dreams with you. This is why you must return and acknowledge your teachers. They're waiting for you. They want to see the effect of what they gave to you."

Mary gently laughed, then instructed Carolyn in what needed to be accomplished in a brief give-away ceremony for Mrs. Thompson. We were assured that no payment was due the Navajo other than our decision to return.

"Why should the give-away be for Mrs. Thompson?" Carolyn asked. "Why not Mary Anthony?"

"Mrs. Thompson introduced you to a weaver's way," Mary Hall told Carolyn. "You must return to her for your give-away. She was the first to put a weaving comb in your hand. She gave you your first threads for a design woven just for you. You see, those people will always be your teachers. They need to meet you again so they'll know how to help you walk along your path in the future. That Thompson family, the Anthonys, I'm sure they are related in some way. Clan relatives. They took you in. They adopted you into the family. They decided where you were going to live. In one way or another, the medicine people will always help you out, even after you have forgotten all about them. Don't ask me why. That's just the way it is."

Mary turned to me with instructions similar to those given Carolyn as to how I was to accomplish a give-away ceremony for Harry Anthony. We were given cigarettes that had been blessed in the Sun Dance lodge. We were advised to purchase good-quality wool blankets. For half a day, Storm and I collected "braided" cedar boughs, which I was told were highly prized as an herb and incense, and widely traded in the old days. The northwest coastal varieties were especially valued. These were to be the essential items for our respective give-aways, along with anything privately chosen we wished to give. After spelling out the details of how we were to approach the medicine man and Mrs. Thompson, Mary Hall again addressed Carolyn.

"The give-away is only a sign for your first teachers, a ritual celebration. Your true give-away was completed when you were actually there, living with the people."

Carolyn asked for an explanation. Mary turned away and bent down to pick up a handful of earth, and Storm responded.

"Your teachers appreciated how you came to them—with your time, your attention, your hands. They tested you because this is what medicine people *do.* Testing is a reflection of the way they honored your coming to them, because you listened and you learned."

Storm lit up a cigarette. "Elk Woman, do me a favor."

I bristled, seeing Storm suddenly become a seducing wolf, a guise he assumed with Carolyn all too often.

"Every time you make a mistake in your weaving," he said, "make that tall drink of water over there do all your unweaving. David still needs to unweave anthropology out of his system. He needs to unweave every trace of conservative academia. Make him do your unweaving. Reversing the threads will help him remember who he is."

The half-Cheyenne hurricane had done it again. Storm was to me what Mary Anthony had been to Carolyn: a tester every step of the way, taking great pleasure in knocking me off guard.

Carolyn and I decided to head for Arizona as soon as the eagle ceremony was over. Obstacles seemed to vanish as we realized our reluctance to return reflected a lack of knowing *how* to return. A few days later we told Storm our decision.

"Good," he said. "Now listen. Do not stay long. You have a purpose. Don't become embroiled in their lives again."

Storm must have sensed the questions forming in my mind. He turned serious, remaining silent for some time. "David, traditional people are having hard times. They are experiencing incredible pain, more now than before. Your medicine family will not want to burden you with the problems. Return and give-away, then leave."

The meeting with the Storms and Halls gave our journey south a sense of purpose. Navajo memories had been renewed, and our relationship with the Anthony family seen in a new perspective. After seven years we finally felt ready for a return. We couldn't swallow the miles fast enough.

Once in Navajo land, however, we were confronted by disturbing changes. Near Shiprock, in an area we remembered for fertile gardens and fruit trees, a coal-processing plant with thirty-story-high towers belched up clouds of black smoke that blurred the sky for miles around. Oil pumps churned away like bobbing steel ducks, the rigs surrounded by dusty flats bulldozed out of former grazing land and mountainsides. In Window Rock, suburban row houses covered the red hills. Shirt-and-tie Navajos carrying black briefcases popped out of look-alike doors and piled into traffic jams on their way to government jobs.

Outside Window Rock, barbed wire fences divided grasslands and plateau country never divided before.

Off the main highways, the land retained the vibrant color and silence unique to northern Arizona deserts and mountains. The road into the Anthony summer camp was as rutted as ever. We parked near the main hogan, waiting in the truck for several minutes to follow the customary gesture of respect. The oldest son Warren came out of the hogan and approached the truck. I rolled down the window. Warren slipped an arm around my shoulder. Tears dripped down his face. The smell of wine was heavy on his breath.

"You finally come back," he said. "My father always say you will come back."

Harry Anthony stood in the hogan door. I climbed out of the truck, sensing something behind Warren's tears I didn't want to know. The news was not to be hidden. We learned that Fred Anthony, the only son interested in his father's medicine ways, the Anthony brother who had been our closest friend in Navajo land, was dead, having been run down by a truck outside a bar south of the reservation line.

There was little time to dwell on the unbelievable news. The medicine man succeeded in splintering sunlight and shadow as he shuffled over to our pickup. Comical as ever, he walked bow-legged, falling over his feet, wearing a rakish wool cap. Blessing Way Man, Keeper of the Pollen Bundles, Harry Anthony welcomed us back to Navajo land.

Mary Anthony received us with open arms and smiles. She reintroduced three of her daughters. Mary Ann had married and moved in with her husband's family, not far away. Maria, a few years younger than Carolyn, who had formerly enjoyed bossing Carolyn around, introduced her one-year-old baby. She readily interpreted every word her mother and father spoke. They asked a dozen questions about Crystal and British Columbia.

After my give-away, Harry Anthony lit up Sun Dance cigarettes and passed them around. He wrapped himself and Mary in the blanket and did a little dance. They put braided cedar on the fire and filled the house with the sweet-smelling smoke. Mary did most of the talking. What Storm had said now seemed entirely clear. Behind every medicine man is a medicine woman. I had the distinct impression that Harry Anthony's powers relied on Mary's support.

There was an invitation to stay, but we did not intend to linger with the family. We gave Warren and Maria a ride to the trading post and back, then left the Anthony hogans.

The next day, puffy clouds filled a hazy sky. A light breeze sang through the ponderosa and spruce forests. The dirt road leading into the Chuska mountains remained unpaved and full of treacherous ruts. We located the narrow side road leading through a mountain meadow into the Thompson's sheep camp. The grass was gnawed to the roots by hundreds of sheep and goats. A stony stream bed held a mere trickle of water, a sure sign of a dry year.

Avoiding boulders and stumps, I followed ruts until the road came to an abrupt end near the sheep corral and cabin. I turned off the engine and we waited for several minutes.

The cabin was badly in need of repairs and appeared deserted. The ground stank of sheep excrement. A solemn-looking dog slunk out of shadows and approached the cabin with its tail tucked between its legs. A couple of chickens squawked out of the corral and scrambled into the brush. A boy peeked around the corner of a shed, then ran into the cabin. We climbed out of the pickup, Crystal clinging to my hand.

No one showed up at the cabin door. We knew that at least one boy was inside. Carolyn tapped lightly on the door frame, but was met with heavy silence. We circled the cabin, and stopped when we saw Mrs. Thompson's oldest daughter, Violet, sitting at her loom. The log frame was wired to pine trees, occupying the same spot as before.

With weaving comb and thread in hand, Violet momentarily turned from her work. Expressionless, she peered our way. Finally, there was a smile, a nod of recognition, a welcoming cry, *"Ya-tah-hey."* But instead of getting up, Violet turned around to face her woven design. She carefully inserted a thread and drummed it solidly into place. "This moment, this meeting, woven in, woven in," the drumming seemed to say. Then she put away comb and batten, pulled herself up from sheepskin cushions, and beckoned Carolyn into her arms.

Holding Carolyn's hand, Violet led the way to the second loom while Crystal and I waited near the cabin. The weaver remained hidden behind a nearly completed, quite large rug. The design contained variations of her favorite theme, alternating columns of white, brown, and black triangles set over a soft grey background, all woven with natural colors of home-spun wool.

Mrs. Thompson had grown ancient. Her tiny thin body was bent like the oak comb in her bony hand. She had loosely tied what was left of her grey hair into a knot at the back of her head. She did not hear Violet and Carolyn approach and did not see them until the drumming of her weaving comb across the woven row led her eye to where they stood.

Staying still, Mrs. Thompson peered closely at her visitor, without apparent recognition. Violet softly giggled, and whispered a few words in Navajo. The old weaver's expression lit up as she tucked her weaving tools into a cloth sack. She struggled up from her sheepskins with Violet's assistance. Crystal and I watched as the three women giggled and talked.

Clinging tightly to Carolyn's arm, Mrs. Thompson made her way to the cabin, walking with a heavy limp. She greeted me and asked who was hiding behind my legs. We introduced Crystal. Mrs. Thompson gently took Crystal's hands and peered into her eyes.

"She's one of us," Mrs. Thompson said. "She has native blood."

Carolyn briefly explained how Crystal had come into our lives. At the cabin door, we shook hands with Virginia, another weaver and a part-time silversmith.

"We move down the mountain soon," Mrs. Thompson said. "When my rug is finished, we go down to the winter camp."

Her words echoed a familiar theme. In Navajo land, the passage of time, including seasonal moves, often coincides with the rhythms of weaving.

"I've been very sick," Mrs. Thompson said. "I almost die they say. Two weeks I stay in the hospital. I ask my relative, Harry Anthony, to help me out. He brought the mountain medicine bundle to me in the hospital so I can come home."

The four weavers entered the cabin. Crystal did not want to go in, so she and I returned to the truck. It was Carolyn's time to be with the old woman. I was content to wait.

Another pickup pulled in, and after a few minutes a heavy-set woman climbed out and headed for the cabin. I remembered the woman was a clan relative of Mrs. Thompson, another excellent weaver. I thought it strange that none of the men were around, that five weavers were together in the dark cabin. Five weavers, each in their own way Blessing Way weavers, familiar with the weaver's spot, where Spider Woman guides the building of woven webs, where dreams merge with the colors of multiple worlds.

The sun was sinking behind ponderosa pines when Carolyn appeared in the dark doorway. Standing with loom-like solidity, she nodded to the invisible four inside, then returned to the truck. Her expression was a weave of joy and tears. We drove in silence down the road away from the sheep camp. Crossing a mountain summit, we stopped for the night in an aspen grove. I gathered dry branches and built a fire. Our respective give-aways were accomplished. It seemed to us another design had been woven, another tapestry was off the loom.

8

A Tree and Two Dreams

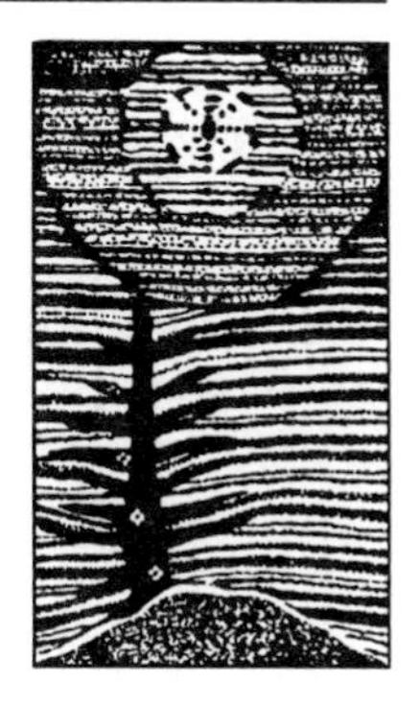

We were on the move again, having learned of a cabin available for rent in northern California on the shores of Lake Almanor.

By this time our possessions were reduced to what could comfortably be packed in the back of the truck. A loom box was perched on top of a carrying rack. With our work foremost in our minds, a rapidly diminishing savings account, and no assurance of how we could afford the next six months, we simply trusted that money would materialize when needed. With winter on the way, the cabin was a reasonable alternative to the back of the truck, which had been our home for nearly three months and six thousand miles.

Four days before moving into the cabin, I headed down a dirt road and found a quiet campsite in a pine forest. That night, after Crystal fell asleep, Carolyn said she wanted to go for a walk by herself. Carolyn entered the forest and found herself searching for a tree.

"Where ever you are, there is a special tree," a medicine woman had once told Carolyn. "In a forest many trees love you, but find the tree that loves you most."

"How can I find that tree?" Carolyn asked.

"You will feel a pull. It's as simple as that. You will feel pulled by the tree that loves you most. Honor your tree like an elder sister. If you find the tree to be male, honor him like an elder brother."

Carolyn found a pine that was just the right size for her to comfortably wrap her arms around. She lay her cheek against the rough bark and pressed her belly against the trunk.

"Talk to your tree, but be careful what you say. The tree listens to the sounds of your words, not the words themselves. Your sounds arise from your body and your body cannot lie, not to a tree."

For a long time Carolyn hugged her pine, wondering what to say. She was feeling vulnerable and full of doubts about the future.

"I began feeling a strange sensation in the area of my stomach," Carolyn told me the next day. "I felt a spot beneath my navel opening. After awhile, I felt I was becoming connected to the pine by means of fibers that seemed to grow from inside me, connecting both ways. I felt created by the tree. I was clinging to it insect-like, but I also thought the tree, from the tiniest tap root to highest needles, emanated from the opening beneath my navel. My insides were joined with the inner fibers of the tree."

"Listen to your tree," the medicine woman had said. "Be patient. Trees breathe much slower than we do. Give the tree time to become receptive to your presence. It's best to return often, but the tree also knows you by what you leave behind. Your sounds, for example, a pinch of tobacco, or corn meal."

Carolyn stayed with her tree. Occasionally she whispered a few words. Most of the time she remained silent. Then, late in the night, a sharp pain struck her stomach. The pain intensified, producing tears and a surge of emotion. Carolyn found herself empathizing with the tree as if it were about to be cut down. In her inner dialogue she asked the tree when it hurt most: when the axe bit into its skin, when the saw worked through the flesh? Was the pain unbearable when the tree fell and hit the ground?

Carolyn clung to the tree, crying softly, feeling the tree's strength against her body. When the tears dissolved, the pain receded. Silver moonlight dripped through feathery branches and fell into the soft bed of needles around the tree. Carolyn turned her ear to the pine trunk and listened.

"Take care of circles," she heard it say.

The words seemed to follow the fibers, flowing like sap, spreading through her body in waves, and bringing images: root power, earth, water, minerals drawn up to create tree growth. Needle power. Sunlight pulled down and transformed into energy. Transformative tree power.

"You and I are linked," Carolyn whispered. "I breathe in what you breathe out. You breathe in what I breathe out. We make a circle, you and I."

With the words and images came understanding. The pain was not so ominous as she had thought. Carolyn returned to camp full of questions about the pain and the crying that had surged up so forcefully. In the first light of dawn, she finally fell asleep and dreamed.

> I am in high school with several girl friends talking about a voluntary "tubal ligation." Most of the girls, including myself, decide to go through with it.
>
> My father walks with me in a hospital hallway asking why I want the operation. "I just do," I answer angrily. "And I don't want my mind changed or influenced by you."
>
> My father and I sit on a bench in the waiting room. I can see the operation in progress as well as a magnified view of the girl's reproductive organs: ovaries, fallopian tubes, uterus, and vagina. The operation is a ritual performed by a severe-looking, white-haired woman dressed in a white surgeon's coat. She uses a large gold cleaver.
>
> My name is called. I do not move. The surgeon calls again. I refuse to move. The surgeon impatiently calls my name a third time.
>
> "No," I shriek. "No!"
>
> Then I am driving a car, with my father beside me. I explain that I was not afraid but felt something wrong with the ritual. "Something about that woman told me the operation was not right." I knew the surgeon was extremely angry with me because it was a serious breach of custom to refuse.
>
> I return to the hospital with David. We find Diana, a beautiful, dark-haired school friend of mine, lying on the floor crippled with pain. The surgeon stands near Diana holding the gold cleaver. I sense the surgeon's hatred of me. I help Diana find a place to rest and ask, "Why have you done this?"
>
> "It is because of my father's culture," Diana answers. "The operation is a Euro-Vedic tradition." Diana complains of pain but says she feels she has done the right thing.
>
> "Few cultures anywhere in the world allow this to be done to a young woman," David says.
>
> The surgeon is outraged by David's statement, but Diana appears greatly relieved.
>
> "Perhaps this horror will stop some day," I exclaim.

We changed campsites, and in a couple of days moved into a cabin surrounded by stately pines, situated on a hillside overlooking Lake Almanor.

Crystal claimed one of two lofts and named the cabin Lake House. We began to arrange Lake House into work and living areas, then went for a late afternoon walk along the lake shore.

An osprey circled down and perched on a pine bough near the cabin. To the north, Mt. Lassen's volcanic cone cast shadows on forested hills. The sun blazed a rippling gold path over the dark green water of the lake. We quickly fell in love with the Lake House solitude, and looked forward to the winter's work. But that night, Carolyn could not get to sleep. She was finding it impossible to dismiss from her mind a white-haired woman with a gold cleaver.

The dream seemed to be a continuation of dreams Carolyn had dreamed before about creative potential—not just Carolyn's, but women's creative potential in general. The dream was stating quite clearly that there are traditions which consciously or unconsciously attempt, and often succeed, to cut away a woman's creative potential.

Eventually Carolyn fell asleep, leaving me wide awake. In the morning, Carolyn woke up with another vividly remembered dream.

> I am with my father, digging in the back yard of my childhood home. Mother is in the house. I dig out a big hole, and with my father's help remove a number of water-damaged bricks which I set aside to dry in the sun.
>
> I realize we are digging out bricks of a grave. We unearth the skeletons of two women and a man. The skeletons stand upright and I wonder if the three were buried alive in a brick vault. I keep digging, and begin to assemble a woman's bones which are caked with gooey mud.
>
> Suddenly I see a half-submerged boat floating in a creek bordering the back yard. My father and I run to the creek for a better look. The boat is beautifully proportioned, a white hull solidly built of wood in lapstrake construction. The boat is self-propelled by a small engine made of pure silver.
>
> Awed by the boat's beauty, I ask my father to rescue it. He wades into the creek, pulls the boat to shore, just in time to prevent it from floating into deep water of a nearby lake.
>
> An exquisite tapestry of white, pastel pink, blue, and green designs is stretched across the top of the open boat. I am able to read the woven designs. They tell me the boat's owner is an Indian from midwestern Saskatchewan. His name is Shannon. His medicine animal is deer. His medicine plants are columbine and parsley.
>
> Father examines the boat, saying he will keep it for himself, but just then I notice a woman's body floating head first downstream, just beneath the surface. The woman's hair and clothes are pure white; her skin is wrinkled and blue. Thinking the

woman has drowned, I reach for her, and with my father's help pull her out of the water. My father lifts the woman to his shoulder and carries her to the back yard.

When he bends to put her down, she walks away. I'm shocked. The woman calmly asks for a drink of water. She helps herself to a drink from an outdoor faucet. After drinking she returns to us.

"I see you have found my boat," she says. "I thank you. And I see you are English like myself. Well then, you will not mind bacon and eggs for dinner, as that is what you will eat when you come to my home in northern Quebec."

I am aware that mother has been watching all this from inside the house. She will be worried about me accompanying this woman to the far north. Crystal will come with me, even if she has to stay up late for many nights. I prepare to go north with the old, white-haired woman.

Carolyn associated the two dreams not only with her pine tree experience, but with the direction North in the medicine wheel. In the terms Chuck Storm had taught us, North in the medicine wheel included the thinking function, the season of winter, the color white, and water in its ice crystal form. By extension we also learned to associate logic, reason, mathematics, and philosophy with the north. After her dreams, Carolyn was aware that the north, personified by the white-haired woman, could also be revealed in two very contrasting aspects.

Carolyn resolved to explore the symbolic north by means of her art. This intention aroused questions. Why, for example, had a dream singled out her dark-haired high school friend, Diana? Diana seemed to symbolize a tendency within young women to sacrifice their creative potential. A starkly cold woman maintained control over the girls by means of the surgery. The dream suggests that the surgeon's ritual derives from traditions that suppress the female creative function, with disastrous results.

Two years later, in Robert Graves's classic study of European mythology, *White Goddess,* Carolyn found references to an ancient goddess by the name of Diana. In Druid times, Diana was a woodland goddess associated with deer cults and sacred oak groves. She was sometimes represented in early artwork carrying a wheel in her hand that symbolized the wheel of life and the turning wheel. Carolyn was reminded of the admonition "Take care of circles."

Diana presided over a Druidic cult that practiced the cutting of mistletoe, a rite symbolizing emasculation of the old king by his successor. In areas of the Druidic world where the mistletoe rite had not yet developed, the king himself was actually emasculated, and eaten eucharistically by magic-making, orgiastic priestesses.[1]

In Carolyn's dream the surgeon operated with a gold cleaver. Druids sliced mistletoe with a gold sickle. The object in either situation was generative organs. The ritual excess seemed the same, but the wheel of life had turned. The sexes had switched, and Diana, in Carolyn's dream, became the object of an operation over which she once presided.

The parallels were intriguing. Carolyn kept digging, and began to examine English family roots, and, at deeper levels, other links with Druidic Britain.

About the same time as reading Robert Graves, we discovered the Evangeline Walton quartet of novels that retell the epic Welsh mythology known as the Mabinogion. In these novels are to be found confrontations between old and new Druidic traditions relating to women's mysteries.

The Druidic Old Tribes venerated woman as the source of life, the embodiment of fertility, productivity, and creativity. This matrilineal, goddess-centered society originally honored Mother Earth according to principles Walton calls Ancient Harmonies. Walton's descriptions of Druidic Old Tribes are reminiscent of Native American traditions, where woman continues to be revered as the Sacred Tree of Life, her womb honored as the source of creative power. But in Walton's account, all this changed with the rise of what she refers to as the New Tribes. Man claimed supremacy over women, regarding himself the supreme creator. The society became king-centered and patriarchal, and gods replaced goddesses. Druids of the New Tribes gave man credit for all wonders worked in the world.

"Woman—she who only receives our seed and carries it while it shapes itself in her darkness—how can she claim then to be Creator," the high Druid said.[2]

As she read, Carolyn rejected the Druid's statement. Her "No" echoed the shriek of her dream, a cry aroused any time a woman feels her creative potential harmed or lost within a male-dominated situation. Carolyn interpreted the image of surgery from another angle as well.

Society itself does not necessarily cut away a woman's creative powers. What Carolyn asks of herself and other women is this: What are the influences encouraging a woman to find her creative potential, and what is it that denies her these capabilities? How does a woman handle the conflict between the opposing influences?

A woman can develop her creative nature by not succumbing to negative attributes of feminine psychology, as represented by the surgeon with her cleaver. In the second dream, for example, the white-haired woman possesses qualities quite unlike the surgeon. Carolyn had to dig deep to find her, then rescue the woman from floating away to unreachable dimensions. The rescue was accomplished with the assistance of a supportive, inner father. And, after drinking the water of life, the rescued woman invited Carolyn to accompany her to her northern home.

A marriage is suggested by the apparent co-ownership of the white-hulled boat. The signs woven into the boat's tapestry cover include the Indian owner's name and medicines. But the white woman also claimed ownership. The dream seems to suggest that Carolyn's journey north might best be accomplished by a marriage of dark and light, masculine and feminine, or, in medicine wheel terms, the directions West and North. In this dream, the Indian man and his medicine ways represent West, the direction which symbolizes introspection, looking within, and dreaming.

Two directions remain. As Carolyn continues to discover inner symbols she recognizes that the direction east includes her personal illuminations, her woven designs. South is her beginning place with each tapestry. South is the place of feelings and summer warmth. As Mary Hall had said, we went to the Navajo with our trust and innocence, qualities that characterize the symbolic south in the medicine wheel. From there, Carolyn's journey in tapestry began, and after her tree experience and two dreams, she knew exactly which direction she wanted to explore in more depth.

Plate 1: Lightning Mountain, 1973, 29″ x 43″

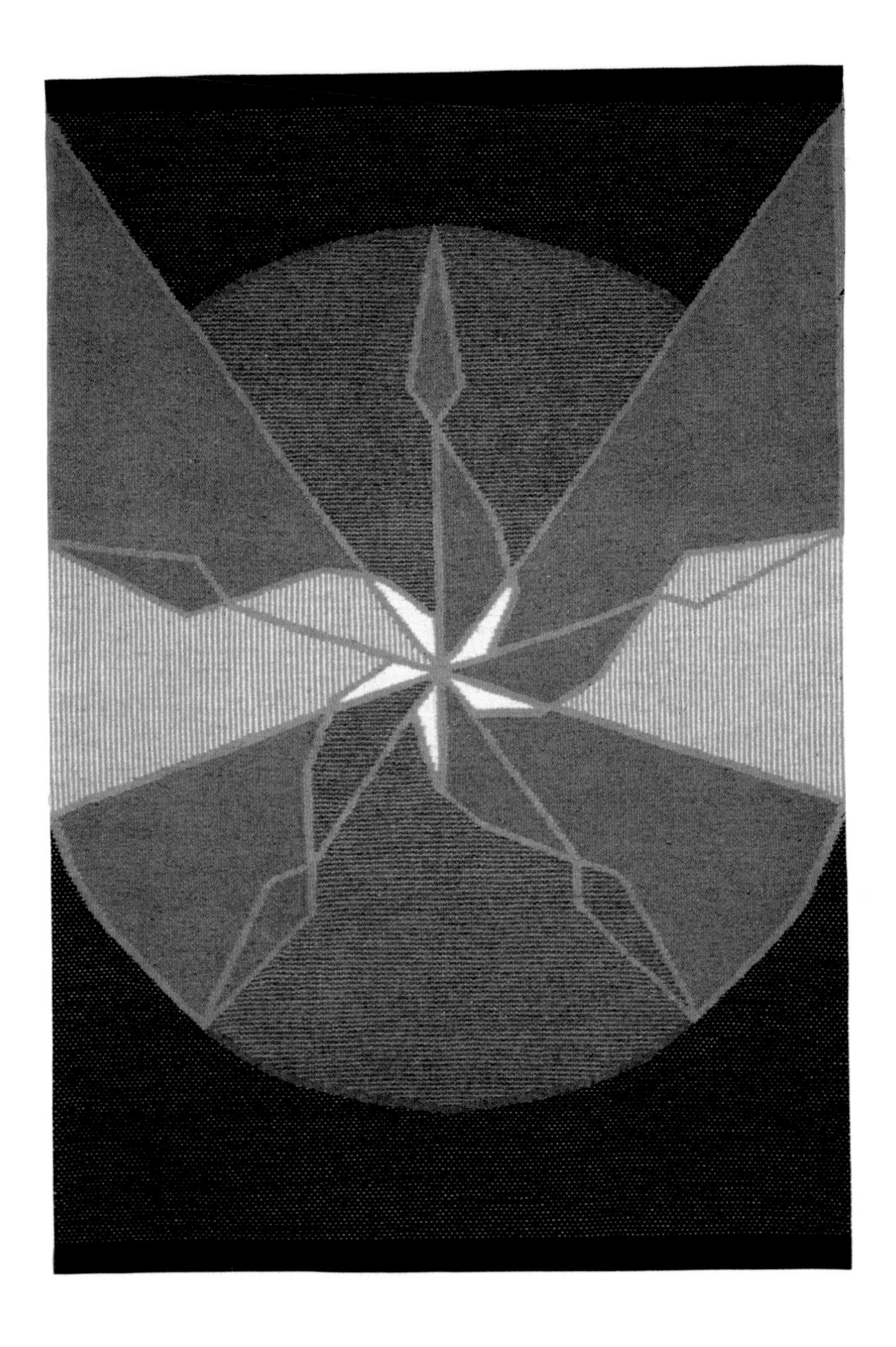

Plate 2: Wings in Gold, 1976, 38" x 55"

Plate 3
Lapis (top), 1977, 48" x 28"
Handsong (bottom), 1978, 48" x 14"

Plate 4: Prism, 1980, 60" x 40"

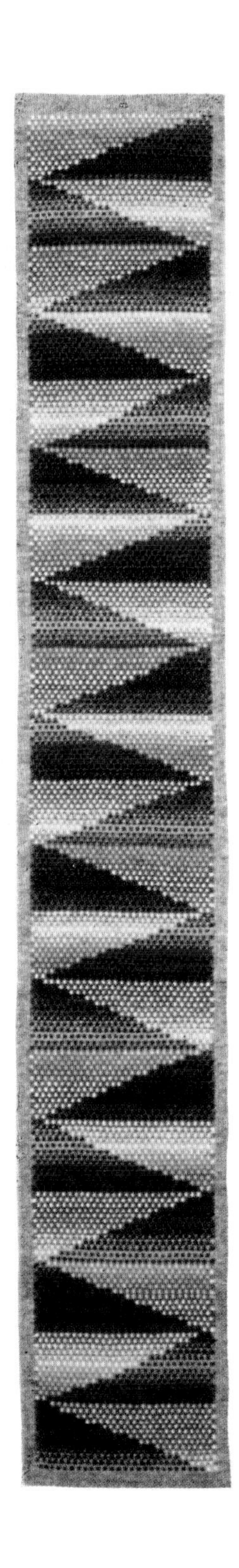

Plate 5
Calendar (left), 1980, 8" x 56"
Lunar Year (right), 1981, 18" x 45"

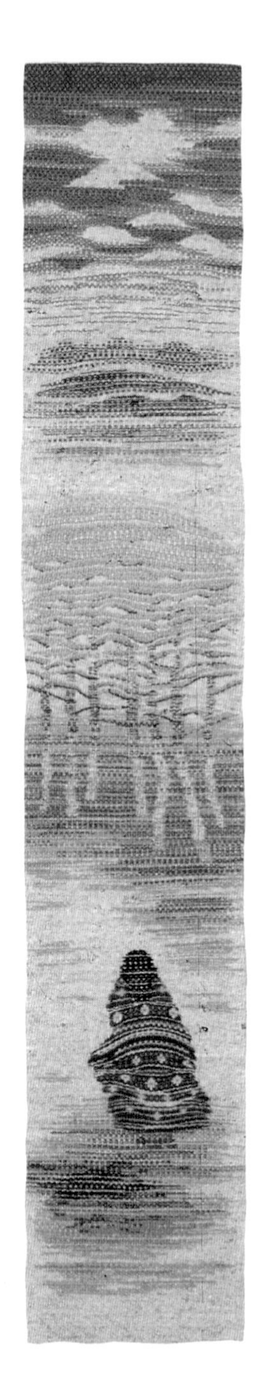

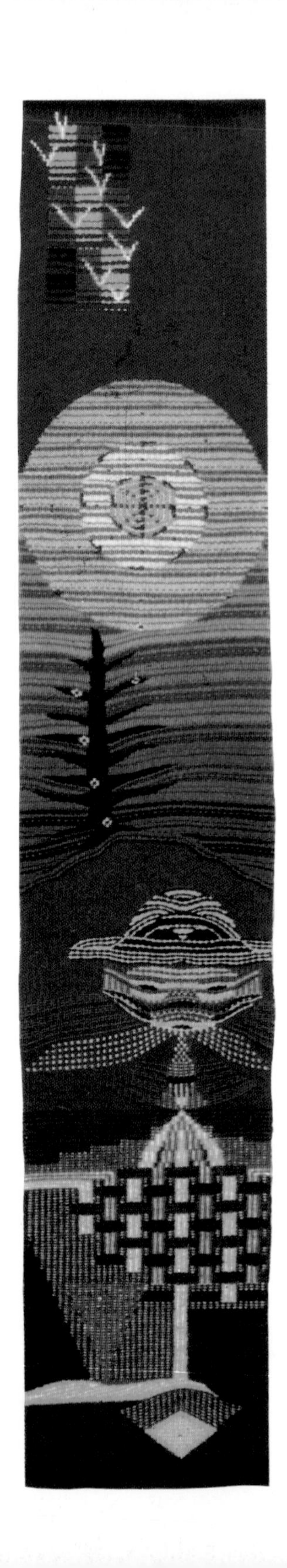

Plate 6
Waiting (left), 1981, 8″ x 45″
Twilight (right), 1981, 8″ x 44″

Plate 7: Waiting detail (facing page)

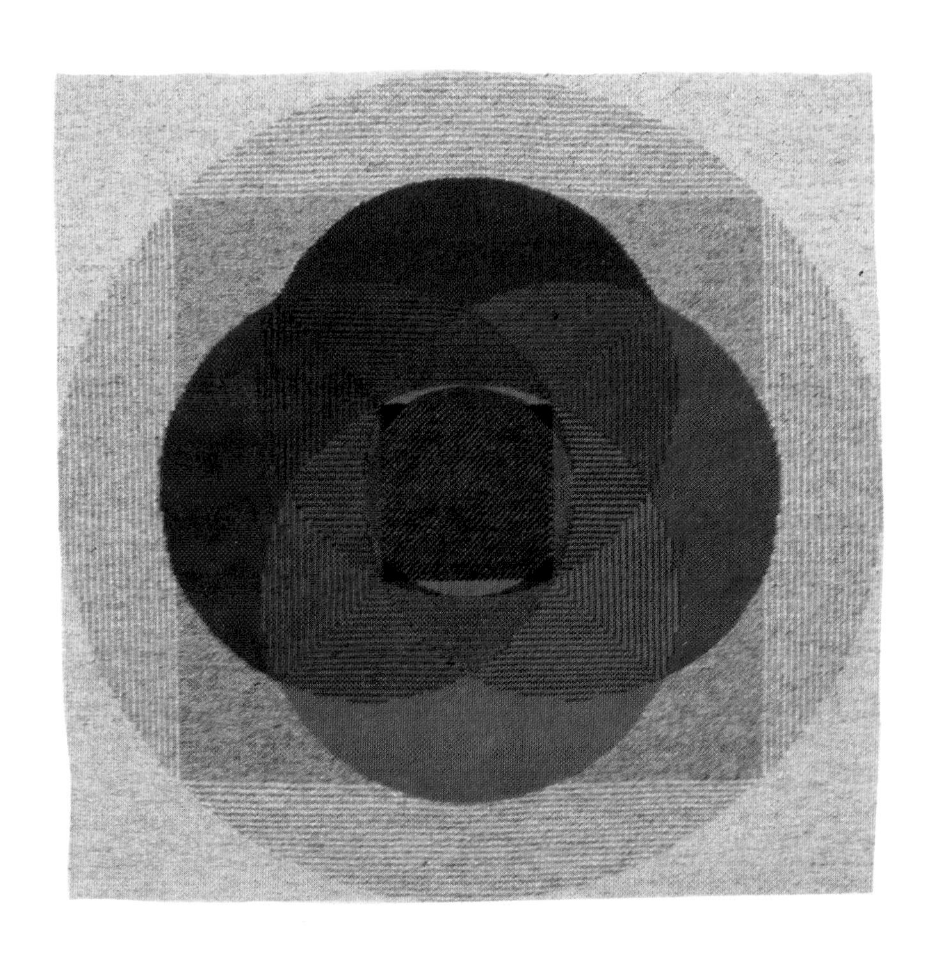

Plate 8: Alchemy, 1981, 28" x 28"

9
The Journey North

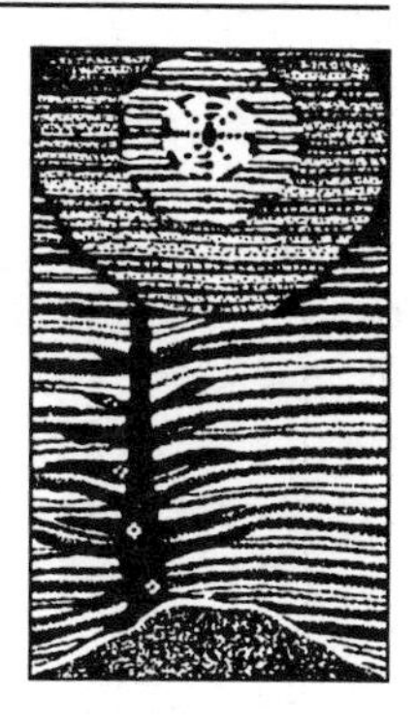

Counting is an exercise of mind basic to every child's education. Counting is also fundamental to the thinking function, which in medicine wheel terms is symbolized by the direction North. Having given her inner consent to follow the white woman of the north, Carolyn decided to weave a series of five tapestries honoring the numbers one through five.

We have good reason to think ourselves overburdened with numbers these days, but in the contemporary tendency to reduce everything to numbers, we actually follow patterns established by the ancients. The difference is that numbers, now used for purposes of quantifying, identifying, and classification, served earlier philosophers and thinkers as a means of reflecting principles of cosmic law. Pythagoreans considered each number a living essence and a supreme power. In early alphabets such as Hebrew and Greek, letters possessed numerical value, and names could be understood in terms of symbolic meanings derived from these numerical values.

Many counting systems include more than quantitative factors to give numbers vitality and meaning. Carolyn and I had learned such a system several months before we moved into Lake House. We had been asked to become children again and learn to count in the Lakota Sioux way.

In the Sioux system, the numbers one through five are called the left-hand count and each of the numbers has symbolic associations. One is the sun, two is the earth, three is plants, four is animals, five is the human being. The left-hand count is associated with the left half of the human being, which is said to be the receptive side, embracing the world of human experience. A drummer, for example, holds a hand drum with the left, or receptive, hand.

The numbers six through ten are considered the right-hand count, associated with the right half of the human, the active, or penetrating, side. The right arm is the striking arm, the coup-counting arm. In the right hand, a drummer holds the drum stick for beating the drum.

For the Lakota drumming itself is a symbolic expression of unity. With the drum stick and drum, drumming unites the receptive with the penetrating. Drum sound is prayer, the unified song of the people, the creative rhythm rising from the reconciliation of opposites.

In Lake House, Carolyn created designs for the left-hand count. The tapestry for the number one was woven with one color, red-orange. White and dark grey were used as background to balance light and dark in the design, and also to relate to the autumn equinox when the tapestry was woven:

> One is the Sun
> Woven with one color
> Circles with all numbers
> To weave within one rhythm
> The Song of a *Sun Drum.*

This poem of mine was inspired by the symbolism Carolyn worked within the first tapestry of her series. Other five-line stanzas followed as each of the number tapestries was completed.

While designing progressed for the number two, winter weather swept across the mountains. Freezing winds whipped over the lake, bringing cold drafts into a glassed-in area where we had set up the loom. I piled armloads of logs into the massive rock fireplace, considering it an achievement on cold days to raise the temperature in the weaving room to 55°. The cabin was not insulated; the electric baseboard heaters were ineffective. While Crystal enjoyed a heated day-school several miles down the road, Carolyn worked at her design table dressed in a wool sweater worn over a wool shirt, thick wool pants, wool socks, and hiking boots.

I supported Carolyn's intention to journey north with the white-haired woman in her dream. Nevertheless, I found our situation somewhat ridiculous. I could readily imagine the English woman with her bacon-and-eggs practicality living in northern Quebec in a toasty warm house. But in sunny California, we had managed to find a cabin that was incredibly cold four of the six months we lived there.

In early December, Carolyn's fingers began swelling, showing symptoms resembling chilblains. Her joints turned stiff, and irritating red sores appeared on her fingers and toes. Carolyn bathed her hands in hot water before sitting down to the loom.

The weather seemed more pleasant outside than in, so we walked down the road, which followed the lake shore. We often called on our neighbors, who lived in a big house sheltered by lofty pines. In this house lived a white-haired woman and a white-haired man. Mrs. Burns was bright as snow and warm as the sun. Dr. Burns was a man of many occupations, and one of them was his ability to guide people into past-life regressions.

Even on the coldest nights, the Burnses' house was warm, heated by burning logs in efficient fireplaces that he had constructed using obsidian rock. We often talked late into the night, and Mrs. Burns served home-made doughnuts and hot English tea, or strawberry shortcake topped with fresh whipped cream and hot spiced apple juice. We borrowed books from their extensive library, which featured editions from literature, philosophy, history, and religion.

In Carolyn's first experience with Dr. Burns of a past-life regression she saw herself as a girl in a village in northern China. The experience was like a wide-awake dream. The little girl wandered away from home down the village's only street. She played in snow beside a stream until her hands were cold. She turned to go home but suddenly slipped and fell into a stream, where she was quickly trapped under a layer of ice. She struggled but was pulled downstream by the strong current. Soon the struggle was over. The girl stopped breathing as she floated head first downstream under the ice.

While describing what she saw, Carolyn shivered violently. Dr. Burns covered her with blankets. Although she was momentarily terrified, when Carolyn woke up she felt waves of warmth passing through her body, accompanied by feelings of well-being.

Carolyn had been reading Mai Mai Sze's wonderful book, *The Way of Chinese Painting.* After the session with Dr. Burns, Carolyn returned to the book with new interest. She found references to pine trees. The Chinese venerated the pine for the graceful lines of its sinuous form. The pine was also regarded as a primary symbol of power associated with the dragon, or yang force, and with the vitalizing spirit of heaven, *ch'i.*

"In my inner journey I move north," Carolyn wrote in her journal.

"It's early winter. *Ch'i* moves like sap sinking into pine roots. My sky wild summer south feelings are not for now. This is root time. I must dig deeper into root darkness so that I can work within a winter way."

The journal entry signaled the beginning of a dark time for Carolyn, but she continued designing. She dreamed of lapis lazuli, then borrowed two books from Dr. Burns, one on geomorphology and the other about jewels and gem stones. Before long, the design for number two was ready for weaving. She worked with blue-green, red-orange, white, and black. Derived from an interpretation of crystal structure, the tapestry turned out to be optically three-dimensional, suggestive of a maze (see Plate 3).

> Two is the Earth
> Woven with complementary colors
> Cold and hot, dark and light
> To weave with twinness in mind
> In a maze of *Lapis* lazuli.

As she did in her dream, Carolyn continued digging in the dark to unearth the bones long buried in her back yard. Dreams piled on top of each other in such numbers that they were scrawled down in nearly illegible hand-writing. One morning Carolyn woke up thinking her hands were caked in mud. After a second look, she found her hands merely blue.

"Cold, cold, cold," Carolyn wrote. "Blue hands. Wrinkled, old age skin. White and red splotches on hands and feet. Numb colors. Cold colors. Constriction. Shrinking. How can I work? Even my mind is freezing."

She opened one of her favorite books, Frank Waters' *Book of the Hopi*. She reread the chapter on the Soyal and Powama ceremonies following the winter solstice, in which a pattern of life is reaffirmed for the new year. During the coldest winter days, Hopi kiva chiefs plant bean seeds in the ceremonial kivas, then keep fires burning day and night while watering the soil. After a few days the seeds sprout. To the Hopi, the emerging green growth symbolizes abundance and successful harvest for the coming year.

During very cold Lake House days, seeds were planted for a design representing number three. Seeds and seed growth inspired the idea. Carolyn knew that within each seed there are meristem cells—the root meristem grows down, into darkness, and the stem meristem grows up, into light. The tapestry design represents the three-fold nature of plants (seed, shoot, and flower), woven within a seed-like elliptical form generated by a Fibonacci spiral progression.

Three is Plants
Three colors and black and white
Woven into seed, shoot and flower
To weave earth linked with sky
In a spiraling *Meristem* memory.

Weaving and dreaming continued to be closely interwoven processes. Designing activated dreams. Dreaming inspired design, with both processes indicating movement in her inner journey north. A dream about dreaming broke the darkness that had permeated Carolyn's moods for weeks.

> I am in a desert with David and an Indian medicine man. The medicine man speaks of the great power in dreaming. He says David has already learned how to be wide awake within dreaming, an ability I am learning also, although my ability will differ from David's because we have different allies. The medicine man tells me, "Your allies will show you how to dream with your hands."

Carolyn looked at her hands with new appreciation. They had been cold for weeks. When hearing the dream I was reminded of the Navajo hogan where an ancient hand had reached out and placed a weaving comb in my hand, seemingly bridging the worlds of waking and dreaming.

"Sitting still within the harmony place," Carolyn wrote. "Weaving comb and threads in hand, I weave my way across a threshold between worlds outside, and worlds behind the loom. My hands dream! Dreaming hands. My hands guide me in the crossover between worlds."

The dream seemed to have a healing effect. The irritating red sores gradually diminished and Carolyn felt the swelling going down. Another dream provided design ideas for a tapestry to honor the number four.

> I am in a hot, red-rock desert expanse. A fresh water inlet deeply penetrates into the desert. I see two snakes, long as I am tall, thicker around than my arm, coiled around each other. The snakes are iridescent turquoise in color, with creamy rose bellies. Suddenly, the entwined snakes upend themselves and slowly roll like a wheel, leaving a trail in the dust. I realize that the snake wheel is also an eye, an eye of the desert I see through as it rolls through the land.

Carolyn woke up with strongly ambivalent feelings. The snake-wheel-eye was a vivid image of primal power, possibly dangerous, potentially healing. She decided that an eye design to symbolize vision would be appropriate for number four. And from the dream, Carolyn chose four colors, in a range from lake blues to hot sand colors. Just as designing commenced, another dream came through with blazing clarity.

> An old woman weaver has put aside weaving tools to take care of her garden. I accompany her to a huge barn where there are milk cows and other farm animals. The place has the feel of the north, possibly Ontario. The barn's earth floor has been tilled and prepared for planting. Wood flats have been filled with dark soil and I notice some green sprouts. Everything feels rich, fecund, fragrant, warmed by sunlight streaming through sky lights.
>
> The weaver-gardener informs me of a tapestry competition and insists I am the one for the job. "The tapestry mural must be a woven labyrinth lattice of eyes," she says. "Eyes that will see the seer seeing the tapestry."
>
> She tells me of another tapestry wanted for a new Children's Mental Health Center. The design is to embody three qualities. First, the labyrinth lattice of eyes. Second, a spider web intersection of lines to reflect pathways in a child's mind, a web that is to be mandala-like, having "fundamental and direct impact in establishing harmony in mental processes." Third, the tapestry is to be a robe wrapped around the headdress, head, and body of a Toltec warrior.

A formidable commission to say the least. Carolyn decided to give it a try. She knew something about principles of harmony, a good start for the project. Recalling her first dream and design impulse, Carolyn was intrigued by the idea of an eye seeing the seer seeing the tapestry.

Carolyn conceived of her tapestry eye as a central circle emerging from a dark blue background. In addition to the eye, she wanted a symbolic representation of her medicine animal. She drew four zigzag lines, indicative of elk trails on mountains radiating out from the center. She also included flight forms, spiraling around the eye, to convey breakthrough from the dark oceanic expanse implied in background colors.

The square is the geometric form related to the number four. The new design was to be woven into a four-foot square. This was the largest warp ever strung up on her loom, and soon after weaving began Carolyn realized that the size itself would be the greatest challenge. The background, for example, was woven with a four-color mix in a sequence that repeated itself every nine rows. This sequence had to be kept in mind while the expansion rate for the circle was determined. Zigzag trails had to be introduced, creating difficulties because

Figure 17: *In* Vision Trails, *Carolyn wanted "an eye that sees the seer seeing the tapestry." The design is inspired by the number Four and includes flight forms and zigzag trails.*

of the steep angles to be maintained. Then the flight forms were introduced with a two-color mix.

The weaving demanded intense concentration at every stage, and Carolyn often left the loom feeling as if she were making little headway. All she gained from a day's work was a stiff neck, a sore back, and twitching eyes. The problem of cold hands had not entirely disappeared.

While writing in one of the cabin lofts, I was constantly aware of the soft, rhythmic drumming of the weaving comb. If the sound stopped for any length of time, my work stopped also. Unfortunately, Carolyn had to put up with the eternal clacking of typewriter keys, which is not nearly so pleasant a sound. One day I was stopped again by eery silence. I turned from my table to see the weaver examining her work. Carolyn suddenly doubled up with a severe pain. Horrified, I half fell, half climbed down the loft ladder while Carolyn stumbled to bed hugging herself. I covered her with blankets and hurried to the kitchen to heat up leftover soup. When I returned, Carolyn was shaking with chills, tears streaming down her face, and mumbling something about her design.

I only had a vague idea of what she was talking about, but I tried to calm her down.

"It's all wrong," she said. "I don't know how it's happened. The nine weft sequence is out of synch. I'll have to rip out a week's work."

Carolyn tried to explain design details which had fallen apart before her eyes. I felt utterly helpless.

"I suggest you stay away from the loom for a few days," I said. "You remind me of that weaver woman you just dreamed about. At least she was wise enough to put away weaving tools for a while to take care of her garden."

That night Carolyn dreamed again. She dreamed she had just finished a stimulating, productive day of work. Excited and happy, she looked forward to jumping into my arms. After undressing, however, she found her body covered from shoulders to belly with nipples, many of which exuded a thick milky goo.

Terrified, Carolyn woke up drenched in sweat, then momentarily thought the sweat was the milky goo. Several months later, we came across a description of a many-breasted goddess in Erich Neuman's book *The Great Goddess.* Curiously, the goddess's name was Diana, and was said to be a highly beneficent aspect of the ancient Mother Goddess. At the time of the dream, however, Carolyn needed a couple of hours to calm down. She finally went to sleep with a somewhat humorous image of herself as the ultimate cow.

But Carolyn dreamed again, about a gang of young hoodlums who were rounding up all her high school friends with the intent to "sever the brain functions in the precise spots responsible for creating symbolic images." Carolyn knew the dream was in part related to books she had been reading, including Lynn Olsen's *Women in Mathematics.* The book discusses women from Pythagorean times to the present whose contributions had been severely suppressed by male-dominated universities and societies. A second book, *Revelations, Diaries of Women,* included excerpts from the journals of famous women and wives of famous men, with much mention of fights for recognition in male-centered situations.

"The world is hungry now for the words and ways of women," Carolyn wrote in her own journal. "Women have begun to rise from the underground to reveal their creative gifts. This emergence is related to what I want to weave in my tapestry eye: my vision trails reaching out to the four directions."

But in reaching out, Carolyn had overextended herself. Perhaps conscious intention was interfering with the pace of unconscious movement. In bed, there was time for reflection. After a couple of days, insight came.

"I see now the pain was not all negative," she wrote. "I had moved out of balance, out of touch with the design. The slow pace bothered me, but each tapestry must progress according to its own time. Beauty, harmony emerge from a place of balance. I must wait for the holding power of integration."

When returning to the loom, Carolyn found the problems not half so bad as she had imagined. The errors were correctable with a minimum of unweaving. What errors there were served to aid in rethinking aspects of the design not yet woven. Carolyn returned to her journal.

> What did I mean by that phrase "holding power of integration?" The tapestry is a mirror of myself. Sometimes, each of us gets tired of being worked on. We wear each other out.
>
> Holding power of integration. I must be tuned in. Too many loose threads have been tangling up my mind. Crystal. David. Money. Cold. Design eye. Trails. Future. Threads outside the work color my progress. Threads must not be woven if *they* control me.

Thread was drummed over thread slowly, carefully. The eye began to take shape. Carolyn became aware of the woven eye watching, seeing her.

One afternoon, Dr. and Mrs. Burns came by for a visit. They quietly stood by the loom. When Carolyn put down her comb, she asked what they thought about the process.

"I'm sure you were a nun in one of your past lives," Dr. Burns said. "All those hours of weaving. This silent, meditative work. You have a nun-like quality, Carolyn. You really do."

Carolyn was surprised by the comment, but it recalled to mind Esther Harding's *Women's Mysteries*. Harding uses the term "virgin" in its original meaning to refer to an inner quality of woman rather than its outer manifestation in sexual purity. Virgin meant "woman at one in herself."[1]

At that time, I was reading a history of the Andean Incas. There was a reference to virgins housed in a building adjacent to the Incas' palace whose sacred life-long task was to weave the Incas' clothing.

The tapestry eye was opening, Carolyn thought. She was having to look at herself in new ways. The insights were disturbing, the more so after another troubling dream.

> People gather in an open area for a feast. A large deer, possibly an elk, walks into the area and begins sniffing in the rubbish left behind. The elk finds a hamburger bun and eats it.
>
> "Looks like she has found a potato," a woman comments.
>
> "Eaten with relish," I remark.
>
> The elk turns around, leaps, attacks me with her legs and dew claws. She kicks me until I cry out for help.

Frightened, Carolyn woke me up to tell me the dream.

"Your medicine animal is starving," I said.

All medicine needs renewal. Carolyn was clearly tired, both inside and out. Weaving was continuing to be ponderously slow, and questions aroused by the mysterious eye brought on sadness that Carolyn couldn't shake. Pressures from the world outside the loom were mounting. Within a few weeks we would have to move, with no idea where to go next. Carolyn's inherent fiscal conservatism was being pushed to extremes. We gave up eating meat, and stretched our dwindling supplies of noodles, rice, and potatoes. We borrowed twenty dollars from a neighbor and made the money last two weeks.

Carolyn put her spinning machine up for sale. The hand-crafted spinning wheel, made of cherry and apple wood, and mounted on a Singer sewing machine treadle, had traveled with us from British Columbia. Carolyn justified the sale by thinking that weaving, rather than spinning, was now her full-time priority. She also decided to sell wool.

I strongly objected. Selling weavable wool seemed an obvious act of desperation. But Carolyn insisted. A few days later a woman left the cabin with the spinning machine and several skeins of wool. The weaving baskets had never looked emptier.

One day, returning from town with Crystal, we found a large doe lying dead beside the road, probably hit by a truck. The deer was still warm to the touch when I loaded her into the pickup. Back at the cabin, we skinned and butchered the animal, discarding the bruised meat and broken bone. There was meat for weeks, enough to give away to the neighbors. Following a Navajo custom, we saved all the bones and returned them to the forest with a gift of corn meal.

Two days later, a telephone call came from a Los Angeles art agent to whom Carolyn had sent slides. The agent announced the sale of *Lapis* for seven hundred dollars. We mailed the tapestry. The check arrived two weeks later. In the meantime, I received payment for some editorial work, with the promise of more. Suddenly our pockets were bulging. I insisted on bacon and eggs for breakfast, a welcome change from porridge.

The tapestry for the number four was finally completed. Carolyn continued to sense an ominous quality in its woven eye. "What is it?" she asked me. "It's a water eye. An eye of the ocean. It turns, spins. There is something powerful about that eye." I could offer no explanations. To avoid its unnerving presence Carolyn rolled up the tapestry and put it out of sight.

Four is the Animals
Woven with four colors
Into movement, a way of perceiving
To weave the seer seeing
Four directions of *Vision Trails.*

The snow melted with spring weather, and design began for the number five. The pain and coloration in Carolyn's fingers finally healed. In tapestry number five, she decided to celebrate the number for the human being by acknowledging her hands, hands that had preoccupied Carolyn all winter. Hands, a human gift. Cold hands, dreaming hands, hands holding the weaving comb to make manifest the designs.

"Manifest," I said, "comes from the Latin *manifestus,* which means—grasped by hand."

"My comb feels light," Carolyn wrote. "Weaving is easy now. I'll weave my hands' song. Sun music. Spring rhythms."

The small tapestry seemed to weave itself and was quickly completed (see Plate 3). The design was composed of a series of undulating lines derived from the sine curve. The lines were built up with mixes of warm colors, including gold tones from wool Carolyn had dyed using marigolds grown in our Cedar Road garden in British Columbia. When the tapestry was off the loom Carolyn decided to fast one day for each of the five tapestries. During the fourth day of her fast she went for a walk in the forest. After washing hands and face in a stream, she noticed a deer drinking from a pool not far upstream. The deer seemed quite tame and let Carolyn approach. She followed a little way behind as the doe slowly grazed uphill. Carolyn stayed with the deer for most of the afternoon.

Five is the Human Being
Woven with five colors
Finding an inner rhythm

To weave with dreaming hands
The drumming of a *Hand Song.*

The day after Carolyn broke her fast, I disassembled the loom and packed the truck. That evening we circled the cabin, visiting our favorite trees. Crystal called out farewells to the ospreys, rabbits, and squirrels. We said goodby to Dr. and Mrs. Burns.

But the story of the five tapestries was not yet complete. Carolyn dreamed a long dream.

I find a familiar place in the forest. I find the same pine tree I had become connected with before our move into Lake House. Instead of one pine, however, there are twin pines in a small clearing. I walk slowly between the trees along a narrow dirt road. The earth is dark, loamy, fragrant. The area is thick with tall, healthy pines.

I discover a cleft hidden in a massive rock wall. I enter a cave and descend a stone stairway. I hear a roar of water coming from far below. After a few more steps down the dark stairway, I sense danger. The roar is very loud, as if I am nearing a torrential force made by a great river.

I decide not to descend further. Then I hear voices. Three women climb the stone stairs, emerging from the blackness below. I join them on the climb back to sunlight. One of the three is a white-haired woman.

"I have met with an old woman who lives down there," the white-haired woman states. "The old woman is a weaver and spinner. It is she who is responsible for the great force of the waters."

Then I am with a younger woman somewhere in Asia, or perhaps northern India. We find a dark young man with black hair. He is in deep meditation and wears a red robe. We understand we have been drawn to the man by the power of his concentration.

The man tells us that when he was two years old, it had been noticed he was unusual in some way. The strangeness stayed with him until he was fourteen, and at that time he found a spiritual teacher, an old man. The old man, dressed in a pure white robe, sits in meditation beside the young man.

The woman says to me, "We know now that this young man who has brought us to him by means of meditation lived many years ago. The record of his life is contained within his art. He is a sculptor, with a great knowledge of animals."

"The sculptures are the stories the man tells about himself," I am told.

> The young man again enters into deep meditation. I know he is a visionary artist, and I know the blonde woman with whom I have come to this place is a highly intelligent researcher.
>
> Then I am in a living room of a beautifully furnished home. I await the arrival of the blonde-haired woman and the black-haired man.

This dream was a focus of conversation for several days, and returned to mind again some year and a half later when we discovered the Mabinogion novels and Robert Graves' *White Goddess.* In Walton's fourth novel, *Island of the Mighty,* the goddess' complementary moods of creation and destruction are beautifully presented in the story of Arianrod.

Arianrod generally uses her powers beneficently, but she is capable of destruction. When her brother Gwidion misuses the magic arts, Arianrod resorts to powers she knows will destroy the Island of the Mighty, and in so doing, destroy also everything known to the Druidic Old Tribes who practice their arts within the context of the Ancient Harmonies.

The outraged Arianrod goes to the cliffs, finds a hidden cleft in the rocks, descends a long dark passage way. She winds through a labyrinth of caves, the ocean roaring in her ears. She digs down and pulls up wet stones one after another. Hands covered with slimy ooze, hair unloosed, Arianrod digs deeper until she discovers a great stone in the center of a deep chamber. She utters the forbidden words, performs the sacred chants, then pulls up the stone to open the Eye of the Deep. Beneath the stone is a well with no bottom but the ocean.[2]

Robert Graves describes Arianrod as another aspect of the ancient Great Goddess, the White Goddess of Life-in-Death and Death-in-Life. Her name means Silver Wheel, and after the Island was destroyed Arianrod returned to her true home, a silver-circled castle beyond the north wind in the constellation Corona Borealis.[3]

We came to see how the dream reflected inner movement related to weaving the five tapestries. The dream affirmed how tapestry art, as well as being a specific record of a time and place, also helps Carolyn find inner teachers to guide her in her psychological journey.

10

Story Belts

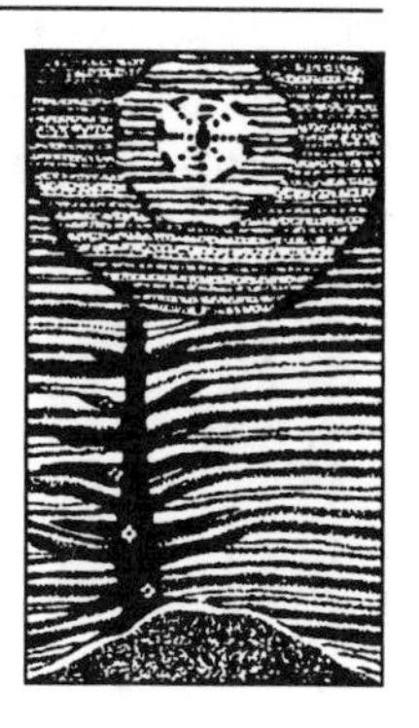

From time to time Carolyn dressed the loom with strange-looking warps, six feet long and only four inches wide. The first narrow pieces were made solely for purposes of practice, to be used like a painter's sketch book. Woven records seemed a reasonable idea. Carolyn wanted to try out geometric, mathematical, and color ideas, and keep a permanent record of her experiments for reference when necessary. What in fact happened to the first practice pieces is quite another story.

The first narrow warp was made several months before we moved from British Columbia to California. At that phase of her technical development, Carolyn wove with two angles, approximately forty and fifty-two degrees, learned from Navajo technique. Thinking that any angle should be possible, she decided to weave a sixty-degree angle. Later research revealed that in traditional European tapestry a wide variety of angles were woven. But without access to such information at the time, Carolyn taught herself. Because sixty degrees is the angle of the hexagon, she decided to weave hexagons four inches wide on her practice warp.

Before weaving, Carolyn found a series of drawings she had done while we were in Yellowstone Park in Montana. I remember the day we followed paths to the foot of the spectacular Upper Falls in Yellowstone Canyon. Carolyn sketched patterns derived from what she saw in the cascading foaming water—interlaced streamers which to me looked like braids. She also drew interconnected concentric circles and ellipses derived from whirlpools. There were hundreds of bluebirds darting along the cliff walls that day, playing in the rainbow-sprinkled spray from the waterfall.

Carolyn wove the first hexagon with a two-color mix to produce a rippling texture. She decided to weave a series of hexagons, more or less braided one above the other, with color mixes to give a watery look. After three hexagons, the practice piece was put away. She had learned the sixty-degree angle, and had experimented with color mixes for *Four Looks East*.

After that tapestry was completed, the narrow warp was brought out again. New angles and color mixes were tried, then the practice piece was put away. Three tapestries were woven in Vancouver, four at the cabin in the redwoods, and five in Lake House before the half-way point was reached in the narrow warp.

When the piece went on the loom again, Carolyn discovered that intricate color progressions could be achieved by means of color mixing techniques. Very subtle patternings could be produced using colors of closely related value. On the other hand, dramatic gradations could be achieved by mixing colors with greater contrast in their values.

Experiments using three, four, or five color mixes filled much of the remaining warp. The last section was a color progression moving through the entire spectrum to produce a rainbow effect.

When the practice piece was removed from the loom and put on the wall, we took our first look at the work in its entire length. We realized immediately that something more than a record of ideas had been achieved. The narrow, vertical dimensionality moved the observer's eye up and down rapidly so as to relate the supposed disparate images. And, if at first glance the geometrical patterns and color mixes appeared entirely abstract, a closer look aroused another perspective.

I saw braided water streamers, canyon walls, birds, whirlpools, even a rainbow. She had translated her Yellowstone sketches into a woven design, as if she had woven a cut-away view, a longitudinal slice of the canyon.

We had returned to the cabin in the redwoods for a short stay when Carolyn put up her second practice warp, intending to experiment with more color mixes. The idea of weaving a catalog of experiments was proving to be increasingly enticing.

Of particular interest was Carolyn's discovery that pointillist effects could be achieved in weaving by using colors in specific, numerically derived combinations. She read about the paintings of Georges Seurat, who had mastered pointillist painting techniques during the last decades of the 1800's.

"A woven row of color can be thought of as a series of points," Carolyn said. "The next row is another series of points, but will not be seen as such unless that second row is a different color than the first."

Carolyn was also studying Joseph Itten's *Elements of Color,* with particular attention to his color wheels, color contrasts, and harmonies. She began applying the ideas to woven color mixes. The results, combined with the perception of a woven row as a series of points, allowed Carolyn to completely rethink her use of color.

For example, a medium blue can be woven as a solid color, but it can also be achieved by mixing combinations of light and dark value blues. The woven mix of light and dark blues becomes a medium blue in the observer's eye. This technique of tricking the eye into seeing a color not actually there was often employed by the Impressionist painters. Seurat was a master of it.

Curiously, Seurat learned his pointillist theory from Chevreil, who in turn had devised his ideas while working as a wool dyer in French tapestry guilds. Woven samples had been used in the guilds to study color gradations and relationships to be used subsequently in woven tapestries.

Experiments with pointillist effects revealed that mixed colors produced richer color tones with more depth than areas woven with a single color. Furthermore, the color mixes, woven by means of mathematically derived progressions, could be used for value and hue gradations in countless design applications.

Half the length of another long narrow warp was filled with color mixes and gradations. But weaving and writing stopped one sunny afternoon when Crystal responded to a knock on the cabin door. In walked none other than the master of surprise himself, Chuck Storm.

Before long, Storm had noticed the first practice piece, which was hanging on the wall next to the loom. He took it down, then slowly passed the images and colors through his hands.

"It's a Sun Dance belt," he said. "You have woven medicine signs: whirlpools, morning stars, animal signs."

He lightly touched several of the designs. "I could think up a story from what I see here. Two stories. One by reading up the belt, another by reading down. Elk Woman, you've woven a story belt.

Storm compared the weaving to a mirror. "Anyone reading the images could come up with their own stories. Ask a hundred artists to conjure from this weaving; you'd hear a hundred stories. Each story would be a mirror image of the reader."

The next day Storm demonstrated his own method of conjuring. He perched himself behind my typewriter. He asked Carolyn to sit beside him. "Relax and focus your attention," he told her. "I'll pull images up from inside you and write them down. The images are yours. You can weave a story belt with them if you want."

The results of these conjuring sessions—he did several—were occasionally poetic, often evocative, sometimes entirely incomprehensible. We eventually decided the poetic allusions had a lot to do with Storm and his use of the language but little to do with Carolyn. Essentially, he was having a good time writing, with Elk Woman by his side. Nevertheless, the idea of conjuring was greatly appealing. Carolyn wondered if the long narrow dimensions of the practice warps might lend themselves to a controlled form of conjured weaving. Weaving spontaneously, allowing images to emerge one after another story-like, was a frightening but stimulating possibility, and a "new angle" well worth exploring.

Two days later, Storm entertained us with horse-stealing stories. He always insisted the Cheyenne were world champions in the horse-stealing trade. I have met several Sioux and Crow who would argue that boast.

Storm began with a few entirely possible, highly probable, perhaps even true horse-thieving stories. After those warm-ups, Storm advanced to several improbable, nearly impossible, but nevertheless believable stories. He was just getting going. I could see horses stampeding through the cabin's back door and raising dust right out the front door. He moved on to totally impossible, conjured fantastic stories followed by a few utterly absurd stories—all Cheyenne horse-thieving stories.

We laughed until our bellies ached. We cried so hard from laughing so much that tears poured down our faces. Nobody has ever made us laugh like Chuck Storm. In the middle of all the stories he said something about great artists being good horse thieves. I didn't give the comment much thought. I was laughing too hard to ask questions.

We recovered sufficiently to eat lunch. Afterwards, Storm surprised us again by preparing to leave. He never says goodby. He just goes. Before leaving, however, Storm carefully removed the first story belt from the wall, neatly folded it, and tucked the weaving under his arm.

"I know a good horse when I see one," Storm said with a smile.

We weren't laughing when Storm walked out the door. There was little either of us was capable of doing except stand there transfixed. An impeccable Cheyenne horse thief was on his way and there was no stopping him. The story belt had not been photographed and we have never seen it since.

Several days later, Carolyn returned to the loom for a fresh look at her second practice warp. Instead of experimenting with color progressions, she sat down in her weaving spot, and conjured. The results excited her, but then ideas for a new tapestry took priority. She practiced a spiral form, then concentric ovoids, then another four-color mix— all potential ideas for tapestries. Then, with only six inches of warp remaining, she decided to conjure the piece to completion.

"I'll begin with this olive color," Carolyn said, thread in hand. "I'll surround the color with its complement, then go on from there."

The idea of weaving a flower came to mind. She would use leftover threads from former tapestries. Instead of a flower, however, the image of a weaver emerged. Carolyn had never attempted pictorial representation, but a figure was evolving nevertheless. She found herself weaving a weaver. The weaver was weaving a belt. The threads passed through Carolyn's hands and into the weaving quite spontaneously, with not much difficulty.

When the second story belt was finished, we brought the piece outside and hung it on the trunk of a cedar tree. Reddish bark framed the images. Tree colors seemed to blend nicely with tapestry colors. We gave the woven woman a name—Cedar Tree Woman.

Carolyn found she preferred reading the story belt in the weaver's way, from the bottom up, while I read the images from the top down. Each of us came up with a story, mirroring our individual perceptions of the images and colors. Then she handed me the belt.

"It's yours," she said. "Providing you conjure with the image of the woven woman and write a story or a poem."

I wrapped the story belt around my waist with the woven weaver snug against my belly. I leaned against the cedar tree, the sun full in my face. After a while, I thought I heard Cedar Tree Woman whispering.

> The mind of the woman is the voice of a kachina[1]
> Her feet-roots feel the depths of the lake
> Her flower-hands weave threads into time
> Her body surrounds an arrow of the sun
> Earth colors clothe her
> Meadow reflections nourish her
> Waters of life flow into her womb
> Pollen paths pour out of her dreams
> Above her is sky
> Beneath her is rock

Behind her is darkness
Before her is the dawn.

Listen, listen
My name is Cedar Tree Woman
My form a dance of light and line
My voice echoes yours
Whispering, whispering
Pleased, yes, that I am with all.

11

The Marketplace

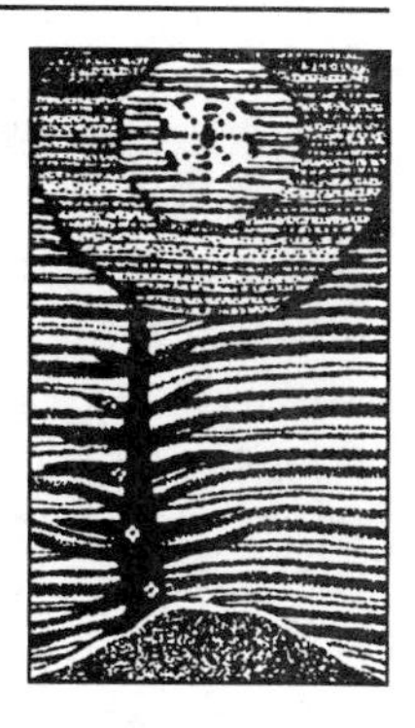

Weaving does not stop when a tapestry comes off the loom. As Carolyn puts it, "A completed tapestry becomes woven into the lives of those who choose to purchase it." Letting go of a piece is sometimes difficult, considering the emotional and physical investment in designing and weaving. We have often kept a tapestry for several weeks or months before letting it go, but releasing a finished tapestry is a necessary and vital part of the process which contributes not only income but incentives to begin another design.

A few tapestries had been sold in British Columbia. By the time we moved to California, Carolyn's confidence in her work had grown, and to some extent her prices reflected the change. But initially, California sales were few and far between, as we relied on word of mouth as a marketing approach. During one period in Berkeley, Carolyn sold two pieces, *Sun Drum* and *Four Looks East,* after no less than fifteen private showings in homes.

The first important market proved to be Los Angeles. When we decided to go there to try our luck, we dreaded what we'd have to face.

At the time, Carolyn and I loved the solitude of our lifestyle and did not like the fact that solitude has its price. We were determined to support ourselves through our art, but at that stage, no one, other than ourselves and a few friends, knew the tapestries existed. Gallery owners and buyers did not come knocking on our cabin door in a remote corner of northern California.

During the next three years we returned to Los Angeles several times and never came away empty-handed. Agents, galleries, and collectors responded positively to the work, but finding them was often a painful, even a humiliating experience. In 1978, we arrived for our first visit with sixty-five dollars, a gas company credit card, and the name of a friend of a friend. Under the circumstances, we knew we could not leave Los Angeles until we had enough funds to support the next few months of work. Our priority was to promote and sell tapestries. In the meantime I would be on the lookout for writing jobs.

We tracked down the friend of our friend in Santa Monica. After brief introductions, Sunset Carson got right to the point.

"How much money do you have?" he asked.

"One hundred dollars," I lied, trying to sound affluent.

"Consider yourself rich," Carson chimed. "Two million artists live in this town and we're all broke. Wonder if you could lend me ten bucks."

This news woke us up. I felt a strange sense of relief learning that we were not alone in our financial straits.

Carson introduced his girlfriend, Anne, who was active in the women's liberation movement and worked as a waitress in a Chinese restaurant. But her real love was clay. Anne was particularly fond of sculpting clay into female figurines she called Betty Buddha. All of Anne's Betty Buddhas were high-breasted and straggly haired, portrayed in full lotus position and wearing nothing except hiking boots and lipstick.

As for Carson, he wrote dirty books. He had a published novel to his credit and another manuscript just finished. I paged through the manuscript and then asked Carson how such a smart man could write such disgusting books. To my amazement, Carson's response was a deep blush. He came off as a rather shy and endearing sort of guy, quite unlike Captain Buffalo and the other heroes of his stories. He told us he had moved to Los Angeles from Oklahoma because he'd heard that a mint was to be made in screenplays. He swung open the garage door to show us his private office. A greasy concrete floor was stacked with bound, rotting bundles of newspapers. A space large enough for a desk had been cleared. He wrote at night under a naked light bulb with the garage door open, unless the neighborhood dogs sniffed him out.

The rooms in the rented communal house were occupied, but we were invited to stay, with a suggestion that we pitch our tent in the twelve-foot square of grass next to Anne's vegetable garden. In spite of Betty Buddha and Captain Buffalo, we immediately liked this Santa Monica couple and gladly accepted their invitation, but instead of camping, we parked our truck in the driveway and slept in the back.

Our initial idea was to meet with art agents. With Anne's assistance, Carolyn made her first appointments. Los Angeles has many agents and Carolyn met several. Some agents tended to be polite but cool, making her keenly aware that her twenty-minute appointment was one of a dozen scheduled for the day. For the first time, we experienced the tyranny of agents' waiting rooms. We entered Los Angeles entirely innocent of the problems young artists face when looking for agents or buyers. It had not occurred to us that for every artist receiving representation by an agent, a hundred or more were turned away, with thousands waiting for first appointments.

We felt very fortunate to find agents who responded enthusiastically and accepted slide records of Carolyn's work. Within a year, one agent sold two of the Lake House tapestries, *Lapis* and *Hand Song,* to Los Angeles banks for seven hundred dollars each. Another agent was especially helpful in arranging appointments with architects and interior decorators who were known to have art budgets for their commercial building projects.

During one of the first appointments I pretended to read a magazine while Carolyn showed her tapestries. The architect appeared to like what he saw.

"Why do you call this one *Rain No Rain?"* he asked.

Carolyn cleared her throat.

"You remember the drought," Carolyn stated, hopefully.

The architect didn't seem to understand.

"The creek dried up," Carolyn said, trying again. "I was studying raked gardens and water molecules . . ."

Her voice faded. Some details needed ironing out before Carolyn would achieve what is commonly called a professional presentation.

"*Rain No Rain* looks like teddy bears to me," he said with a big smile.

The architect told us he did not have tapestry art in mind for the buildings he was working on, but that as it was a question of timing, we should call him again the next time we were in town. He gave Carolyn a written recommendation to a Beverly Hills gallery. We soon learned that such recommendations carry considerable weight, and we made no further appointments without one.

The gallery accepted three tapestries on consignment and included the work in a group exhibition, which received good reviews. No tapestries sold in the exhibition, but the owner seemed patient and supportive, telling us that it would take time for her clientele to accept the idea of tapestry art being sold in a fine arts gallery.

There was another problem with galleries.

"You're too unpredictable," one gallery manager said. "Your designs are bound to be successful here, but how do I know what you'll be weaving a year from now? Weave me six variations of *Lapis* or *Sun Drum* and another six of *Rain No Rain* or *Wings in Gold,* and I'll be happy to give you a one-person show."

Tapestry weaving takes time. Carolyn weaves as few as four tapestries a year, rarely as many as ten. Whether four or ten, she has not been inclined to repeat designs when other ideas call for her attention. Nor has she contemplated setting up a production studio with apprentice weavers working on editions or variations of a theme. Galleries, in fact, have not proved to be her most viable means of selling. Carolyn is not in a position to turn down sales that occur privately so as to have enough pieces available for a major exhibition, which in any event require at least two years of advance planning. Instead, Carolyn shows her work in selected group exhibitions, juried shows, and invitationals.

During our first trips to Los Angeles, however, there were days when we felt our efforts were getting us nowhere. Someone would recommend someone else who in turn had other people for us to call or see. Travel time in the city made it impossible to arrange more than three or four appointments a day. Since we were living in our truck, scheduling created interesting problems. We ate our lunch and supper in the cab. I often drove through streets looking for a telephone booth or parking spot while Carolyn changed clothes in the back. Sometimes I stayed with Crystal while Carolyn made the rounds, but in later visits to the city, Crystal played with new friends, leaving me to volunteer my services for Carolyn.

At the end of exhausting days, Carson was usually around to reassure us.

"Stop feeling sorry for yourself," he told Carolyn. "They'll knock you down and hit you where it hurts but you've got to be strong. You've got to be a warrioress."

You'd never know by Carson's red hair that he has a strong dose of Choctaw Indian blood in him, but he liked to use the language he'd learned from Indian people he had grown up with.

"Use your tapestry like a shield," he said. "Let your art ward off the blows that the dealers throw at you, but hold your tapestry high anyway. You've got your medicine signs woven into your designs and they tell people who you are and what you're capable of doing."

"I'd rather hide," Carolyn said.

Experience improved Carolyn's presentations. Even when she was not as polished as she would have liked, she did find she could trust her work to do her talking for her. And with experience came new questions. What kind of commission was Carolyn willing to work out, and on what terms? When would she agree to release a tapestry on consignment to a museum store, gallery, or craft shop? How often and under what circumstances would she agree again to give a private showing for a friend of a friend of a friend? And, after a particularly bad day, we found ourselves asking what had we done to deserve a particularly insensitive interior decorator.

I pushed the elevator button in a plush lobby. It was my job that day to carry the tapestry bag. As usual, Carolyn had prepared for the appointment by neatly rolling each tapestry she intended to show, surrounding the tapestries with a linen sheet, then putting the bundle into a big bag. The bag had been hand-woven of alpaca wool in the Peruvian Andes, originally for the purpose of carrying potatoes.

The interior decorator who met us wore plastic alligator skin shoes and held a plastic ebony cigarette holder. Almost immediately, his eyes turned cartwheels.

"Honey, did you weave this marvelous bag?"

"It's a Peruvian potato sack," Carolyn said.

The decorator turned pale. Carolyn held up a tapestry.

"Vision what?" he asked, blowing smoke rings.

"*Vision Trails*," Carolyn repeated.

"Mystical influences, right deary?"

Carolyn quickly unrolled another tapestry.

"Some potatoes you have here," he said, loving his joke. "Yes, well, that is marvelous. *Rain No Rain* looks like record discs to me. I have a friend with Columbia Records, I'll recommend they hang your tapestry in the lobby."

He made a phone call and arranged for an appointment, but we canceled it the next day. We decided to keep the tapestry for our private collection.

When least expected, somewhere in the maze, a tapestry would sell. The first Los Angeles buyer knew the moment she saw *Vision Trails* that the tapestry had been woven for her. I recalled Carolyn's dream of the weaver-gardener who had need of a tapestry having a labyrinth lattice of eyes in the design, spider web intersections, a tapestry robe to be worn by a Toltec warrior. The buyer did not appear to be Toltec, although her father had done archaeology in Mayan and Toltec sites. She did not appear to be a warrior either, but who am I to question how a tapestry weaves its way into the vision trails of a young actress, a black-haired woman by the name of Dhanna—a name which like its sister name Diana can be traced to the ancient white goddess?

Our fourth marketing visit to Los Angeles brought fresh surprises, not the least of which was finding Carson living with a Beverly Hills woman in her spacious canyon house.

"How'd you do it?" I asked.

Carson pulled on his monogrammed leather boots. He buttoned his silk vest, donned a pair of smoke-blue shades, and adjusted his black cowboy hat.

"David, my friend," said Carson. "In this town I've witnessed miracles that'll put the Second Coming to shame."

"But what happened to Anne?" I asked.

"Betty Buddha was a smash hit in Japan," he said. "Anne moved to Tokyo."

Later that day, we stopped at the Santa Monica beach. We found a spot of sand, unpacked our lunch, and watched the beach parade pass by.

"Look at the warps," Carolyn said.

Carolyn sees weavings everywhere She's in the habit of watching warps which populate the streets. She's called me a warp.

"We're all warps," she said. "We are all walking, breathing, living warps on our way to becoming completed tapestries."

She imagines inserting threads into incomplete tapestries walking by. She can find dangling threads in any crowd, uneven edges, loose ends, irregular dimensions, lines lacking color, designs needing centers. She knows a broken warp when she sees one, and noticed several on the Santa Monica beach.

"So how do you repair damaged warps?" I asked.

"It takes care. You need a new piece of strong string which must be joined to the original warp with two knots, one at the top, the other at the bottom of the break. It's essential the knots hold. They must be tied in such a way as to give the repaired warp strength equal to all the others."

I took her word for it. She proceeded to study the scene from another point of view. She pointed out unusual color progressions, vivid geometric patterns, undreamed-of design possibilities. In every moment, in one way or another, Carolyn interlaces weft and warp, drumming thread after thread into place.

During that visit to Los Angeles, two tapestries were placed on consignment in a prominent gallery, and another agent accepted a portfolio and slide record for promoting the work. The most memorable meeting came the day before we left, when we were introduced to a man who was a composer, conductor, film scorist, song writer, and record producer. Carolyn described to him the conjuring process used in weaving sections of my story belt, *Cedar Tree Woman.* The composer was immediately taken by the work. He draped the long belt over his hand and slowly drew the piece towards him in such a way that only a small portion of the weaving was visible at a time. He began to hum. He appeared to be "hearing" the colors and forms, and finding rhythms in the color progressions as if they were his musical score.

"Your story belt is a composition," he said. "Instruments of the orchestra could be assigned to each color or color movement and then we would find a woven musical composition."

He gave Carolyn a check for a down payment and asked her to improvise a story belt for him.

"Weave with music in mind," he said.

12

The House of Waters

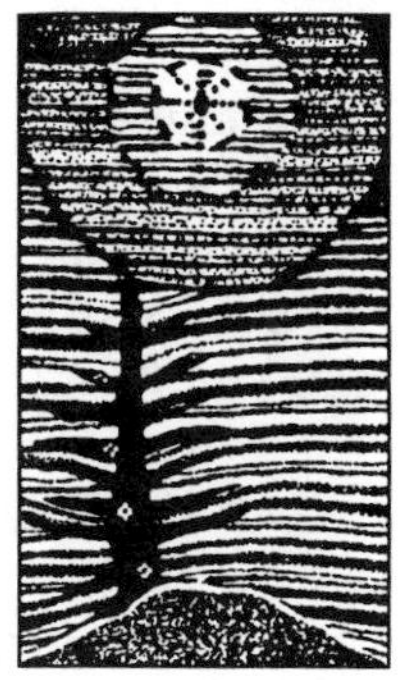

For years I had wanted to meet Frank Waters, a writer who lived near Taos, New Mexico. His *Book of the Hopi* had been annual reading for both Carolyn and me, and an important resource for my comparative religions course when I was teaching. His book *The Man Who Killed the Deer* is essential reading for any student of native American life and philosophy. When *Mexico Mystique* appeared, I welcomed his provocative analysis of meso-American myth and symbolism, especially the interpretations of the Mayan sacred calendar. During a camping trip in the Southwest, I finally decided to give him a call. He answered the telephone with a hearty hello and, after an introductory conversation, asked us to come by when we passed through Taos.

I approached the meeting with some trepidation, imagining a solitary person, a man of dreams inclined towards mysticism. With instructions to follow a dirt road uphill toward Taos Mountain, we found the appropriate driveway, skirted by towering aspens. A sage-scented atmosphere surrounded the house. We were invited inside by a tall blonde woman, Waters' wife, Barbara, a teacher and writer. Once again our travels had led us to a white-haired woman of the north.

Waters was not half so remote as I had imagined. He seemed very much at ease in his favorite rocking chair. He filled a pipe with Golden Burley tobacco and soon the pungent smoke was swirling around his greying hair. We discussed his books and he asked about our Sun

Dance experiences and our time with the Navajo. He seemed very calm; yet he possessed a wry sense of humor. He impressed me as being unusually careful, a veritable wise old man of the mountain.

We camped in the mountains nearby and joined Frank and Barbara two nights later for dinner. Then we left New Mexico and returned to northern California for Carolyn to complete preparations for a one-person exhibition in a San Francisco gallery. After the month-long showing, we intended to leave California, but had not planned just where to go.

When the time for the move came, I decided to give Frank Waters a call and ask if he knew of a place for rent in the Taos area. Waters' command of silence comes across even on the telephone. After a long pause he came up with an astonishing suggestion. He said he and Barbara planned to move to Tucson for the winter, and asked if we would care to live and work in his Taos home.

We packed up and moved in late November, arriving in Taos on a cold day. The air was breathlessly clear and invigorating. We circled the large adobe house before entering. Taos Mountain, with its snow-tipped blue folds, surged up east of the house. To the northeast, less than a mile away, were the rocky crags of a split mountain. To the south and west stretched a vast expanse of high desert plateau. A mountain stream flowed through a grove of cottonwood and aspen in front of the house. Near the entrance, in a yard blanketed with gold leaves, seven graceful aspens stood like silent sentinels.

Inside, daylight streamed through the windows.

"Why does Frank have so many feathers?" Crystal asked.

Feathers filled little bowls and hung from the light fixtures. Fire-blackened adobe fireplaces occupied a corner in every room. Navajo rugs carpeted the floors. There were Indian ceramics on the shelves, paintings by southwestern artists on the walls, books filling shelves in every room except the kitchen.

"Almost as many books as there are feathers," Crystal said.

During our first night we found that the house of feathers and books was also a house of dreaming. Carolyn's dream included some intriguing riddles.

> I see a large man's head. His wild dark hair is filled with feathers. His warm smile welcomes me into the house. He appears to be a caretaker, a kachina caretaker, and I love his inviting, friendly disposition.
>
> I study a painting opposite the bed. I feel the painting was done by Frank Waters and portrays a woman who has died, perhaps his former wife. The white-haired woman looks up over

the curve of the earth's surface. Her face is as large as the earth. Both face and earth are pure white. She peeks over the edge of the curve and I believe she is preparing to return to earth. Four large plants grow in front of her eyes, three green plants and one red.

The dark wild man with feathers in his hair returns. He has a spider's body. He is Spider Man. His smile continues to welcome me. I sense his great wisdom. He speaks a few words in a soft clear voice. He repeats what he has said, but with a changed word order. He repeats himself again and again, always emphasizing each phrase as if it's a unique concept he wants me to understand.

Spiders are the soul of water.
Spiders are the water of soul.
Soul is the spiders of water.
Soul is the water of spiders.
Water is the soul of spiders.
Water is the spiders of soul.

Then I swim under water, and look at the night sky through bubbles. The bubbles rise from my mouth, surface, then rise to become stars, fixed in their places in the sky.

Spider Man asks me, "What is essential for making hydrogen and oxygen atoms into water?"

"It is in the linking," I answer.

Carolyn awoke to find moonlight casting a pale blue ambience through the room. A line of kachina dolls on a shelf next to the bed seemed to be listening as we talked about this kachina-like dream, a dream about essences or inner forms, especially of spiders and water. The dream reconfirmed a relationship established in earlier dreams between medicine ways and the white-haired woman, a goddess-like figure who peers over the edge of earth's surface preparing to return.

I gazed at a strange old shield ringed with hawk and eagle feathers hung from spruce vigas above the bed. We allowed ourselves to be swallowed for awhile by the incredible silence in the house, until Carolyn whispered, "David, what are we doing here?"

"I'm not sure," I said. "We're here for six months, but then what? We'll move again, who knows where. All this moving. Maybe it's another test of some kind. What do you think?"

Carolyn remained silent. I thought she had gone back to sleep, until she said, "I believe we are here because for now this is absolutely the best place for us to be."

I felt the same way. In the next few days we set up our respective work areas and looked forward to beginning. We had not enjoyed so much room since our farmhouse years on Cedar Road. We sensed an energy in the area, a vibrancy that was there to be tapped and transformed by creative work. A sense that the house was held in a beneficent and protective embrace never left us all the time we were there.

Carolyn prepared a story belt warp for the composer's commission, and I helped her dress the loom. The intent was to weave with sound in mind and conjure an entire design. But she needed guiding ideas.

One morning, Carolyn pulled a book off the shelf beside the bed. The cover was a faded red. The pages were well thumbed and marked. Carolyn had never heard of the author and was unfamiliar with the subject suggested by the title. She slowly paged through Lama Govinda's *Foundations of Tibetan Mysticism,* and her eye settled on the following paragraph:

> The word *tantra* is related to the concept of weaving and its derivatives (thread, web, fabric, etc.) hinting at the interwovenness of things and actions, the interdependence of all that exists, the continuity in the interaction of cause and effect, as well as spiritual and traditional development, which like a thread weaves its way through the fabric of history and of individual lives.[1]

In her dream, Carolyn had responded to Spider Man's riddle with the answer, "It's in the linking." Carolyn's links with her own artistic medium were expanded by learning the meaning of weaving in metaphysical terms. In Tibetan Buddhism, and, as we would later discover, in many religious traditions, weaving is a primary symbol relating to the inherent interconnectedness of all life.

Tibetan mystics describe five psycho-physical body centers called chakras. The centers have physical locations in the body, and also many symbolic associations. Govinda stresses that the associations are far from arbitrary, obeying rules inherent to the system. Each center is associated with a seed syllable of sound, a color, and a geometric form.

Carolyn conceived of her story belt as having five weaving areas based on "body centers" of the Tibetan chakra system. For example, the first center or chakra is known as the Root Center, located at the base of the spine and associated with the square, the color yellow, and the seed syllable LAM.[2] Carolyn studied the five centers, especially the colors and geometry associated with each, then sat down at the loom.

Weaving was slow. Five weeks were needed to bring the piece to completion. When the belt was off the loom, it was clearly a significant departure from anything woven previously. Aware of her unfamiliarity with the spontaneous approach, Carolyn harbored uncertainties, and was reluctant to send the belt off to the Los Angeles composer.

She decided to use the belt as a means of consulting the *I Ching, Book of Changes.* This book of Chinese mythology and ancient knowledge is organized into sixty-four hexagrams, each of which reflects some aspect of the Tao. Carolyn had conceived of her belt design in terms of the five chakras, but to determine the belt's overall dimensions she had used an approximation of six six-by-ten-inch golden rectangles. So now she folded her belt into sixths, then read each rectangle in terms of its relative lightness or darkness. A light or yang area could be noted as a solid line in the making of her hexagram. A relatively dark or yin area could be noted as a broken line. The six areas, read one above the other, could in this way be interpreted as the six lines of a hexagram.

She consulted the *I Ching* and the hexagram turned out to be number sixty-four, the last in the book. The central idea for that hexagram is called "Before Completion," indicating a time when transition from disorder to order is not yet complete. Of particular importance to Carolyn was the image associated with the hexagram. The image, Fire over Water, suggested the importance of finding how forces of fire and water can be beneficially integrated.[3] In the *I Ching,* fire is related to warmth and light, and upward moving, with its highest manifestation the fire in the sky, or the sun. Water on the other hand, is associated with the cold and abysmal, the low place. Viewing the story belt as a representation of the "present moment" of her psyche, Carolyn found in the hexagram clear warnings to be careful, as well as pointers to potential success. She would proceed with her new approach to design, but with caution and patience.

The story belt was mailed, beginning a time of anxious waiting. Several days later a check arrived, along with a letter bearing a logo of the Tibetan *vajra,* or diamond scepter, which in Govinda's discussions is associated with the second floor or navel area of the five-layer temple of the body. The composer asked Carolyn for a description of her sources for the belt's design. Carolyn responded with a lengthy letter, then received a telephone call and learned that Lama Govinda's book had been an important source of inspiration to the composer for years.

The response encouraged Carolyn to continue with her conjuring; the house seemed conducive to her new approach to designing. A house of feathers and books and dreams, the House of Waters was proving to be absolutely the best place for us to be.

13

The World Behind the Loom

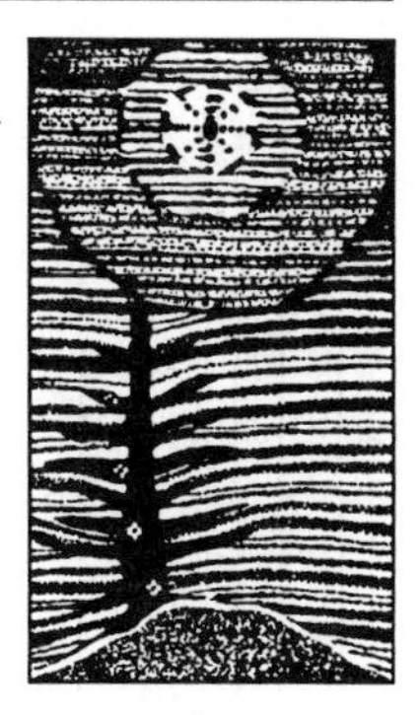

"How can forces of fire and water be integrated most beneficially?" Carolyn asked.

She dreamed of swimming towards an island with Crystal clinging to her waist. Huge waves built up, so she swam deep under water, fish-like, and made her way along the bottom. She surfaced, but found monumental waves bearing down. She dove down, breathing like a fish.

Astrologically, Carolyn is a triple Pisces, definitely a water person. The dream suggests she is very familiar with her element, but Carolyn woke up thinking that water had become overpowering, threatening Crystal also.

"Perhaps the inner child is threatened," I suggested. "Your creative energies are in transition. They need special attention."

Carolyn sat behind a new warp waiting for ideas. The empty strings appeared impatient, as if demanding action. For several days Carolyn's journal writing was virtually illegible, with angry twists to her words. "Transition to new order? What order? What do I do now?"

> Snakes emerge from my belly—a long black one, a yellow one, then a short blue snake with red spots. The snakes crawl beneath the surface of my skin and come out through my navel and crotch. Many snakes, some tiny, some large.

> I look up and see Mary and Solomon Hall (the Lakota Sioux medicine people). I ask them what I should do. "Walk with *huichols* in your hands," they say. The *huichols* are small disks that reflect the sun, move the air, create little winds. They are blue and red. *"Huichols* synthesize fire and water," Mary says.

There was a horrifying aspect to this dream when Carolyn recalled the snakes. But later, when she could return to the images with a degree of objectivity, Carolyn found that she was especially attracted to the blue snake with red spots. She asked me what I knew about *huichols*. I remembered this to be the name of an Indian people living in northern Mexico, who were known for their annual peyote hunt and their brilliant yarn paintings. I also recalled that deer were especially sacred to these people.

A few days later we purchased a book called *The Art of the Huichol Indians*. Carolyn opened the book to a photograph of a "god disk" with incised red and blue wedges radiating from a center. The reverse side of the god disk depicted, in red and blue, two deer and three fish.[1] Another page showed what the Huichol Indians call *nearika,* a term pertaining to the mask likeness or aura of gods, fire, water, deer, corn, or shamans. A pen-and-ink drawing depicts a Sun *nearika,* another drawing of a fire deity, both shown as circular, mandala-like images terminating in spirals. We could imagine the god disks and *nearika* rapidly spinning, blurring the colors, effectively creating a synthesis of red and blue.

Ideas were coming. To integrate forces of fire and water in weaving, the colors red and blue could be interrelated. But how?

To find solutions to design questions, Carolyn moved into the world behind the loom, the sitting still place where she reviews her resources and considers her alternatives. At this point, Carolyn could rely on either calculation or conjuring. She felt herself on safer ground with calculated designing. Conjuring was still a frightening new approach, but full of possibility. When these alternatives were pondered, it was revealing to view calculation as essentially a thinking-centered, ordered approach to design. Conjuring seemed feeling-centered, yielding, an intuitive approach. Perhaps the two approaches could be blended or synthesized, mirroring the idea that the next tapestry was itself to represent a synthesis of red and blue, fire and water.

Speculations were intriguing, but no design was emerging. Not knowing which way to turn, Carolyn waged an inner battle that lasted for days. And then once again, dreaming provided clues for a solution.

> I am in a war. Two lines of soldiers fire at each other, with me between them, stringing a new warp on a small Navajo loom. I do

my work, untouched by bullets that whine by my head.

I discover that my loom is a gun. I stand, loom-gun in hand, ready for battle, but I can't decide which way to point the gun. Fortunately, no one seems to be getting hurt in this war. I see a soldier raising his rifle, pointing at me, firing. The entire gun rockets through the air, hitting the earth and kicking up dirt beside me. Whipping my loom-gun around, I smash the rifle to pieces.

I strike a match, set the rifle pieces on fire, and somehow pack them into a small container, something like a matchbox. I hurl the box to the other side, where someone catches it and throws it back. But I'm ready. I pick up a Navajo High School Year Book and hold it like a baseball bat. I bat the burning box to the other side.

My effort stops the war. Soldiers on both sides stare at the burning box, which then explodes, shooting metal fragments in every direction and injuring soldiers on both sides. For a while the battle rages again, and I'm standing in the middle of criss-crossing rifle fire.

Then it's time to eat. Everyone puts down their weapons and enters a long narrow building, talking about an anticipated feast. "It's very difficult for women and children to participate in this war," I say, gazing around a room full of men.

Long narrow tables are set, with a corncob on each plate, along with a glass of water. Solomon Hall sits beside me, and tells me he's been very sick—so sick he finally had to ask himself, "Do you want to live or do you want to die? So I got better," he says. "I learned my medicine name, recovered my pride, and practiced strong discipline of mind."

Then I see women soldiers at the tables. Solomon Hall tells me, "Soon it will become unimportant for people to be distinguished as male or female. What will be important is people knowing they are like me or not like me."

I understand him to mean that people will be distinguished by whether or not they know their medicine name.

Dreams have a rather bizarre humor. Nevertheless, absurd as the images seemed, there was a strong suggestion that Carolyn is impervious to attack when she sits in her weaving spot. The dream was indicating that the sides of battle, either left or right, are of no consequence. Maleness or femaleness was also of little importance. What mattered was discipline of mind, knowing one's medicine (which is to say, knowing one's personal perceptions while adhering to a creative path).

With this dream, Carolyn knew her design would be woven into a long narrow belt form, combining calculation and conjuring. She worked out a color progression with several hues in the dark purple to red-orange area of the color spectrum. Each new hue was to be introduced in stepped increments determined by the Fibonacci series so as to achieve a blend of colors in precise steps throughout the sixty-inch length.

Frank Waters' *Mexico Mystique* stimulated an idea for a foreground design. Waters discusses a sign the Aztecs were to expect before building their sacred city. The sign which determined the location of the island city in the valley of Mexico was an eagle perched on a cactus with a serpent in its beak, and a fountain gushing forth a red stream and a blue stream. The streams were said to have given rise to the hieroglyph *atl-tlachinolli,* or burning water. The glyph is a stream of fire, uniting with a stream of water. As a symbol for the Aztec Blossoming War, the hieroglyph represents internal wars in the human heart which can be resolved by reconciliation of the two opposing forces.[2]

Carolyn represented the two streams by means of a pictographic helix of intertwined red and blue. The helix becomes dominant or recessive in relationship to the background color progressions. In the belt's last section, Carolyn chose yellow threads to weave another Fibonacci series against a dark background. The resulting image is a yellow globe, a kind of symbolic resolution of the belt's theme.

Many of the tapestries create a particular resonance within me as well, as I find myself drawn into the web which a piece represents. Not long after the completion of *Red-Blue Belt* I dreamed I was living in a village, anticipating a flood caused by a tidal wave. I climbed an earth mound and in my struggle to achieve the top I was assisted by an old man. He told me the earth mound "has something inside it." I took him to mean that we were climbing Mayan temple mounds, perhaps an ancient pyramid. At the top, there was an old house with a latticework surrounding the front porch. The land below was soon flooded, but we were safe on the mound. I had the distinct impression that by hand weaving with blue and red-orange threads, I could weave in such a way that my choice of threads controlled the flood.

Several days later the theme of integrating red and blue appeared again. I dreamed of a kiva, one of the circular ceremonial chambers such as those found in Indian Pueblos on the Rio Grande River. Mural paintings covered the kiva walls. Many images were unclear, as if time or erosion had worn parts of the images away. But two figures were quite clear. Streams of color (apparently living rather than painted), made of intermingled blue and red-orange points, flowed both ways, into and out of the open mouths of the two figures. Upon waking I immediately thought of the *atl-tlachinolli,* the Aztec intermingled streams of fire and water.

After a tapestry is finished, I'm often in a mood for preparing a festive dinner. When the main course is served, I watch the weaver woman pick up her fork. I know by a slightly glazed look in her eyes that, even though she is eating, her attention is elsewhere.

After dinner I ask Carolyn to describe the world behind the loom, for it's quite clear she has not yet fully emerged back outside the loom.

"It's a land of meadows," she says, "rivers and lakes, wild columbine, mountains, a herd of elk, a soaring eagle. A land rich in signs of ancient cultures. Petroglyphs incised in stone. Kivas and ceremonial plazas. Pottery shards, omphalos stone, geodetic markers, stone circles, calendar stones, cave walls filled with signs and symbols."

"Fascinating country," I say. "A land where one might find wings of gold, for example, rain no rain, sun drums, hand songs, vision trails, vivid dreams."

Her smile tells me I'm on the right track. Eventually, I get the picture that with each tapestry, the world behind the loom expands in relationship to the weaver's inner life, with colors, images, and perceptions increasingly more alive and clear. Each new tapestry reveals trails leading deeper into the personal landscapes. And I realize that with each entry into that world, the weaver must clear the land of as many personal enemies as possible. To accomplish such a task, Carolyn has come to rely on the assistance of inner world Grandparents.

"The Grandparents are the Keepers of the world behind the loom," Carolyn says. "Spider Man. The white-haired woman. They are the Keepers. In time I have learned to recognize their relationship to me and their ways of opening and expanding my perceptions."

So now I understand that when Carolyn goes to work at the loom she enters into a kind of contract with her Grandparents. In exchange for protection from the onslaughts of personal enemies, the Grandparents insist that Carolyn come to the weaver's spot disciplined and receptive, taking full responsibility for the tools she holds and the threads drummed into the design. And Carolyn makes demands of her own.

"I want the right colors, the right points and lines, the right seed ideas with which I can fulfill my commitments. I ask to be given full freedom in exploring new landscapes. I ask that guiding voices be clear. I demand dreams. Dreams reveal an archaeology of mind, exposing deeper levels the further I dig down."

In Navajo land, weavers cover the looms with layers of blankets after a day's work is done. Blankets keep away dust and protect the weaving from outsider's eyes. We often wondered if blankets served other purposes as well. While weaving, Carolyn keeps a light yellow, cotton flannel sheet draped over the loom.

"I need a backdrop," she says. "A curtain that helps pull me into the weaving and keeps me there while I work."

The sheet has become the first veil of protection for the world behind the loom.

When the weaving day is over, the sheet is pulled across the entire loom to help protect the warp. Then Carolyn unfolds an old, finely woven Mexican blanket and neatly drapes it over the cotton sheet. This blanket is made of black and white bands intermixed with bands of vivid bright colors, including a radiant central design.

"A rainbow blanket," Carolyn says. "A protective rainbow guardian for the loom and for the world behind."

The third covering is a softly tanned, gold elk hide.

"The elk hide hides the elk," Carolyn laughs.

"But how is the world behind the loom linked with the world outside?" I ask.

"To enter an inner world, I release the world outside. In so doing a part of me must die. My outer world must die, especially that part which includes rationalizations, fears, any obstacle which prevents free exploration of the inner dimensions. When this outer world fades away, then the inside worlds open up alive and vibrant and I weave within the world revealed by the Grandparents."

"But there must be a transition zone between your outer and inner lives."

"The weaver's spot is the threshold. In the place where I discipline myself and become still, I experience movement back and forth, release of one world, openness to the other. On some unconscious level, the weaver's spot allows a continuing experience of death and rebirth."

"But inner and outer are never entirely separated. So what is it that links the worlds?"

"Colored threads. While weaving I hold threads from the outside world. I do not, and cannot, take the outside world itself with me. I do not take you, for example, or Crystal. I take threads of you, threads from the teachers I have found outside. Threads of you become woven with threads from dreaming, threads from the Grandparents, threads from teachings and teachers revealed behind the loom. Weaving links. Everything I do, on either side of the loom, becomes interrelated by means of weaving."

"Why can't you leave your loom attitude behind when reemerging into this world?"

Carolyn explains that her loom attitude is in fact a life attitude. In a sense, she would prefer to sustain the loom attitude, but this is rarely possible or even desirable. The loom attitude is rigorous, highly demanding in terms of time and attention.

"Nevertheless, I would think that the completion of a tapestry would facilitate your reentry. But often you seem trapped by the other side, even when your tapestry is off the loom and on the wall."

"I still remain attached to the process. It is not easy letting loose of a design that has occupied me for weeks. When I finish a piece, I end a certain relationship with the world that is revealed by the design. But the threshold for any piece is not really crossed until I give the tapestry a name and prepare for its give-away."

When possible, we live with the finished piece, for a while appreciating the view it reveals of Carolyn's discoveries during her designing and weaving. Carolyn studies the finished design and derives ideas for future designs, or discovers ways to refine her technique.

When new warp strings were attached to the loom, and Carolyn was again sitting within her threshold spot, a seed idea emerged for a new conjured design.

"I will weave wind by weaving a tree."

Her aim was to improve loom attitude, to allow intuitive processes to guide the choosing of color and image. Carolyn reread selections from George Rowley's *Principles of Chinese Painting,* then wrote in her journal.

> I sit down to weave. I pick up threads. As I place threads between warps, I must learn to "breathe" design into being. I do not know what the design will be. I have my colors. I have my seed idea. So now I conjure, reflecting what I find in the moment.
>
> The word is *chi,* life movement, essence or spirit of movement. I must find *chi,* allowing this movement to flow through heart-mind-hand into design. Doing so requires utmost clarity of mind and freedom from distraction.

In traditional Chinese painting an artist strives to find an inner resonance that will manifest itself in the tip of the brush, activated during the very moment of applying paint to paper. Painting in such a way requires disciplined, undisturbed receptivity so as to awaken what the masters call *chi yun,* or spirit resonance, said to grow out of the search of the heart/mind and to be achieved through and inspired by the artist's guiding spirit. The artist strives for naturalness, effortlessness, a high state of creative readiness obtained through concentrative, meditative receptivity.[3]

"I will not try to weave a tree I see out the window," Carolyn wrote.

"I must catch an essential idea of treeness, which emerges during the meditative moment of inserting thread into warp."

Carolyn conjured only when a deep sense of quiet had emerged. She was accustomed to weaving up to six hours a day, but the degree of concentration required for the new piece, *Tree,* could be sustained for only two hours at a time. Always, the seed idea, wind in tree, guided her. Her discipline often wavered. She knew Chinese masters apply paint to paper with a sense of certainty, a sense of correct form. Paint applied to paper cannot be erased. Fortunately, a woven row can be unwoven if necessary.

In the last section of the tapestry, the sky area, Carolyn chose to include a poetic statement expressing the loom attitude she had felt during the weaving. She wanted a woven ideogram to be an integral part of the design concept in much the same way a calligraphic poem is included in a traditional Chinese painting. In Mai Mai Sze's book, *Way of Chinese Painting,* she found word-ideas she wanted. The first was *I,* expressed in two images: *hsin* or heart-mind, and *yin,* referring to sound or utterance. The second was *Ch'i,* Breath of Heaven, also expressed in two images: *ch'i* or breath, and *mi,* the cardinal directions.[4]

Woven one above the other, the four ideograms expressed Carolyn's intentions for *Tree:* "united heart-mind sounding the breath of *ch'i* to the four directions."

Then, like the Chinese artist's stamp, Carolyn devised a personal signature, a woven symbol which is to her "elk antlers within the circle of the sun."

When the tapestry was removed from the loom, we discovered that the carefully woven images suggested other images which were entirely unforeseen and unplanned. Within the tree roots there appeared the image of a child. The clouds seemed to be in the shape of a woman, enfolding the tree in her arms. The image of a man was woven into the sky. The elk signature was his head, the poem his body. By weaving *Tree,* Carolyn had woven her family: roots child, tree woman, sky man.

"In this *Tree,*" I said. "I see the sounds of your breathing."

14

Prism

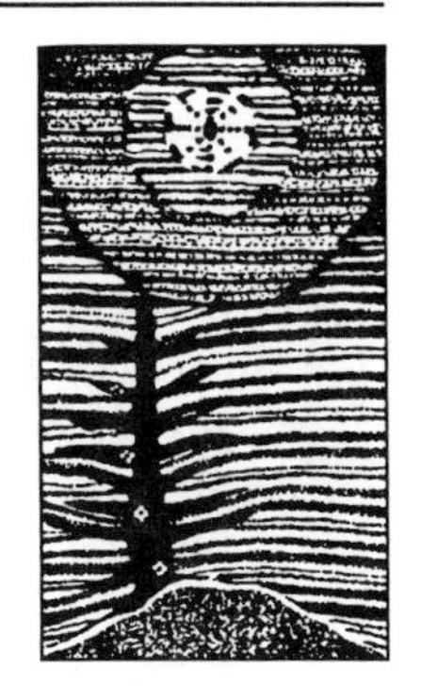

Frank and Barbara Waters returned from Tucson. It was time for us to move. Five story belts had come off the loom; the first draft of a novel was finished. But with no clear plan of what to do next, our accomplishments seemed overshadowed by indecision.

Late in the summer I found a small house in Santa Fe available for rent for a few weeks. I worked on a story treatment for a commissioned screenplay. When Carolyn and Crystal returned from a trip to Ontario I set up a design table, but Carolyn found she could not concentrate on new design work. With no loom, and still no plan for the months ahead, she felt disoriented and clouded with doubts.

For a few weeks, Carolyn took on a job of dressmaking for a Santa Fe woman. It was a welcome focus of attention for restless hands and mind until we decided what to do. But design ideas were brewing, even if not finding immediate translation on the drawing table. She was reading de Santillana and von Dechend's *Hamlet's Mill,* a vast study of the origins of myth. The authors follow clues found in astronomy, mathematics, verse, and music, and discover an ancient world order, based on cycles of time, to be a source for the cosmological framework of myth. During this period of delving into *Hamlet's Mill,* Carolyn dreamed of story-telling robes, wrapped around figure-forms. Each robe contained woven inscriptions, "Runes, an ancient Celtic vocabulary."

Is Celtic myth my source?
Symbols from this land, with its Indian heritage,
work for me,
But I am an old one.
I love the ancient philosophers,
Old mathematicians who plotted
The course of stars
And laid out plans for constructions,
Temples on the earth that mirror
Movements of the stars.
Yes, I would weave the night sky.
I wonder about the moon's course,
The stars and constellations,
The fantastic galaxies.

Wanting solitude, we left Santa Fe to set up camp in the Sangre de Cristo mountains. We went for long walks, and at night gazed at the blazing sky full of stars.

"This is the way it is," Carolyn wrote. "We wander. We wobble with discomfort because of fears of no money. This, though, is not what motivates us. Money-no. We choose another way. We do not wander unguided. I choose to know more about my self."

Then, in a decisive hand, she wrote:

The new weavings will include
Sharpness of focus,
Gentleness of atmosphere,
A foundation of brightness,
Calculated proportions.

Time answers questions for me. I seek a guiding symbol for my design. Time becomes the woven weft. The warp strings define the space. All else is intersection. Into this web I must venture to unravel the stories of my movements.

We continued to wait. The pressures generated from not knowing what was next continued to mount. "Can I be clear of my purpose?" Carolyn wrote. "There is too much that is tenuous right now. Where is my pointer—my direction, my own point of reference?"

We were no less surprised than the first time when Frank and Barbara Waters came to the rescue with an invitation to stay in the house for another winter. We heaved sighs of relief and within a few days were ready for another season of work.

The move elicited an expansive atmosphere for the weaver's designs. Carolyn chose not to be constrained by the narrow dimensions of the belts. Instead, she designed for a warp using the entire sixty-inch width of the loom. The design was to be planned in advance, instead of conjured.

The first step was to divide each side of a golden rectangle by means of *phi* proportions. Squared spirals were then drawn from the four corners of each of the four inner golden rectangles in an expansion rate determined by the Fibonacci series. This produced a web of intersecting lines and points. The outermost points were joined to establish a color area, then lines were drawn to link the next set of points inside the former, and continuing, until eight color areas had been determined.

Scores of drawings were discarded before Carolyn was satisfied that the right points had been linked to define the color areas. During the stages of designing, Carolyn recorded several dreams, but one seemed of particular importance.

> I dress to go out, but have trouble finding what I want to wear. Suddenly a strange human-animal appears. She beats on a wide rimmed basket that is covered with a dark hide stretched tight. A finely woven net is wrapped around the basket drum.
>
> I see a polished, light yellow stone or wood carving in the human animal's navel. It looks like a scarab beetle, with four turquoise stones inset into its yellow back. The scarab grows. It's a moving form that grows upward as I look upward. The scarab becomes the human-animal's mask. But then I see the mask is a gourd, shaped like the snout of a large deer. Light yellow, tear-shaped eyes are painted on the gourd deer head. When the deer lowers her head I see two tiny dark, shiny, inset stones. These are the deer's "real" eyes, and they are closed. The tear-shaped painted eyes are in fact tears, falling from the closed eyes.
>
> I touch the web-net drum cover. The entire body of this human-animal form is self contained, solid, impervious to what goes on around her. I know she has ceremonial deer medicine. She is a Deer Mother and has the power to draw people to her.

The strange images stayed with Carolyn for days. There were no clear clues to the dream's meaning, only the feeling of an indelible bond with the Deer Mother and her woven net-covered basket drum. The dream prompted research into Egyptian mythology. In one reference, Carolyn learned that the scarab, or *kheperer,* was associated with the rising sun and the human soul, and symbolized transformation.

A month had passed in design time alone. There was still a warp to prepare. This in itself proved to be a time-consuming task. When the loom was finally ready, Carolyn wrote, "Heddles of an immense loom

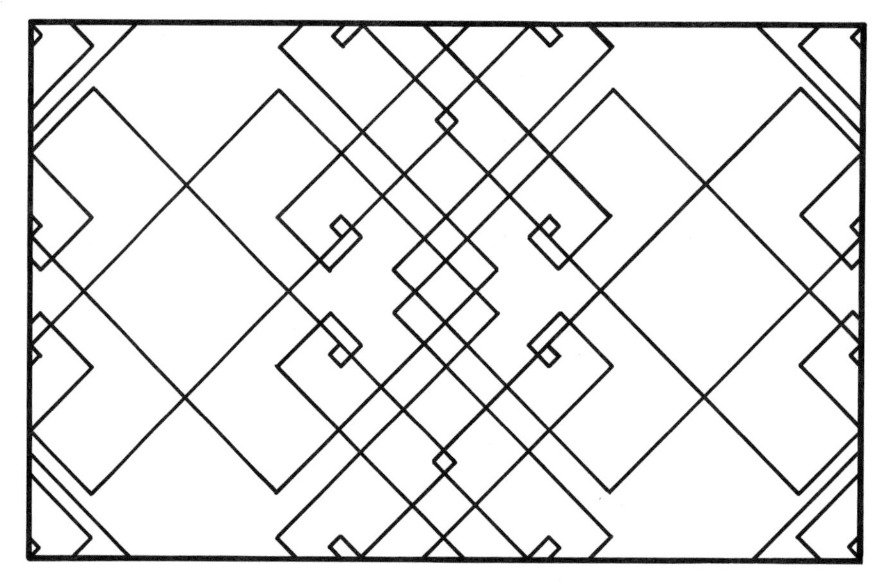

Figure 18: *Carolyn's design sketch for her tapestry* Prism. *Squared spirals were drawn from the four corners of each of four inner golden rectangles in an expansion rate determined by the Fibonacci series.*

open wide the shed of infinite space. The sheds open into a vast expanse over which I must now weave my web."

Before actually weaving, however, Carolyn spent two weeks experimenting with color mixes. She wanted a color spectrum to fill out the eight areas, moving from dark to light in six steps of increasing brightness, then two steps deepening in value for the center design areas. She experimented with color mixes of two, three, or four hues, so as to achieve the vibrancy she had found so effective in previous color mixing. At long last, she settled on the color combinations she wanted. She entered her first threads into the enormous warp, and within a few days she dreamed an enormous dream.

> David, Crystal, and I walk uphill on a road during the night. David suddenly shouts that he has seen a brilliant flash of light beaming from sky to earth. Then I see it. Straight shafts of light, coming closer. A beam flashes into an ovoid shape pointed at top and bottom, looking like the yellow globe in *Red-Blue Belt.* I hold Crystal close, not knowing what will happen, but feeling we are about to be taken away.
>
> We are then sitting by a roadside. Many men work with machines around a huge truck or moving van. The men come to us and put instruments on our bodies. They talk and work quietly.

Then we are somewhere else. All my perceptions have changed. We are in a wide, spacious, high-roofed building, with many rooms adjacent to a central hall. Everything is white. We walk down a long hall alone, although I notice several men who are not earth people—not men from the same place as ourselves.

We are given more tests. Tourniquets are wrapped around our arms, large silver needles inserted into our joints. I am afraid, but the tests are done painlessly.

An old, white-haired man, wearing a white coat, a scientist-philosopher, says he wants to show us around. He takes us into a Room of the Galaxy. We see various sculptural dioramas of the galaxy, but it is a "functioning representation of the Galaxy" he wants us to see.

We climb on to the Galaxy. It's an enormous loom, with a warp stretched from one cross-beam to another over a vast distance. The warp is wound onto each beam in opposite directions.

The walls of the room disappear and dark space surrounds us. The loom now is the Galaxy rather than a representation. The man explains the workings of the Galaxy loom, but then the warp begins to vibrate and shake violently. We have to hang on to avoid being thrown off. We are so tiny compared to the warp's immensity. Then I see a large knot of threads hanging in space, a Gordian knot formed by tangled and broken warp strings.

We return to the room of the Galaxy. Crystal finds a stick-figure doll made of cloth-covered wire. I tell her it belongs to the scientists, but she takes it anyway.

As we walk down a large central hallway, Crystal is attracted to a small room. I see she is being invisibly pulled into the room, as if the stick-figure doll led her there without her being able to do anything about it. Then Crystal is gone. I'm concerned, but notice the number 19 over the door. I have the feeling the rooms and entire building move around and change locations, but I feel that if I keep my eye on the number 19, I'll find Crystal again.

I talk with a man who works in the building, and show him a mark on my index finger. It's a pink dot in the center of my fingernail. The dot is in a little divided circle, half white, half green. The white-haired man tells me the mark indicates a measure of "one man-space." He shows me how to outstretch my arm and finger, rotate my body, making a circle that describes a "time" containing a circular "space." This is the true "human measure," he tells me.

Crystal reappears from the small room without the doll and I know she had gone somewhere with the old man who showed us the Galaxy.

> As we leave the immense building I notice a child's toy truck. The truck had fallen to the ground from the back of a huge moving van near the place where the men first put instruments on us. "I know what's in that toy truck," I think to myself. "No one would know it, but the immense building, all the scientists, the Room of the Galaxy, everything we saw, is inside the tiny truck. Looks insubstantial, doesn't it?"

This was a formidable maze of images seemingly unrelated to the dream of the Deer Mother. The first dream was earthy and warm, full of browns and golds, evocative of ancient mysteries. The second dream was stellar and cool, filled with white and light, and futuristic images. Yet both were completely in character with Carolyn's psychological journey in tapestry. The Deer Mother and her net-covered drum appeared at an early stage in the designing of *Prism,* reflecting the source of Carolyn's designs, whereas the second dream, which came during the actual weaving, suggests the direction of Carolyn's journey. On the one hand, Carolyn's work is rooted in ancient traditions; on the other, her search is towards the mathematician/philosopher who reveals his Galaxy loom.

Carolyn's two dreams suggest a marriage of Mother Earth and Father Sky as perceived by the Navajo in the inner form of the loom. On the loom, time past is linked with time future during the moment of weaving. Sitting still with weaving comb in hand, the weaver experiences interconnections of threads in both a physical and metaphysical sense.

Prism (see Plate 4) is calculated design, but woven with a discipline learned from conjuring, holding *chi,* striving to maintain balance between numbers and proportions, lines and forms, dark and light. Carolyn's intent was to achieve fluidity in the weaving, to find the right balances, then to let go. When the tapestry was off the loom, after three months' work, we resisted taking it to the marketplace so that Carolyn could study the optical effects and light-generating properties she had produced by using the full color spectrum.

I noticed in the central design area, or what might be called the navel of the tapestry, an image that was very similar to the scarab form Carolyn had sketched from her Deer Mother dream. No image was intended in the tapestry's inherent geometry, and that I perceived a scarab form was less important than the fact of being reminded that the tapestry has its own mysterious inner form. Shine a beam of light into a prism and the light is transformed into a rainbow-like spectrum. If I think of my focused attention as that beam of light, and I turn my attention to the tapestry *Prism,* I have the opportunity to see facets.

Somewhere in those colors, for example, the Deer Mother with her drum is self-contained, suggesting an attitude Carolyn tries to achieve while drumming threads into place at the loom. I see also the image of Carolyn standing with arms extended, index fingers pointing, her body rotating, establishing a space within a time, and creating a human measure, which recalls a Leonardo da Vinci drawing where an idealized human body in similar pose is diagrammed entirely in terms of *phi,* the same proportion which underlies *Prism's* design. And there is also a somewhat amusing image of a toy truck falling to the ground and Carolyn knowing what's in that little toy.

"What is really inside me?" Carolyn asks. "What's inside my work? I like that little truck which has the appearance of being so insignificant, so insubstantial. Yet I somehow know that what's inside is a Galaxy Loom, with vast worlds being woven together."

15 Weaving Time

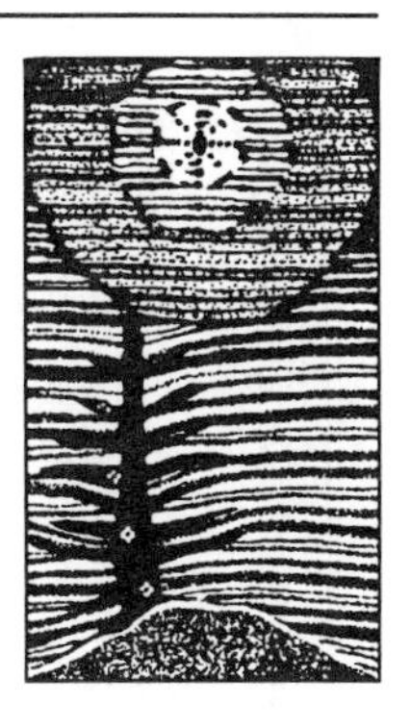

"So unusual," Frank Waters said to Carolyn one summer day. "Maybe it's because weaving is such an ancient craft that the process allows you to touch the archetypes. These images you weave seem as old as they are new. Your designs appear to have been long buried in the depths below our thinking selves, then brought to light on your loom."

Waters thought the work with golden sections, Fibonacci numbers, and the mysterious *phi* in part accounted for the evocative quality of Carolyn's art. He was particularly intrigued by a story belt called *Landscape.*

"You've woven a cut through time," he said. "Who would ever have thought of tapestry as a medium for recording passing eons of geologic time?"

The comments made a deep impression. Waters suggested Carolyn continue to work with the idea of time in tapestry. Carolyn was already familiar with "weaving time" in the sense that it was essential for her to come into harmony with the particular tempo required by each piece of work. But now she came to understand woven time in quite another sense.

Carolyn pursued the idea in a journal entry:

> Weaving is an exploration of interconnecting pathways. All the connections shuffle up the spaces in my mind. I walk along

inner pathways in country I have not yet charted, looking for new directions, new linkings. Weavings are maps. I look at the paths, see connections, then ask, "Which path do I follow now?"

Health. Harmony. Rhythm. Relationship. These are the keys to a Pythagorean philosophy founded on an esoteric knowledge of numbers. I have learned that numbers contain more than quantitative functions. Numbers are living powers. And weaving is a numerical language. I must devise weaving codes which convey my moment of being, my time. I must find a woven poetry of time.

Carolyn strung up a long narrow warp with the idea that every row of color would be entered according to specific numerical sequences designed to convey astronomical cycles. The idea was appealing, but calculating the sequences for weaving was quite another thing.

Within a few days Carolyn came up with a numerically derived color progression using four colors to represent the four seasons of the year. Each season was to be woven in eight steps of a two-color progression, with blues, for example, representing winter and slowly changing to spring greens. Overlaying this color progression would be a second progression, derived from the ratio of hours of light relative to hours of darkness in each month of the year. The proportion of light to dark in the latitude of Taos at winter solstice is about nine hours to fifteen in the twenty-four-hour day. Spring and vernal equinox have equal hours of light and dark, and the intervening months change by approximately one hour per month. This changing proportion during the four seasons was to be represented by a black/white progression.

Apprised of this complex design plan, I tried to look agreeable, and helped set up the warp. Having worked out a thread progression, and knowing that weaving would progress at the rate of thirty rows per inch, Carolyn knew that the design would require just over fourteen hundred rows of weaving to represent the four seasons. It was essential that each row correspond exactly to the interrelated progressions. Any row woven out of sequence would upset not only the color plan but the cycle of the seasons.

When *Seasons* was completed, we were intrigued with the result.

"You need to weave more time," I suggested.

Carolyn decided to weave the Mayan calendar.

Frank Waters had often discussed with us the Mayan obsession with time. The Mayans had devised meticulously accurate measurements of time, indicating a highly advanced system of stellar observation and computation. As Waters states in his *Mexico Mystique,* no one has yet come up with a full interpretation of the Mayan 260-day calendar, which apparently combines Sun, Moon, and Venus cycles, and possibly Jupiter and Saturn cycles as well.

The calendar links thirteen numbers with twenty day signs. The Mayans, like the Lakota whose number system we had learned, attribute special qualities to each number and regard them as sacred. The twenty day signs were each ruled by a particular deity who influenced events for good or bad depending on the attributes of the god. As Frank Waters writes, the linking of numbers and gods has been likened to two enmeshed wheels, one with thirteen cogs and the other with twenty. The smaller wheel makes twenty revolutions while the larger makes thirteen, so that the same god sign and number could reoccur together only every 260 days (20 x 13). The cycle then repeats endlessly.[1]

The sacred calendar was consulted in much the same way as the *I Ching,* to assess propitious planting days, ceremonial days, and marriage dates, or to divine the nature of birth dates, deaths, catastrophes, or fortune, in terms of how a sacred number links with one of the god signs during the time in question.

To weave a twenty-day count, Carolyn chose five colors, mixed in four combinations. To represent the numbers, she devised a black/white pattern, with white increasing and black decreasing through a thirteen-step pattern. The idea was to weave the black/white pattern of thirteen steps twenty times, interwoven with the twenty-step color progression, which would be repeated thirteen times. Each woven equivalent of a day in the calendar required nine rows. To complete one 260-day cycle, exactly 2340 rows would have to be woven—with no mistakes.

Once again, Carolyn's powers of concentration were tested. And one day, she found a mistake. She retreated from the loom, and recorded the event in her journal.

> The other day I came to the last section of *Calendar* and noticed the patterns were not meshing correctly. I finally located the mistake, and not one mistake, but two, in two different "days," near the beginning of the tapestry.
>
> What happened? An attention lapse? Why didn't I establish a checking system? Now I have no choice. It all must be unwoven. The mistakes are at least one hundred Calendar days back. It'll take me two full days to unweave all that length.
>
> When I described the mistake to David he said he would help

> with the unweaving. I sense his disappointment, mirroring mine. In the past I might have lambasted myself for such an error. Now it's different. It's simply a mistake which I will correct when I am ready.

I sat at the loom, unraveling threads of a calendar. It was not my first experience unweaving time. Thread after thread fell from my fingers.

Perhaps woman is the weaver of worlds, I thought; man the unweaver. The psychology in this thought was depressing, so I decided to postpone searching into history for verifications. I took another look at the threads. Perhaps the weaving of it all must necessarily take into account the unweaving of it all. This felt better, an abstraction I could relate to, a symmetry I could appreciate. I paused in my work long enough to notice spider gossamers floating in the air. If only the web-maker and I could share the same eyes, I thought, maybe I would know what I was doing in the woven web. But the spider went about its business, linking threads, and I went about mine, unweaving threads of time.

Several days later, after the tapestry was completed and off the loom, I realized we could have taken note of the exact day in calendar time when the mistake had been made. Perhaps a sacred number, ruled by a certain god, linked in the process of weaving, had been resurrected from the depths to influence the weaver in such a way as to break her concentration. And later, during a day ruled by another linked number and god, insight had come, the mistake found.

When Frank and Barbara returned to Taos in the spring, Carolyn gave them the woven *Calendar* (see Plate 5). They responded enthusiastically, asking for all the details as to how Carolyn had related the thirteen-number and twenty-day sign counts. Now *Calendar* travels with them during their moves between Tucson and Taos.

Thanks to the Waters, we were in Taos eight or nine months a year. During the summers we rented elsewhere or traveled. Every autumn we harvested apricots, plums, and apples, and hauled in truckloads of oak and pine wood for the fires. In the winter we took care of the Waters' horses. Crystal was soon comfortable on a saddle and held tight while our neighbor led the frisky mare around the pastures. This annual rhythm very much suited us. It lasted for seven years.

The design work on *Calendar* made Carolyn aware of relationships between tapestry time, seasonal time, and calendar time.

She joined an amateur astronomy group that met once a week on top of a house just up the road. In addition to weekly observations, Carolyn studied a guide for amateur astronomers, Guy Ottewell's *The Astronomical Companion.*

When half the moon's disk is illuminated in the first quarter, one would think it sends out half as much light as the full moon. But as Ottewell shows, the moon's reflective characteristics don't work that way. The moon fades in brilliance further out from the middle of its surface, owing to the angle of sun rays, and because the moon's surface is rough, its reflected brightness is reduced to a considerable degree.[2]

These lunar qualities intrigued Carolyn. She found a fancy formula relating to brightness ratios that she was determined to translate into woven form. It required reeducation in the use of logarithmic scales. After several days of work, with piles of papers and graphs accumulating on her desk, she came up with several weavable design ideas.

To represent new moon darkness gradually changing to full moon brightness, Carolyn devised a numerical progression of black moving into dark grey, light grey, then white. She allowed one lunar day to equal one and a half inches of weaving, with each day containing a scaled amount of brightness to correspond to the brightness curve. Since a lunar month is twenty-nine and a half days, the tapestry length was established in advance at forty-five inches.

A second progression—a color series—was used to represent the ratio of change in the illuminated fraction of the moon's disk each day. The dark portion of the moon was depicted with a mix of dark blue and rose, while the part of the moon reflecting sunlight was represented with a combination of yellow and bright blue.

Two changing factors of the moon were thus interwoven by means of interrelating two number cycles. The first cycle was related to relative brightness; the second to the illuminated portion of the moon's disk. The design depended on each color, and the black, grey, white series being introduced according to each of the numerical cycles. Interestingly, the weaving time for the tapestry was about one lunar month. When removed from the loom, *Lunation* revealed its narrow band of greatest brilliance through the middle, corresponding to the moon's greatest brightness, which occurs during less than one full day in an entire lunar month.

Every week, the group of star gazers met on a house-top observation deck that was furnished with telescopes, binoculars, benches, and cushions. At an elevation of 8200 feet, during clear and often very cold winter nights, these intrepid star watchers wrapped themselves in goosedown sleeping bags. Nevertheless, they maintained their vigil most of the night, watching the constellations, which seemed to lift off the mountain then swirl through the sky.

Carolyn continued to study the sphere most closely linked with the earth. She was interested in the fact that the 354-day lunar year is eleven days less than the solar year. In the course of a lunar year, the moon circles the earth twelve times in revolutions of about twenty-nine and a half days each, known as the synodial month. The 354-day cycle is the lunar synodial year. The sidereal lunar month differs from the synodial by a factor of about 2.2 days. Sidereal refers to the time required for the moon to revolve around the earth and return to the same point relative to a fixed background of stars—a period of 27.3 days. Because of the earth's movement around the sun, the moon must move the extra 2.2 days to arrive at the place where it is once again directly between the earth and the sun. So in one lunar year, there are twelve synodial, but thirteen sidereal months.

For the design of her second astronomical tapestry, Carolyn derived a color language based on numerical sequences. She chose to weave twelve columns for twelve lunar months. The sidereal number, 27.3, was woven with a color combination using the three primary colors mixed in nine steps. The synodial number, 29.5, was made with five colors mixed in six steps, with the half day taken into account by dividing the thirtieth step between adjacent columns.

There had to be a beginning place for the calendar, and this was easily decided. The "first day" in the design corresponds to the day she began to weave her lunar year, which happened to be the new moon before winter solstice, 1980. As this is the darkest time of the year in terms of sunlight, the darkest color combinations represented that day. In terms of moonlight, however, full moon at winter solstice is the year's brightest, so the brightest colors reflect that time.

The color code of the design, *Lunar Year,* can be read as a lunar calendar (see Plate 5). Astronomically, the new moon before the December solstice is in Sagittarius and the full moon is in Gemini. With these guides, the constellations of the Zodiac can be found in each of the column-months in their respective color combinations. In column-month one, Gemini turns out to be yellow mixed with the full moon color, orange. The full moon colors for each of the zodiacal signs can be found by reading across the column-months.

Lunar Year reads "serpentwise," down column-month one, up column two, down the next, and so on. Like all of Carolyn's numerically derived designs, each thread in each column had to be woven in correct sequence. There was no room for error. "The synodial and sidereal cycles intermesh and return to the same point relative to each other only once every nineteen years," Carolyn explained. "To put it another way, the full moon in Gemini will not coincide with winter solstice again until nineteen years from now."

Translated, this means that *Lunar Year* is a calendar for 1980, 1999,

2018, and 2037, or, reading into the past, 1961, 1942, 1923, etc. If the "woven first day" were changed by just one phase of the moon, the tapestry would become a calendar for different years, with the color combinations producing an entirely different effect. Here was another design lending itself to innumerable variations.

We might have thought that translating astronomical information to woven design was quite new. Later, however, Carolyn learned that Peruvian weavers have been weaving time for centuries. According to ethnoastronomer Zuidema, a Huari textile dating from pre-Inca times apparently contains an accounting of all the days in a solar year, using colored circles organized in groups along diagonal lines. The number symbolism indicates that the textile also contains lunar information.[3] Quechua Indians in the Lake Titicaca area even now weave calendar belts divided into twelve sections, one section for each month. Each section contains a variety of symbols related to agricultural cycles and used for purposes of divination.[4]

Peruvians share with the Navajo and other traditions a perception of the loom as a construction which relates sky and earth. The warp is often perceived as sky threads, and the weft as earth threads. From the intersection emerges the created design. This realization leads inevitably to the symbolism of the cross. Every weft intersecting with a warp forms a cross. Every point in every tapestry forms the center of such a cross. The cross contains the vertical dimension, referring to the transcendent, and the horizontal dimension, the place of earth and human experience. In many philosophies, including the Upanishads for example, the vertical dimension refers to direct light or sunlight, the spiritual dimension, complemented and crossed by reflected light or moonlight, related to the human sphere. The cross is also an intersection of masculine and feminine principles, or, in Taoist doctrine, yin and yang, which Taoist commentators also liken to "the to-and-fro motion of the shuttle across the loom."[5]

Carolyn continued to weave herself deeper into weaving symbolism. Other designs related to the stars came off the loom in the next years, including a tapestry called *Galaxy*, but there were times when other voices called, other threads picked up, bringing her back to earth.

16

Waiting

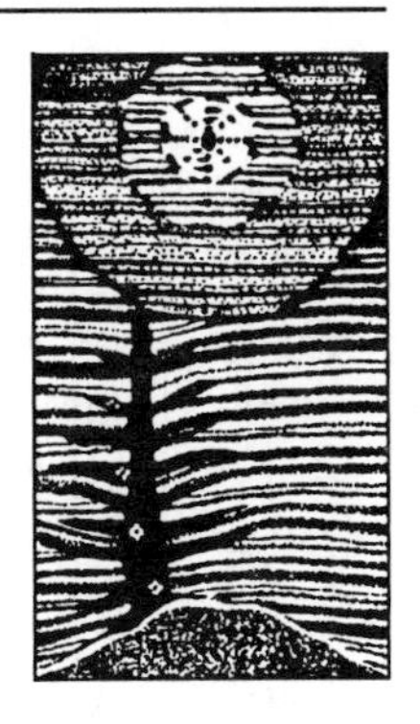

In several tapestries, Carolyn had used a color contrast technique to produce an unusual labyrinth effect. She decided to devote an entire tapestry to the idea.

Classical labyrinths were created using properties of numbers and principles of geometry associated with the square, rectangle, pentagon, octagon, and circle. After preliminary study of classic forms, Carolyn knew her experience with numbers and geometry could readily be applied to woven labyrinths. Surprisingly, she did not design a labyrinth in advance of weaving. She sat down at the loom, waited for the right moment and right mind, then conjured.

Complementary colors of equal value, a sky blue and an earthy yellow ochre, were drummed into place. After a few days, the first suggestion of labyrinthine trails was clearly evident, but Carolyn had no idea she was weaving her way into a maze of problems. Initially, all her attention was focused on the intricate process of alternating colors in specific arrangements to produce the desired effect. Inherent relationships of warp and weft impressed her more than ever.

> Here I sit weaving with warp strings stretched out before me. With a heddle system I change positions of alternate warps to create the shed. I insert my threads, weave a row, use heddles to alternate the warps to form a second shed. I insert other threads,

> weave a second row, once again change the warp in preparation for another row. In this way I am constantly working with a dyad fundamental to my art. One, two. Front, back. Odd, even. Vertical, horizontal. Left to right, right to left. Opposites, coordinates, always present before me. I weave into relationship the odds and evens of things.

After several days, weaving became difficult. Having moved deeper into the design, Carolyn was finding the process more arduous. She had found ways of conjuring her way into the maze, but was uncertain how the woven trails would lead her out. Recalling the story of Ariadne's thread, given to Theseus when he entered the maze of the Minotaur, Carolyn began thinking she needed a magical thread, but a new thread laid in seemed to allow no way for the weaving in of another. The thread was removed, a new pattern tried and taken out. Nothing worked. The trails had closed.

Over three feet of empty warp remained stretched out before her. I was called to the loom. "What do I do now?" the weaver asked.

"It's your labyrinth," I responded, wary of being led in.

Carolyn considered unweaving everything and starting over with a pre-planned design. Another alternative was to cut the warp and consider the piece finished. Fortunately, she did neither. Waiting seemed a better option than pressing ahead when uncertain. The impasse was temporarily resolved by setting up another loom.

It was summer. We were staying in a small adobe house about a mile up the dirt road from the Waters' place. The adobe was beautifully situated on forested slopes near the foot of El Salto Mountain. We found a clearing near the house where we set up a small loom. The clearing was shaded by a lofty pine and surrounded by oak and juniper trees.

On the new loom, Carolyn wove sashes for Martha of Taos, a fashion designer renowned for her broomstick skirts, Navajo blouses, and other southwestern styles. The prospect of commercial weaving was not initially appealing, but Carolyn measured her doubts against a predictable income. In time, other shops also wanted Carolyn's sashes, and occasionally orders came in for twenty or more at a time.

It was also a summer for gardening—our first since Cedar Road years. Water turned out to be as much a problem in New Mexico as in British Columbia, except that in British Columbia there had always been too much. In New Mexico I watered the garden by carrying buckets from an irrigation ditch a hundred yards away. We collected rain water in barrels. There was no running water in the house, so I hauled more buckets from a pump house near the irrigation ditch.

By this time Crystal had developed the heart of a hunter and gatherer. She knew every trail to a waterfall a mile from the house. Every day she visited berry patches and birds' nests. In the evenings, she received a few weaving lessons on a small table loom. Crystal soon learned to pass bright threads of her own choosing through the warp to make a scarf for her dress-ups. One day Carolyn gathered leftover warp strings and braided them into the body, arms, and legs of a doll. Crystal described what she wanted for a head and face, so Carolyn embroidered little sunshine-burst eyes, a crescent moon smile. Black yarn served for hair.

"What's her name?" I asked Crystal.

"Pearl," she answered without hesitation. "My baby Pearl."

Carolyn returned to the tapestry loom, which had been left covered and untouched for weeks. Taking weaving in hand, she studied the woven trails. Crystal joined her at the loom, with Pearl in hand.

"What have I woven here, Pearl?" Carolyn asked.

"Water," Pearl responded in a high-pitched voice. "Water, water, water."

Carolyn looked at her design again. She called me to the loom. Pearl was right. Within her labyrinth, Carolyn had woven a virtual lake. Woven water rippled in sunlight, appearing as if it might spill to the floor at any moment. The sky color, interwoven with the earth color to form trails, now appeared to be waves in a meandering water maze. We noticed fish forms swimming before our very eyes. Carolyn had apparently entered her design by way of the element closest to her Piscean nature.

The woven design is entirely abstract, representing nothing, affirming no image. When at the loom, Carolyn is working with threads and colors, building up design with the use of vertical, horizontal, diagonal, and curved lines. Yet beneath the pattern formation lies her guiding idea or guiding image, which by means that are largely unconscious informs her conjuring. An analogy with dreaming is again apparent. Waking reality affects dreams, and dreams can affect our perception of waking reality. Similarly, conjuring influences pattern in weaving and colors, and patterns influence conjuring. Within her woven abstractions Carolyn did not find merely any image, she found indications of where her conjuring had led her so far. The suggestion of a water maze showed Carolyn that she was not finished with the tapestry after all. Then a dream helped her see what had to be done next.

> I dream of a lovely ten-year-old girl with short blond hair. She has found something in common between two stories she has

> read—one about Isis and Ishtar, the other about the Celts.
> She opens one of the books to a picture of a mermaid sculpture, her body inset with jewels. The image was sculpted a very long time ago, and I notice the mermaid is similar in appearance to the girl. Both appear young and old, male and female.
> The girl asks, "What does this mean?" I see the mermaid, and think of the ocean. "She lives within her dreams," I say. "She creates her world by way of her dreams. She makes the world beautiful because she dreams of beauty. She is completely at one with the world of dreams."

Carolyn woke from this dream with a positive feeling for the mermaid figure and reaffirmed in her relationship with dreams. She was disappointed to find, however, that in psychology literature, the mermaid was often described in negative terms. Carl Jung saw the mermaid as an example of the negative anima who infatuates young men and lures them to their deaths in the water depths.[1] Carolyn returned to her journal.

> Mermaid, who are you? Why do you occupy the chambers of my psyche? Are you showing me a capricious, sleuthing, immoral side to my character? Are you mocking my fluid nature?
> I believe you are a symbol of unity and duality within my Self. Spiritual, physical, at one with life-giving water. Water is my source. Because I trust the water depths, consciousness may emerge. The mermaid gives me a glimpse of the deep. She lives within her dreams.
> The monster side is there,too. I don't deny the existence of the shadow. But I feel the monster qualities of mermaids and mermen emerge from people who are alienated from nature.
> The mermaid would be at home in the native American world. Elk Woman. Eagle Man. Corn Pollen Girl. Fish Maiden. Humanity in harmony with the natural world.

If the mermaid had lured Carolyn into a woven water maze, then she had also revealed a way for Carolyn to weave a way out. "I must emerge," Carolyn said. "I have to find dry land."

In advance of further weaving, Carolyn designed a geometrical labyrinth which was to become the tapestry's central image. With new threads introduced, a central vertical axis was woven which Carolyn thought of as her *axis mundi.* The *axis mundi,* or world axis, appears in creation mythology around the world and connects earth and sky, or lower and higher levels in the cosmos. The axis is found in many forms in different cultures, as a sacred mound or mountain, a world pillar or tree. Carolyn used a vertical axis in her design, surrounded by a receding water pattern, to lift her out of the water maze below, into the formal labyrinth that was to appear next.

A series of concentric ellipses then appeared on either side of her axis. These ellipses resembled whirlpools, but also reminded Carolyn of another symbol she was reading about called the *mandorla*. A *mandorla* is the "eye" formed by the intersection of two circles having the same diameter, with the circumference of each circle passing through the center of the other. From earliest times, this symbol has been thought to represent the marriage of heaven and earth, spiritual and material. In the early Christian mysteries, the symbol was known as the *vesica piscis,* the "vessel of the fish." It's one of the earliest recorded astrological signs, representing the Piscean fishes swimming in opposite directions and returning to each other. In the *Dictionary of Symbols,* Carolyn found other associations of interest. *Mandorla* refers to the spindle of the Magna Mater, or the Great Mother archetype, and in a related reference, *mandorla* refers to the magical spinners who spin the threads of life.[2]

Another book facilitated the next steps in Carolyn's design. In his book *The Tewa World,* Alfonso Ortiz, a cultural anthropologist and a native of San Juan Pueblo in northern New Mexico, describes labyrinths found in his peoples' mythology and cosmology. According to the people of San Juan Pueblo, labyrinths form the interior of each of the four sacred hills surrounding the village, guarded by beings popularly known as Whippers or Whipper Kachinas. Once a year during the winter Turtle Dance which we often attended, the Whippers are impersonated by masked dancers who appear in the plazas.

Reading the Tewa book gave Carolyn the idea that her formal labyrinth needed guardians. So Carolyn's central image was surrounded by eight *mandorla*-like forms, which she related to as the guardians of her labyrinth. These eight elliptical forms were woven with the use of the familiar Fibonacci series.

After completing her guardian *mandorlas,* Carolyn once again relied on conjuring for the last section of the design. Colors were chosen throughout the tapestry that were closely related to each other in value, a technique that continued in the final inches, when all six colors used from earlier sections were blended in sequence according to Fibonacci numbers.

When the tapestry was removed from the loom we found a place for it on an adobe wall where the design received maximum light. We were excited by how the whole design worked out. The colors seemed to vibrate and shimmer. With all the ideas and associations that had evolved during the weaving, the piece still held together as an integrated whole, with completely abstract designing at one level, yet so suggestive and full of imagery when looked at in a different way. The lower section still seemed watery, while the final section looked like lightning patterns, with the formal labyrinth in the center.

Carolyn wrote a few of her impressions in her journal.

> When I weave, warp threads become sky/time threads. The woven wefts are earth/space threads. Weaving relates warp and weft, sky and earth, time and space, tapestry weave and labyrinth design.
>
> The weaver's spot is a place where linking is accomplished. That spot is the place where I center myself, the place where I prepare myself to take threads in hand and weave them with my guiding idea.
>
> The center of this tapestry is a woven labyrinth. To find the design for the tapestry center, it seems I had to draw energy up from the water maze below, and pull energy down from the lightning above.
>
> In the weaver's spot, where I am sitting still, where I am centering myself, I weave within the movements of energy that comes from below and above.

In *Labyrinth,* Carolyn found relationships between the meaning of the maze and processes of weaving. Ancient initiates entered the maze to test discipline, to awaken intuitive awareness of how to proceed when searching for the labyrinth's center and then returning without getting lost. Often such a task can only be accomplished with the aid of a guiding thread. Creative weaving seems to embody a similar search, and Carolyn found that the task was certainly no easy one. She was lost more than once, and needed many guiding threads.

Essential to the search is the ability to wait. Sitting still at the loom requires a knowing how to wait, knowing what to wait for, trusting the right thread will come at the right time.

Carolyn has woven very few representational tapestries. One, a long narrow conjured piece, is called *Waiting* (see Plates 6 and 7). A guiding idea for the design comes from Mai Mai Sze's discussion of a principle of consonance in her book *The Way of Chinese Painting.* According to the traditional Chinese approach, when properly applied, consonance unifies in one image, blending all parts within a whole, and is achieved by rhythmic repetition of a theme, whether a color theme, image theme, or number theme. Another important source for Carolyn's tapestry came from her toss of the coins to consult the *I Ching.* The hexagram turned out to be the number five, *Waiting,* and the image for the first line was "waiting in the meadow."

Following is my poem for the tapestry *Waiting*.

A woman stands waiting
Beside a still pool reflecting.
Star-water is woven into her robe.
Her vision waits within the trees,
Her promise within the clouds.
The woman is prepared,
Accepting what must be.
Nourishing rain will come in its own time.
It furthers one to abide in what endures.
Waiting is woven,
Woven in, woven in,
Waiting is woven.

17

Twilight

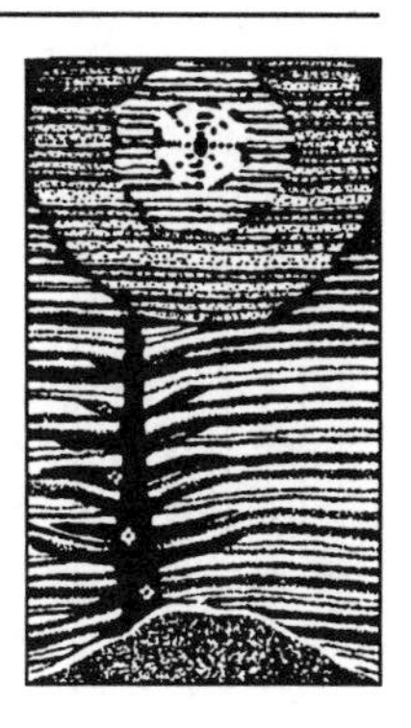

Twilight begins with a band of black. The design was conceived during a stormy day in early March. A heavy snow was falling, bending cottonwood and aspen branches to the ground and knocking out power lines. Carolyn was experiencing hand problems again. Her fingers swelled with red sores. She was also suffering from severe stomach cramps that persisted for days in spite of a special diet, relaxation exercises, and bedrest. I was in Los Angeles at the time, working on a film project.

Carolyn tried weaving her way out of her despair by conjuring, using number symbolism as her guiding idea. During her years of weaving, Carolyn had become increasingly aware of the importance of numbers in her art. Counting functions often formed the foundation of her design ideas and woven images. For the tapestry that was to become *Twilight,* she set up a forty-five-inch-long warp, equal to the sum of the numbers one through nine. The idea was to weave one inch for the number one, two inches for two, three for three, and so on. Each woven area was to be conjured from qualities associated with each number.

"I cannot consciously consider associations with numbers every time I repeat a numerical sequence," Carolyn says. "But I try to remain receptive to numbers as qualities, as well as quantities. I am beginning to believe that by counting threads over and over during the process of weaving, I am tapping into elemental powers rooted deep in the unconscious. I often wonder what constellation of events is being activated within me every time I repeat the numbers one, two, three, four."

One. When Carolyn picked up her weaving comb and threads, there was no indecision or doubt about the choice of color. She simply sat down and quickly completed one inch of black. But after peering into this band of darkness for a while, Carolyn left the loom and went to her journal.

"Why have I woven black in the beginning?" she wrote. "Am I being tricked by illness? Should I be resisting this black? Apparently, my work on the loom now must begin in my own darkness, and I'll thread my way through the numbers into light."

Carolyn was reading John Anthony West's *Serpent in the Sky,* an evaluation and presentation of Schwaller de Lubicz's reinterpretation of Egyptian philosophy, with regard to the temple of Luxor. Like the Pythagoreans, Egyptians considered numbers neither as abstractions nor as entities in themselves: "Numbers are names applied to functions and principles upon which the universe is created and maintained."[1] Egyptian number systems proved to be Carolyn's primary source for the new tapestry, and so she began by realizing that her band of black was woven for the Egyptian symbol for the Absolute, the principle of Unity, unpolarized energy.

Two is an expression of division and opposition, a state of primordial tension. Of interest to Carolyn was Schwaller de Lubicz's proposal that the "primordial scission," or first division from the principle of Unity, is not necessarily a division in half (One divided by Two), which implies static division, but rather a division according to properties of the *phi* proportion, a dynamic division (One divided by ø).[2]

Carolyn chose yellow and white threads. She divided the black woven for the number one with an axis, rising on the right-hand Golden Mean of the warp width.

Three is the number for the first geometric planar form, the triangle. In West's discussion of numbers, Three is an expression of the reconciliation of opposites, the force of attraction and inspiration that draws together opposing elements.[3]

The woven axis continued to rise. A third color was introduced for the three-inch section, interwoven with the other two to build a triangular form.

> I weave slowly, finding the way the threads of this number lead. I wait for an inner consent which clears the way and then I *know* the way to move. But I must weave very slowly, with details worked in, taken out, woven in again.

Four. When Carolyn sat down at her loom to weave for the number Four, a maze of associations passed through her mind. The four directions, the cross, the square, earth with its four quarters, the number most closely related to the process of weaving in the sense that weaving continually creates intersections and crossings. In the Egyptian numbers, Carolyn found that Four was associated with the physical matrix, the principles of substantiality and materiality.

Carolyn chose four colors and wove a mesh design of interlaced bands. But her preoccupation with the meaning of numbers took another turn. Her mesh design recalled the net-covered basket carried by the Babylonian god Oannes, a fish-tailed man whose net-covered basket signified a geodetic mesh, a network of crosses.[4]

The reference to Oannes was found in Robert Temple's *The Sirius Mystery.* In the same book, Carolyn also learned about the Dogon of West Africa. According to Dogon mythology, the people are descended from the Nummo, spirit beings from the Sirius star system, who on earth appear as sea-green water beings, fish-like with forked tongues, having the essence of water.

Once again, star and water. Carolyn set aside her weaving tools to learn more. She found that according to Dogon myth, when the Nummo ancestor emerged, he spat out eighty cotton threads. The threads were distributed between his upper teeth to make the uneven threads of a warp. The Nummo did the same with his lower teeth to make the even threads, and when he opened and closed his mouth to talk, he made the movement necessary for weaving. As the threads crossed and uncrossed, the two tips of the Nummo spirit's tongue pushed the weft threads back and forth, and the woven design took shape. In this way, the Spirit imparted the Word of Creation by the process of weaving.[5] For the Dogon, the Weaver is the Word, the Word is in Weaving, and the Word *is* Weaving.

The association of weaving with the word is found in other traditions as well. Knotted cords were used in the place of writing in ancient China. In Peru, knotted cords called *quipus* were used for recording sophisticated numerical information related to agriculture and astronomy, and also to record complex ideas expressed poetically. In Sanskrit, *tantra* means thread or fabric, and *sutra* also means thread. Both *tantra* and *sutra* also refer to the written word or collections of writings.

Five. When weaving for the number Five, Carolyn recalled the five-pointed badge of the Pythagorean brotherhood. There were many other associations, but West's discussion was of primary interest at the time. By incorporating principles of polarity (Two) and reconciliation (Three), Five was the number of potentiality and creative vitality. To represent this potentiality, Carolyn chose to allow her mesh design to culminate in an opening flower bud. Despite her progress, weaving was taking its toll.

> Why does this loss of heart happen every day? Why is my weaving energy slipping? Some inner being needs to flower. She lies hidden, like a bud beneath closed petals. Why not leave her hidden? What do I wish to reveal? What is hidden in this number Five?

Old doubts and fears crowded into her weaving time. Money matters were always easy to worry about in dark times. Carolyn became concerned about her relationship to Crystal, and she brooded about my working in Los Angeles for an extra week. Weaving did not seem to be improving the situation.

Six. In West's analysis, One through Five relate to metaphysics; six presents a framework for actualization and the perception of the material world by means of our senses.[6] Six, as the six sides of the cube, implies volume, space. Six, and six times sixty or three hundred sixty, implies the circle of time. Six represents manifestation in time and space. Carolyn picked up her threads.

The pattern woven for the number Five changed into a bowl form. A small dark ellipse emerged within the bowl, which Carolyn took to be a mouth. The pulse pattern woven before now appeared to be sounds emanating from the mouth. Carolyn wrote:

> Someone is coming. Someone to tell me about the other side of joy. What do I really feel now, weaving these threads of my imaginings?
>
> I must quietly reflect. Center. Heart must guide. I enter more threads. Someone is emerging from the other side of the world. I see her now. Why is she so sad?

Thread followed thread, with small areas built up, taken out, and tried again, with only a finger's width of work to show for an entire day's effort. The pain in her hands intensified. Never had Carolyn known such deliberation in the choosing and inserting of a thread.

> Crystal came home early from school today brimming with her usual high-energy happiness. How incredibly beautiful she

> was. Yet as soon as I saw her I closed in. I didn't say as much, but whatever I did say might as well have been, "Don't touch me. I don't want your world." I became the condemning monster. Crystal broke into tears. I left the house for a long walk in the snow. When I returned I climbed inside the world of the loom for another two hours work.

After another day of weaving, the enigmatic portrait had been woven in. When I arrived back in Taos, Carolyn removed the loom coverings, allowing me a preview of what had been conjured.

"I've woven a teacher," Carolyn said.

She was masked. Her hat looked like an inverted basket. She appeared to be a masked Haida Indian personage from Crystal's heritage.

Seven. In the Egyptian numbers, and in Native American as well, Seven is the number of transformation and transcendence. As Three plus Four, Seven is the union of reconciliation and materiality. But the quality of Seven that Carolyn related to most strongly was its shamanic associations. In Native American traditions, Seven includes the four horizontal directions of the earth plane, plus the below, the above, and the center of the vertical dimension taken by shamans or medicine people in journeys to other worlds.

To symbolize her own sense of transcendence, Carolyn wove a seven-inch-tall black tree, with seven branches on either side of the trunk. The tree established a new vertical axis in the design, woven on the left- hand Golden Mean of the warp's width.

> Something is happening, like neural sparks connecting. I know the tree is there somewhere. I have woven, unwoven, and rewoven it three times already. Some weaving law, a law of seven, underlies this tree pattern. I must find that law.
>
> I begin with ideas, like little lights casting shadow and light patterns on the walls of my mind. With these sparks, I begin to see what is there to be seen. I am unfamiliar with the territory I am now scanning. It's an awesome place. I must *see,* then go with the thread. In the right moment the law is revealed which I must obey.

Carolyn's black tree was woven as a silhouette against a fiery sky, achieved by a sequence of bright colors. In this sky sequence, Carolyn found a law of seven by weaving a color progression derived from the decimal 1/7, or .142857.

Eight. In the Egyptian system, Eight is the number of renewal and regeneration, the wheel of life and death. Carolyn wove a circle. Within the circle, she wove an eight-fold division, which gives the circle the appearance of a wheel. But the wheel is also the sun.

Nine is the number that unites all the numbers because Nine is One plus Eight, Two plus Seven, Three plus Six, Four plus Five. Nine is the metaphysics of structure, the fruition of pattern and form. When Nine changes it becomes One again.[7]

Carolyn was discovering that the study of numbers could become a vast undertaking. Each of the numbers, with its many associations and related symbols, pointed to complex systems of thought. Carolyn could have been overwhelmed and stopped weaving, thinking her imagery inadequate to such complicated and intricate systems. But Carolyn followed her threads, knowing it was better to do something she knew than to do nothing. To complete her design, Carolyn chose white threads and wove them into angles taken from G.I. Gurdjieff's symbol of the enneagram. P.D. Ouspensky, in his *In Search of the Miraculous,* describes the nine-pointed enneagram, as a universal symbol, a schematic diagram of perpetual motion, and a symbolic representation of the philosopher's stone of the alchemists.[8]

The white angles Carolyn wove were intended to be white birds in flight. *Twilight* began in darkness and it ended with spirits soaring (see Plate 6). The white birds reminded us of a dream dreamed years before in our Cedar Road farmhouse, when white birds had flown out of a garden where a woman told Carolyn she would protect a large white egg. We saw in the egg a symbol of creative potential, and now, it seemed, that potential had taken form and been given flight.

Conjuring is a means of catching glimpses of oneself within mirrors of myth and symbolic images. It's a curious fact of tapestry weave that threads hanging down from an unfinished warp represent the working side of the weaving process, the side that the weaver is always facing. The finished side faces out. What she sees from where she sits is the mirror image of what she actually weaves. To study a section of a design she has finished, Carolyn often uses a hand mirror. If she chooses, she can hold the mirror in such a way that she sees herself as well as a portion of the finished design. What she sees, to take this image another step, is a moment of herself within the designs of a continuously evolving personal mythology. She sees the patterns which in time reveal a much larger design.

All tapestries need finishing touches after being removed from the loom. There may be small details to correct. A wobble in a curved line may require adjusting. The tapestry may need a bit of stretching to straighten an edge line. Wool ends protruding through the design will be carefully removed. To smoothe the surface, Carolyn steam-presses the back side.

"Tapestries are like people," Carolyn comments. "Never quite finished even when the weaving is done. The first thing to do now is to sew in a hem line with strong binding tape."

"Why don't you sew your signature on the front?" I ask. "You're always hiding it on the back."

Then we set up the tungsten lights and take photographs for our permanent slide record of the work.

The day we found a place on the wall for *Twilight,* Crystal burst into the room in one of her painted paper-bag masks, her pink tutu, and a dozen scarves tied to her arms and legs. Seeing that we were absorbed by the new design, she took a good look at the four-color mesh design.

"Looks like plumbing," she said. "Here's a bathtub. Water comes in here. Goes into the tub and drains out over there."

"Tell me about the woman I've woven," Carolyn said, pointing to the figure in the design.

"She's an old Indian woman," was her immediate response. "She wants to wash in the water. She's standing at a window looking at the green hill and tree. She's watching the birds fly through a cloud. Why did you weave all that?"

"I weave my story," Carolyn said. "But anyone else seeing this tapestry will have their own story to tell. Just like you."

"You sure weave funny-looking bathtubs," Crystal said.

Later, Carolyn looked again at her design, wanting to understand more about the darkness in the beginning, and the upper sections flooded with light. The enigmatic masked woman, woven within the number Six, seemed to have led her from one to the other, from dark into light.

"If she's sad," Carolyn told me, "her sadness is for me, for anyone caught in the physical dimension. I was trapped in a world that prompts questions like 'Why do my energies ebb? Why my loss of heart? Why are my hands so sore?' She led me on. She stands within the Six of Time and Space, between the Five of potentiality and the Seven of transcendence. She shows the way to the sun and beyond."

18

Alchemy

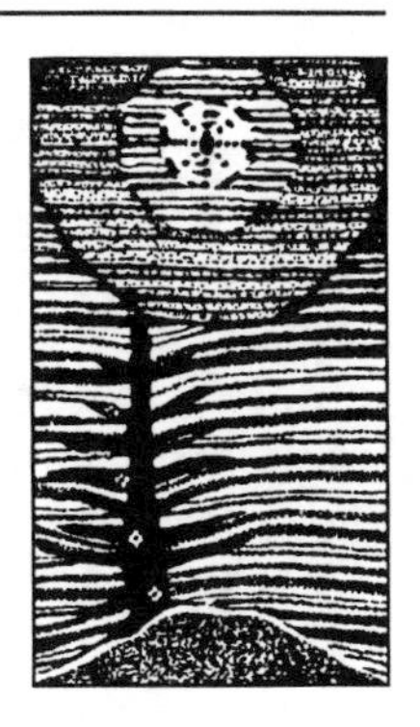

Every weaver, when engaged in the act of interlacing one thread with another, participates in a process that for countless generations has been a primal metaphor for creation, including creation of the world itself.

When Carolyn asked Navajo women how to weave she did not know she was being introduced to a metaphysical process as well, whose dimensions would become increasingly apparent as she worked to master the physical requirements. While reading Dogon mythology during the weaving of *Twilight,* Carolyn found fresh reminders of the richness of the weaving metaphor, and how symbolism permeates every aspect of the process. The Dogon associated weaving with the spoken Word of Creation. Lébé, an ancestor representative of the Word, introduced through the Word the mysteries of weaving. Lébé taught the Dogon how weaving is associated with the sacred marriage and the fruitful womb, that making of fabric is the multiplication of mankind, and that weaving is also the tomb of resurrection.[1]

Early in her weaving career, Carolyn realized that she wanted her designs to have meaning and to find symbols relating to her own life. The Navajo gave her a strong push in that direction.

"By giving me weaving tools," Carolyn said, "Navajo weavers placed me on a trail of exploration and discovery that has led me into inner and outer worlds, and back and forth through time."

After *Twilight,* Carolyn wanted to renew her use of geometry to reflect the sense of wholeness she looks for in her life and in her art. A design idea soon presented itself. The new idea, as so often occurs, was in fact extremely old. She decided to give woven representation to a question that was considered sacred in Pythagorean times, was rediscovered in Medieval art and cathedral construction, and continues to fascinate mathematicians and philosophers today. The question, which contains both metaphysical and mathematical dimensions, is this: How can a circle be described relating to a square in such a way that the circle's circumference is equal to the square's perimeter?

An arithmetic solution to the squaring of the circle is impossible because perimeter is expressed in terms of whole numbers, while circumference must be found in terms of the irrational number *pi.* The metaphysics of the question is discussed by many writers, including John Michell in his *City of Revelation.* Michell states that "the original function of the Great Pyramid, to promote the union of cosmic and terrestrial forces by which the earth is made fertile, is clearly stated in the symbolism of its geometry, for the Pyramid is above all a monument to the art of squaring the circle."[2] Michell sees the squared circle as the most crucial exercise of sacred geometry, and the key also to St. John's description of the New Jerusalem as found in the Book of Revelation.

The question can be solved geometrically, and drawings of a geometric solution appear in Keith Critchlow's book *Time Stands Still.* Critchlow's research led him to believe that squaring the circle was fundamental knowledge applied by ancient builders to prepare the ground and establish a sacred space for constructing stone circles or monuments, including Stonehenge and many other sites in Britain.[3]

With the Critchlow drawings as a guide, Carolyn returned to her design table and picked up a compass. She drew a circle. Using a straight edge, she drew the circle's horizontal diameter. She found herself remembering the medicine wheel.

"This circle is my Self," she said. "The diameter line is my East-West axis."

In medicine wheel terms, the diameter line represented movement between introspection on the West point of the circle, and intuition on the East. How had the journey begun? As Carolyn visualized herself twelve years younger, just finishing a science degree, it seemed a matter of sheer coincidence that she had learned to weave in the first place. What was the nature of the impulse that had carried her off to Navajo land? Why had she been so insistent on learning the very difficult Navajo weaving techniques? And why had the process of weaving, and woven designs, taken on such enormous meanings? The use of the tools, the preparation of a warp, the insertion of weft threads, choosing colors, building designs with horizontals, verticals, diagonals, curves—all of it seemed so much more than mere technique. Why?

The products of the loom now reveal a clear link between Carolyn's need to design and weave and her need for self-exploration. Outwardly, working with the loom, Carolyn wanted to master the craft. This in itself involved a discipline. Yet, with each new challenge to her technical facility, more opportunity presented itself for inner work. Carolyn discovered that weaving could be a form of self-study. It seemed as if each thread she chose to weave with had potential to lead her into the threads of her own life. And as the thread was drummed into place, there was an opportunity to glimpse a slowly unfolding inner design. When she paid close attention to her dreams, she found they often related to work on the loom. And because dream images could not always be comprehended in terms of her everyday life, she looked to mythology. In myths, she found frequent references to weaving, to the loom, and to all aspects of using thread and making fabric. All of it seemed to fit, to form a pattern of some kind, but Carolyn knew there was much more.

She returned to her drawing, compass in hand. The diameter line she had drawn intersected the circle's circumference in two points, which became centers of two new circles having radii equal to the diameter of the original circle. The intersecting circles form the "eye of the fish," the *vesica pisces,* or *mandorla* image Carolyn had used as guardians of the central maze in *Labyrinth.*

Again, she found herself remembering. How was it that as work on the loom progressed, and her techniques expanded and improved, the inner journey had become increasingly multi-dimensional? Attention to an inner life brought an even greater need for producing something tangible—physical fabric to mirror inner fabric. She found that the inner work influenced designing, and woven design influenced the direction of her inner journey.

Carolyn proceeded with the design. Having drawn the two intersecting circles, she drew the line linking the points of intersection below and above the original circle. This vertical line intersected the circumference of the original circle in two points which became centers for two more circles.

The original circle with its cross was now a completed medicine wheel. Carolyn saw the vertical line as her North-South axis, a line

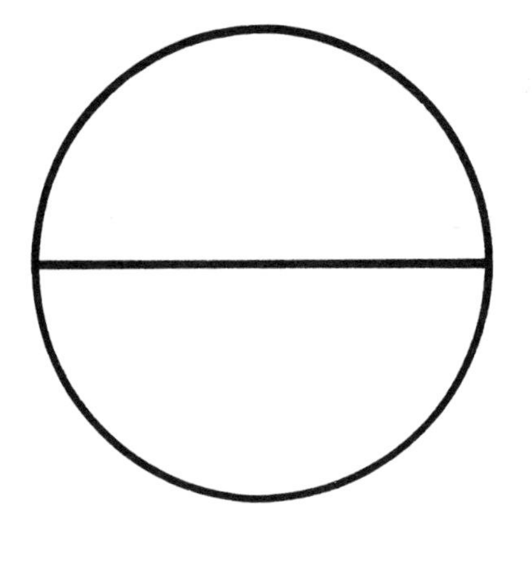

***Figure 19:** The first step in the design for* Alchemy. *For Carolyn, this is also the first step in the making of a medicine wheel. The circle represents Self; the diameter line represents an east-west axis.*

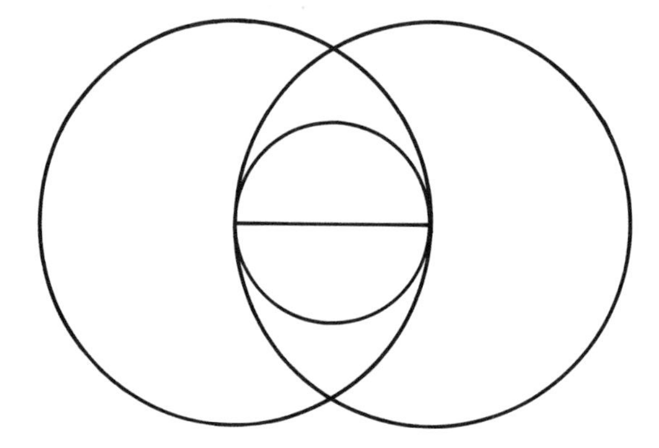

***Figure 20:** Two new circles are drawn with radii equal to the diameter of the original circle. The intersecting circles form the* vesica pisces, *or* mandorla, *image Carolyn had also used in other tapestries.*

representing movement between the thinking function in the North and the feeling center in the South of the medicine wheel. The axis brought to mind questions regarding her affinity for geometry and mathematics.

Even in high school, Carolyn had been aware that the coherency and precision of geometric forms appealed to her. In a university paleontology class, she had been deeply impressed by the spiral symmetry of fossil seashells. Then when seeing Navajo rugs, Carolyn saw how wool texture and choice of colors added depth and beauty to even the simplest of geometric shapes. And in her own weaving and designing she found geometry and mathematics to have an even larger appeal.

"Geometry gave me an anchor for my work," Carolyn says. "Geometry made sense as a language of form. It's comprehensible, precise, and orderly, yet geometry is also mysterious and readily lends itself to symbolic and metaphysical associations."

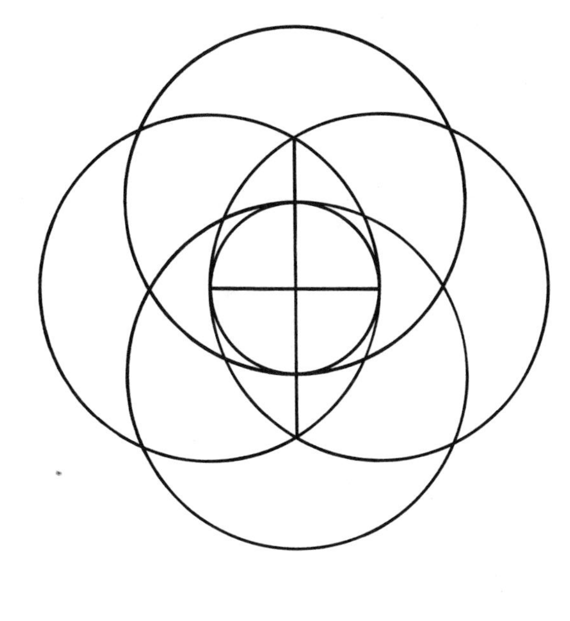

Figure 21: *The design for* Alchemy *continues with a line linking the points of intersection below and above the original circle. This vertical intersects the circumference of the original circle at two points which become centers for two more circles. The original circle is now a medicine wheel.*

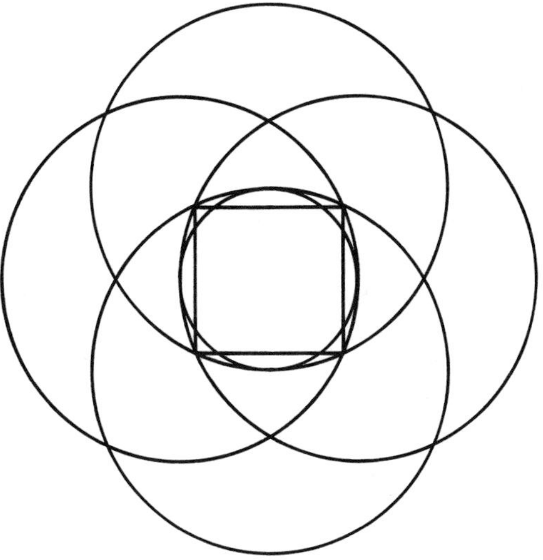

Figure 22: *To complete the design, two* mandorlas *intersect at right angles in four points. Lines drawn between the four points form a square that has a perimeter closely approximating the circumference of the original circle. The circle is squared.*

Furthermore, geometry and mathematics are inherent to the weaving process. Carolyn found that weaving involved numbers and counting at every stage and that weaving technique is essentially work relating horizontal, vertical, and diagonal dimensions. Geometric forms and number systems seemed to work at many levels. They lent themselves to the demands of weaving technique, they satisfied Carolyn's need to find her own beauty/harmony equations through tapestry design, and they provided symbols to give form and direction to her inner search.

"If these forms and numbers had no meaning for me," Carolyn says, "then designing and weaving would be mechanical functions devoid of life. I want to be open to something larger than myself and let my art be more than self-expression. How is it possible to find more, to reveal a sense of the sacred? I see this as a life-long quest. It comes back to inner responsibility and discipline."

The design for the new tapestry was nearing completion. The North and South circles intersect the East and West circles to form two mandorlas, which intersect at right angles in four points. Lines drawn between the four points form a square, which has a perimeter closely approximating the circumference of the original circle. The circle is squared.

As Carolyn studied her drawing, she realized that the medicine wheel had taken on an entirely new dimension. She had been relating to her East-West axis, then the North-South axis, but the squared circle symbolizes the possibility of the physical dimension manifesting a sacred dimension. The square represents the earth, the material plane, the physical body. The circle represents heaven, the metaphysical or spiritual. The squared circle is a marriage of the two, the above and below, the spiritual and physical. Recognizing these qualities in the drawing made a deep impression.

Carolyn had often been aware that design work inspired an inner dialogue, as if one part of herself questioned or commented to another part of herself, and sometimes clarified intentions for a particular problem. During the designing of the new tapestry, an inner voice took on unusual directness, a voice that came with such immediacy and impact that Carolyn often wrote in her journal as if recording a conversation. She asked the voice where it was coming from and heard the following reply: "You are tapping on the door which is an eye of consciousness. I tap on the door also; the tap is a tapping both ways. Your call calls me, and my call calls you. When the door opens, you allow me to enter, compelling my presence to manifest in you."

Carolyn did not worry about this voice or question the division between "I" and "You," but she sensed that the conversation was between her everyday "I" and a higher "I." Later she felt that the clarity of the voice was related to heightened sensitivities because of her way of working with the *Alchemy* design (see Plate 8).

Weaving is an intensely solitary, inherently repetitive activity demanding careful concentration. The new design tested Carolyn's skill to even greater levels, in that she wanted perfect curved lines for her circles. And Carolyn was also keenly aware that she was working with a design that to Pythagoreans represented an esoteric alchemy, a sacred marriage of heaven and earth. To Lama Govinda and the Tibetan Buddhists, united circles represented inner conversion, the turning about in the deepest seat of consciousness. Weaving the squared circle was an inner request for transformation, and when the colors were chosen, the first threads drummed into place, Carolyn was in a state of readiness.

Sitting still, threads in hand, Carolyn waited, poised to allow part of herself to rise up, ready to receive energies she wished to pull down. The meeting point between this rising up and pulling down was in herself, to be made manifest in woven design. After weaving for a while she took a break and opened her journal. During a period of three weeks she filled pages with conversations and commentary spoken by the mysterious but compelling inner voice. For the most part the journal entries are clear, written slowly and deliberately.

One day, resting in the shadows of the seven aspens in the front yard of the Waters' home, Carolyn wrote the following:

> Receptive to trees,
> You hear trees speak.
> Five years ago a tree touched you.
> Time now moves through trees.
> Lift your antler-branches and listen.
> Tree time is root time.
> Tree breathing is tuned to all life
> Within the circle of the Great Wheel.
> Remember what the pine tree said,
> "Take care of circles."
> Remain open to the silence in these words.
>
> Your body is a sacred tree.
> Your eye holds a vision.
> Lightning, striking open the eye of the tree,
> Opens your eye also.
> Use this strength well.
> Be carried by your tree-branch antlers
> Into higher wisdom.
> As tree, see yourself
> Growing rising,
> Rooted waiting.

Returning to the loom, Carolyn approached her emerging circles with new insight. Four circles, surrounding a central circle. She saw the South circle as her Navajo experience, the discovery of native teachers and an ancient craft, the place where the journey had begun. The West circle represented dreaming, the relationship of dream images to her creative energies. The circle in the North represented her research and work with geometry, mathematics, astronomy, and mythology—the direction in which much of her journey had taken her. The East circle included her intuitions, her moments of clarity and understanding, the woven designs themselves. And now Carolyn perceived that in the central circle stood her sacred tree with its tree-branch antlers lifted towards the sky. This was the circle of change and transformation, the place allowing the possibility of aspiring to spiritual dimensions.

She had chosen four colors for the four circles and utilized color mixing techniques achieved in earlier work. Where two circles intersect, two colors mix. Where three circles intersect, three colors mix, and in the central circle, all four colors mix, creating a fifth color in the viewer's eye.

She wove during the day, often writing during breaks and at night. One morning Carolyn woke up with an image of a white woodlands bear, who told her a name.

"Listen to me," the white bear said. "Albion. This is a name for you to know. The teachings hidden within your art are old; you have no idea how old."

There was a long pause, but Carolyn knew more was coming. She continued writing.

"Albion is a matrix of energy, an atunement particular. You have touched a source."

For several days, while weaving, Carolyn tried giving a face to the name. No clear image came to mind. She found herself thinking of qualities rather than images. She sensed that Albion was distinctively feminine, yet also masculine. A womb-man.

"You have seen an aspect of Albion in your garden," Carolyn wrote. "The woman who protects the egg. You resurrected Albion from the river in your own back yard. A spaceship carried you to Albion's realms, and you weave Albion into your designs."

Carolyn could not recall ever hearing the name prior to these internal revelations, but she went to Robert Graves's *White Goddess* and found reference to another aspect of the white goddess in Celtic times, Albina by name, the root form of the name Albion.[4] This was the name given to the islands now called Britain. It seemed that once again Carolyn was being led to her English roots; yet she sensed that the message included more than family ancestry. "Breath builder behind forms, measurer of time and space, Albion is the keeper of forms founded on principles of harmony," she wrote.

Carolyn continued weaving. At times, demands made by the design seemed technically impossible, and work progressed slowly. Several days after advancing past the tapestry's midpoint, Carolyn woke up with a dream image of an open eye in the palm of her hand. The image preoccupied her for several days. Then, after a time of quiet meditation, Carolyn opened her journal.

"The open eye in the hand is the creator's symbol," she wrote. "The eye sees the universe in part and in whole. With an open eye in your dreaming hand you build woven mirrors of ancient harmonies."

Later, Carolyn recorded the following words as if receiving a set of instructions.

> Weave the sound of Albion into your design.
> See the sounds.
> Keep the eye in your hand open.
> Retain your solitary mind.
> Work on yourself always.
> Respond to guidance from within.

After the last thread was woven in, Carolyn carefully removed the tapestry from the loom. She gave the tapestry a name.

Alchemy. Woven to convey a sense of marriage. Uniting the above and below, sky and earth, form and content, masculine and feminine. Uniting the part with the whole.

After a few finishing touches, *Alchemy* was ready for a place on the wall. While studying the design, Carolyn found herself becoming quiet again. The inner dialogue which had resounded through days of weaving had stopped. Apparently the other voice had been woven in, contained within the colors and lines of the tapestry.

To Carolyn, weaving *Alchemy* completed a circle, one revolution around the medicine wheel. She soon felt the urge to move on and find a new beginning. Where would the journey take her next?

For a while, her move out from behind the loom returned Carolyn to the marketplace. As usual, she entered the market with mixed emotions. A newly opened gallery in Taos offered Carolyn a one-person exhibition. We gave much time and energy to the show, and the opening drew a crowd of enthusiastic friends and local gallery goers, but at the time Taos was not a town where art buyers were purchasing tapestries. One piece sold. Nevertheless, over the next few months, several tapestries found good homes for good prices.

Her work was included in several invitationals and group shows in Los Angeles, Albuquerque, Santa Fe, and Taos. An article about her work was featured on the cover of *New Mexico Magazine.* Carolyn was asked to give slide and lecture presentations, and she taught workshops. Approached by students, Carolyn began giving private instruction. She found she enjoyed teaching design principles as well as tapestry technique, and she always encouraged students to find their own threads of inquiry.

Before Carolyn disappeared behind the loom again, we went for long walks. It was spring. The aspens surrounding the Waters' place quivered with fresh greenery. We followed a road uphill, then left the road by way of a trail to the mountain foothills. We rested beneath the branches of our favorite tree, a ponderosa pine that commanded an expansive view of mountains, sage flats, and the high desert plateau. Clearly visible seventy miles away, a flat-topped mesa known as the Pedernal turned purple in the late afternoon light. We stood silently, but I couldn't help wondering what threads Carolyn found in that vast and open view of desert atmosphere. She's a weaver of worlds. She knows how to make manifest the invisible, finding designs in the elemental forces of Mother Earth and Father Sky.

Endnotes

CHAPTER 4: *Beauty Equals Harmony*

1. Gary Witherspoon, *Language and Art in the Navajo Universe* (Ann Arbor, Michigan: University of Michigan Press, 1977), p. 151.
2. See, e.g., Margaret Link, *The Pollen Path* (Palo Alto, California: Stanford University Press, 1956), p. 155.
3. Gladys Reichard, *Spider Woman* (Glorieta, New Mexico: Rio Grande Press, 1968), Frontispiece, from a Navajo legend.
4. Witherspoon, *Language and Art in the Navajo Universe*, pp. 26-27.
5. Peter Tompkins, *Mysteries of the Mexican Pyramids* (New York: Harper & Row, 1976), p. 262.
6. H. E. Huntley, *The Divine Proportion* (New York: Dover Publications, 1970), p. 30.

CHAPTER 8: *A Tree and Two Dreams*

1. Robert Graves, *White Goddess* (New York: Farrar, Straus and Giroux, 1948), pp. 65-66.
2. Evangeline Walton, *Prince of Annwn* (New York: Ballantine Books, 1970), p. 109.

CHAPTER 9: *The Journey North*

1. Esther Harding, *Women's Mysteries* (New York: Harper & Row, 1971), p. 103.
2. Evangeline Walton, *Island of the Mighty* (New York: Ballantine Books, 1970), pp. 312-314.
3. Graves, *White Goddess*, pp. 98-99.

CHAPTER 10: *Story Belts*

1. The term *kachina* refers to the inner essence or spiritual component of mountains, clouds, natural forces—all animal and human life. Kachinas are personified in masked dances and also represented in dolls given to Hopi children so that they can learn the names and qualities of these essences. For further information see Frank Waters, *Book of the Hopi* (New York: Viking Press, 1963), pp. 165-166.

CHAPTER 12: *The House of Waters*

1. Lama Govinda, *Foundations of Tibetan Buddhism* (York Beach, Maine: Samuel Weiser Inc., 1969), p. 93.
2. Lama Govinda, *Foundations of Tibetan Buddhism*, p. 145.

3. Richard Wilhelm & Cary F. Baynes, trans., *The I Ching* (New York: Bollingen Foundation, 1950), p. 249.

Chapter 13: ***The World Behind the Loom***

1. Kathleen Berrin, ed., *Art of the Huichol Indians* (New York: Fine Arts Museum of San Francisco/Harry N. Abrams, Inc., 1978), p. 147.
2. Frank Waters, *Mexico Mystique* (Chicago: Sage Books, 1975), pp. 181-182.
3. George Rowley, *Principles of Chinese Painting* (Princeton: Princeton University Press, 1959), pp. 34-35.
4. Mai Mai Sze, *The Way of Chinese Painting* (New York: Vintage Books, 1959), pp. 431-434.

Chapter 15: ***Weaving Time***

1. Frank Waters, *Mexico Mystique*, p. 220.
2. Guy Ottewell, *The Astronomical Companion* (Greenville, South Carolina: Department of Physics, Furman University, 1979), p. 36.
3. R. T. Zuidema, *"The Inca Calendar,"* in A. Aveni, ed., *Native American Astronomy* (Austin, Texas: University of Texas Press, 1977), pp. 221-225.
4. Moh Fini, *Weavers of Ancient Peru* (Bath, U.K.: Tumi Press, 1985), pp. 32-35.
5. Rene Guenon, *Symbolism of the Cross* (London: Luzak & Co. Ltd., 1975), p. 67.

Chapter 16: ***Waiting***

1. C. G. Jung, *The Archetypes and the Collective Unconscious.* Vol. 9, *Collected Works.* Bollingen Series XX (Princeton: Princeton University Press, 1959), p. 25.
2. J. E. Cirlot, *Dictionary of Symbols* (London: Routledge & Kegan Paul Ltd., 1962), pp. 203-204.

Chapter 17: ***Twilight***

1. John Anthony West, *Serpent in the Sky* (New York: Julian Press, 1979), p. 45.
2. Ibid.
3. Ibid, pp. 47-48.
4. Robert Temple, *The Sirius Mystery* (Rochester, Vermont: Destiny Books, 1987), p. 206: Plates 6-9, p. 139.
5. Marcel Griaule, *Conversations with Ogotemmili* (Oxford, U.K.: Oxford University Press, 1970), p. 28.
6. West, *Serpent in the Sky*, pp. 54-58.
7. Ibid, pp. 67-69.
8. P. D. Ouspensky, *In Search of the Miraculous* (New York: Harcourt Brace Jovanovich, 1949), p. 294.

Chapter 18: ***Alchemy***

1. Marcel Griaule, *Conversations with Ogotommeli*, p. 73.
2. John Mitchell, *City of Revelation* (New York: David McKay & Co., 1972), p. 60.
3. Keith Critchlow, *Time Stand Still* (London: Gordon Fraser, 1979), p. 31.
4. Graves, *White Goddess*, pp. 67-68.

Bibliography

Berrin, Kathleen, ed. *Art of the Huichol Indians.* New York: Fine Arts Museum of San Francisco/Harry N. Abrams, 1978.

Bronowski, Jacob. *Ascent of Man.* New York: Little, Brown and Co., 1973.

Castaneda, Carlos. *Tales of Power.* New York: Simon and Schuster, 1974.

Cirlot, J. E. *Dictionary of Symbols.* London: Routledge & Kegan Paul Ltd., 1979.

Critchlow, Keith. *Time Stands Still.* London: Gordon Fraser, 1979.

Fini, Moh. *Weavers of Ancient Peru.* Bath, U.K.: Tumi Publications, 1985.

Ghyka, Matila. *The Geometry of Art and Life.* New York: Sheed and Ward, 1946.

Gorman, Peter. *Pythagoras, A Life.* London: Routledge & Kegan Paul Ltd., 1979.

Govinda, Lama. *Foundations of Tibetan Buddhism.* York Beach, Maine: Samuel Weiser, Inc., 1969.

Graves, Robert. *White Goddess.* New York: Farrar, Straus and Giroux, 1948.

Griaule, Marcel. *Conversations with Ogotemmili.* Oxford, U.K.: Oxford University Press, 1970.

Guenon, Rene. *Symbolism of the Cross.* London: Luzak & Co. Ltd., 1975.

Harding, Esther. *Women's Mysteries.* New York: Harper & Row, 1971.

Homer, William Innes. *Seurat and the Science of Painting.* Cambridge, Massachusetts: M.I.T. Press, 1964.

Huntley, H. E. *The Divine Proportion.* New York: Dover Publications, 1970.

Itten, Joseph. *Elements of Color.* New York: Van Nostrand Reinhold, 1970.

Jung, C. G. *The Archetypes and the Collective Unconscious.* Collected Works, vol. 9. Princeton: Bollingen Series XX, Princeton University Press, 1959.

Jung, C. G. *Man and His Symbols.* New York: Doubleday, 1964.

Jung, C. G. *Memories, Dreams and Reflections.* New York: Vintage Books, 1961.

Link, Margaret. *The Pollen Path.* Palo Alto, California: Stanford University Press, 1977.

Matthews, W. H. *Mazes and Labyrinths.* London: Longmans, Green & Co., 1922.

Michell, John. *City of Revelation.* New York: David McKay & Co., 1972.

Moffat, Mary, and Painter, Charlotte, eds. *Revelations, Diaries of Women.* New York: Random House, 1975.

Neumann, Erich. *The Great Mother.* New York: Bollingen Series XLVII, Pantheon Books, 1955.

Olsen, Lynn. *Women in Mathematics.* Cambridge, Massachusetts: M I. T. Press, 1974.

Ortiz, Alfonso. *The Tewa World.* Chicago: University of Chicago Press, 1969.

Ottewell, Guy. *The Astronomial Companion.* Greenville, South Carolina: Department of Physics, Furman University, 1979.

Ouspensky, P. D. *In Search of the Miraculous.* New York: Harcourt Brace Jovanovich, 1949.

Reichard, Gladys. *Navajo Shepherd and Weaver.* Glorieta, New Mexico: Rio Grande Press, 1968.

Reichard, Gladys. *Spider Woman.* Glorieta, New Mexico: Rio Grande Press, 1968.

Rowley, George. *Principles of Chinese Painting.* Princeton: Princeton University Press, 1959.

Sandner, Donald. *Navajo Symbols of Healing.* Rochester, Vermont: Healing Arts Press, 1991.

de Santillana, and von Dechend, Hertha. *Hamlet's Mill.* Boston: Gambic Inc.,1969.

Schwaller de Lubicz, Isha. *Her-Bak, Egyptian Initiate.* Rochester, Vermont: Inner Traditions International, 1978.

Schwaller de Lubicz, R. A. *Temple in Man.* Translated by R. and D. Lawlor. Rochester, Vermont: Inner Traditions International, 1981.

Storm, Hyemheyhosts. *Seven Arrows.* New York: Ballentine Books, 1972.

Sze, Mai Mai. *The Way of Chinese Painting.* New York: Vintage Books, 1959.

Temple, Robert. *The Sirius Mystery.* Rochester, Vermont: Destiny Books, 1987.

Thompson, D'Arcy. *On Growth and Form.* New York: Cambridge University Press, 1961.

Tompkins, Peter. *Mysteries of the Mexican Pyramids.* New York: Harper & Row, 1976.

Tompkins, Peter. *Secrets of Egyptian Pyramids.* New York: Harper & Row, 1971

von Franz, Marie-Louise. *Number and Time.* Evanston, Illinois: Northwestern University Press, 1974.

Walton, Evangeline. *Island of the Mighty.* New York: Ballantine Books, 1970.

Walton, Evangeline. *Prince of Annwn.* New York: Ballantine Books, 1970.

Waters, Frank. *Book of the Hopi.* New York: Viking Press, 1963.

Waters, Frank. *The Man Who Killed the Deer.* Chicago: Swallow Press, 1942.

Waters, Frank. *Mexico Mystique.* Chicago: Sage Books, 1975.

West, John Anthony. *Serpent in the Sky.* New York: Julian Press, 1979.

Wilhelm, Richard, and Baynes, Cary F., trans. *The I Ching.* New York: Bollingen Foundation, 1950.

Witherspoon, Gary. *Language and Art in the Navajo Universe.* Ann Arbor, Michigan: University of Michigan Press, 1977.

Zuidema, R. T. "The Inca Calendar," in Aveni, A., ed. *Native American Astronomy.* Austin: University of Texas Press, 1977.

Index

Acknowledgments

I wish to express sincere and grateful thanks to Frank and Barbara Waters who encouraged me to write this book and who have remained supportive in so many ways. Grateful acknowledgment is made of our Navajo teachers and the medicine people who helped us along the way. My special thanks go to Donald Sandner. Thanks also to Hillis Garlick and Rachel Brown, to Margaret Lloyd, to the late Helen Aufderheide and Francis Tidd, and to all those who contributed time, comments, and support. I especially wish to remember the efforts of Christopher Bamford, and I thank the people of Inner Traditions International who have produced this book, especially Leslie Colket and Susan Davidson.